D0512199

Mine

3013021852834 6

Mine

EMILY MERRILL

SALAD
PAGES

A NEW AGE OF BOOKS

A note. *Mine* contains some short scenes of domestic abuse.

Salad Pages Ltd.
89 Leigh Road, Eastleigh,
Hampshire, England, SO50 9DQ

Published by Salad Pages Ltd.
© Salad Pages Ltd. 2019
The author asserts the moral right to be
identified as the author of this work.

A catalogue record of this book is available
from the British Library
ISBN: 9781913067038

Cover designed by Kate Rowland

For my mum, who taught me to love stories, and for my grandad, who has always believed in me. I love you both to the moon and back.

Prologue

"I don't belong to you. I don't belong to anyone!"

His eyes flashed. For a moment, all I could hear was his breathing. It could only have been a second that passed, but it felt like a lifetime. A standoff: me and him. Two people once entwined, now on opposite sides.

For a moment I wondered if he had finally heard me.

And then his eyes narrowed and his hands were on my throat.

"Yes. You do, Avery. You are *mine*."

One

I pushed on the glass, leaving the coffee shop and stepping out into the bright, winter sun. York in January was my favourite thing; when the light peeked through the crowds and the spires of the gothic York Minster shone golden amidst the rooftops. My friends were waiting, huddled in their coats on the grass opposite the cathedral, their faces turned toward the sun. Connie was applying lip gloss, half-listening to Maia who was chatting animatedly, probably about our new assignments. They couldn't have been more different, but I loved them for it. I loved everything about York and the way it made me feel. Especially – I looked down at my phone, seeing a text from him and smiling – today.

"I'm pretty sure I've remembered this right." I settled the cup holder onto the grass. "An iced soy caramel latte for Connie." Maia rolled her eyes and I stifled a laugh, passing the reusable cup to my friend. "A black coffee for Maia, and hot chocolate for me."

"I *need* that. My hands are freezing. What? It may be sunny but it's still cold!" Maia had moved from the south to come to university here, so she complained about the weather way more often than Connie (a proud Liverpudlian) or I ever did.

The three of us had just left our first English Lit tutorial for the year; twelve students packed into a tiny seminar room, eyes wide as the assignments for the term were relayed to us. I'd been tapping my foot the entire time, unable to concentrate on what the seminar leader was saying. Usually, I was on top form: drinking in the words. Today, the butterflies in my stomach were suspending all other thoughts but those about Luke.

"I *still* haven't started unpacking. I swear I'll have to re-iron all my clothes." Connie pouted.

"Avery's a dab hand with an iron, just bribe her with hot chocolate." Maia was pointing at me, simultaneous chugging her americano.

"She's joking, but I will happily comply if there's chocolate beverages involved."

I caught a glimpse of Maia's phone screen, no longer paused on Scrabble, but the seminar timetable for our module on medieval literature. I jabbed her in the ribs and pulled the phone from her hands. "And you, missy, can delay starting that deadline for at least an hour."

Maia relented, pulling the pencil out of her hair and braiding it over her shoulder. "As soon as I'm finished here I'm basically moving into the library. My mum packed a twelve pack of energy drink in my suitcase."

Connie snorted. "I'm pretty sure my big sister snuck a bottle of vodka in mine. There are two types of students, clearly."

I laughed along with them. My sister Stella had tucked some shells into my suitcase; a reminder of home. I imagined Dad and Stella now, probably fighting over the TV remote, Dad eventually caving in and letting Stel watch her reality shows. They were getting less and less emotional every time they dropped me and my luggage off in York, but that didn't mean I was finding it any easier to deal with.

Connie was waving her hand in front of my face, and I jumped. "What time are you guys coming to the house party tonight?" Connie shared a student house with five other girls from her accommodation in first year. "You're bringing Eliza, right?"

Maia, ever the most conscientious of our group, interrupted Connie. "Avery can't. Tonight's the big night."

I couldn't help it. I squealed.

"Whoops. How could I forget? Never mind the lager and cheap wine then. Are you excited?"

"I literally could not be happier. Luke can't wait to see you guys again. He's been asking when we can go on another pub crawl."

"Did you know that there are enough pubs in York to go to a new one every single day of the year?"

Connie shoved Maia. "Where do you even find these facts? Anyway, I can't imagine having a man fall that far in love with you that he'll move his whole life just to live in the same city. I don't think I've ever kept a boyfriend for longer than two months."

Whilst Maia tried to console her, I let my mind drift off again. I was like a child on Christmas Eve, unable to sit still. Of my friends I was the only one in a relationship; Connie was notorious for coming on strong, and Maia was more into textbooks than people. I, on the other hand, had Luke. My best friend. Luke coming to live in York was a dream come true. I glanced between my friends and sipped my hot chocolate, my cheeks aching from my smile. Everything was perfect.

A few hours later I checked my reflection in our shared bathroom mirror, pinning the tiny braid around the back of my head and running a brush through the ends of my black waves. I'd decided on a coat of mascara and some lip balm, confident enough without the foundation I sometimes wore. I knew he preferred me without anyway.

Luke was arriving in five minutes, and I wanted everything to be perfect. I could hear Eliza shuffling around in her bedroom, and I knocked on the wall, knowing she'd be able to hear it. There was some movement, and then she popped her head into the bathroom, crazy blonde hair looking a little slept on.

"I'm going, I'm going! I sat down to my calculus like three hours ago, and just woke up with dribble on my pillow. So that's how that's going. But I promise, I'll be gone in like two seconds." She saw me raise my eyebrows. "Maybe three."

"You know you don't actually have to leave the flat. Just don't burst in unexpectedly on my candlelit picnic." I wiggled my eyebrows, making her laugh.

"I said I'd go to Connie's party later, so don't worry. And I've got dance practice with the team in thirty so I'll be completely out of your hair.' She stopped. 'You know,' she said, making a fake annoyed face. 'It's only two days into term and I've already been roped into another group dance competition."

"What a *chore.*" We both knew she loved getting up on stage. There wasn't a chance that she'd fall asleep at practice. Eliza had been my best friend since day one, and it had been obvious that we'd move in together in our second year. So far, living with my best friend was proving to be the right choice.

The doorbell rang and she squealed, grabbing my hand. "Right, I'm out of here! Don't forget me after your big reunion."

I watched her scurry down the hall and walked into my bedroom, aware that she'd direct Luke in here on her way out. I'd spent the last couple of hours procrastinating my first course assignment and getting the perfect setting ready to welcome my boyfriend to my university city. He'd made the decision back in October and had gone to his dad for help. As the director of an accountancy firm with a string of offices all over the north, his dad had eventually agreed to put Luke in an entry-level accounting role in his York branch. The ease with which Luke's father had set up his son's future intimidated and impressed me in equal measure.

I moved one of the tea lights I'd bought away from the edge of my shelf just as the door opened.

Luke.

I raced over to him.

"Avery." His expression immediately softened as he hugged me. I breathed in the smell of mint and the faintest hint of aftershave that I knew so well, resting my chin in the crook of his neck.

"I missed you."

"Missed you too. But hey, no need to miss me anymore!" He beamed down at me and then finally took a moment to look around the room. "This looks amazing." His eyes clocked the pizza in the centre of my bed. "And that looks especially amazing, I'm starving."

"I can imagine. How was moving day?"

"Moving boxes into the flat has taken the majority of today. Never mind unpacking them."

"What's your flatmate like?"

"I haven't met him yet, although knowing the people that work for my father's business, he's probably in the office from dusk til dawn." He sat on the bed, shaking off his shoes and grabbing a slice of ham and pineapple, dripping grease onto my bedspread. I didn't want to say anything to ruin the moment, but popped a napkin under his hand, making him smile.

I knew he was nervous to finally be making steps towards his future. The past year since we'd finished our A-Levels he'd been doing admin in his dad's office with his dad watching him carefully until he was deemed ready to start working towards his accountancy qualifications. I knew he was hoping that proving himself in the York office would give his dad the confidence he needed to let Luke start his training. "How're you feeling about starting work?"

"Fine,' he said, quickly. 'Did you make these?" He gestured to the little canapes. I'd made two batches to get them just right.

"I did."

"You're a genius. Now come here." He pulled my chin towards him with one finger, kissing me lightly on the lips and looking around my room at the neatly organised books on my shelf, and the bright white duvet that I made sure to wash every week. "I should have just moved in here with you."

"Right this second I can't see why I said no." Luke was kissing my neck, making me laugh. "But you know I just wanted the genuine university experience. Plus, this way you get to really know Eliza."

"I know, I know. I'm just excited for us to start our future together." He rubbed my chin with his thumb and forefinger.

"Two more years of university and then I'm all yours. We'll take London by storm." That was the plan, and when

I looked at my boyfriend – tall, blonde and muscular, with the bluest eyes I'd ever seen – I was completely sure of it. We'd get a flat in London and I was going to get my PGCE whilst he finished his accountancy training. I had an image of finally settling down with my boyfriend of four years, and it was my favourite one to visit when I closed my eyes at night. My homelife had been rocky, but there had always been a raft to hold onto: Luke. I looked into his eyes.

"Love you millions."

He grinned through his second slice of pizza. "Love you more."

It was about an hour since Luke had arrived and I was lying on my back, staring at my glow-in-the-dark stars on the ceiling. "I don't think I will ever eat again."

Luke laughed, and we both looked at the debris on my bed. I'd probably gone overboard with his favourite foods: ham and pineapple pizza, canapes, crusty bread from the bakery down the street and about five different types of cheese, strawberries dipped in chocolate and glasses of Eliza's homemade lemonade that she kept stocked up in the fridge.

"I appreciate the effort." He kissed my forehead again, crossing his feet at the end of the bed and snuggling into me. "How does it feel to be back in York?" I knew what he was referring to. Every time I went home, it was hard to force myself to leave again. Westby was only two hours away, but it felt like forever.

"I thought it would have been easier by now."

"They don't mind. They love you."

I imagined Stella on her own at the kitchen table, in the tiny house we had in Westby. It was a small seaside town, but I loved it with my whole heart, as well as the people in it. My friends hardly visited home, but they were all aware of how my situation was different, and the guilt I felt when too much time passed between trips. My dad and Stella were my number one priority. If Luke was my emotional support, I was theirs. And I hated leaving them to their own devices. It never stopped hurting when you were the one left behind. I would know. I'd been there and relived it ever since.

"And having me here," he said, moving his mouth over mine. "That'll make everything feel much, much better."

Two

The toaster popped, and I heard the click of the peanut butter jar as Eliza moved around the kitchen. It was still the first week back, but already our assignments had begun. I had three poems to annotate for tomorrow's tutorial, and from the stack of notes by Eliza's laptop, I could tell her workload was the same.

Eliza shoved a plate in front of me. "I really need to stop going out. That's three times this week, and I keep dreaming about Pi in my sleep. And not even the good kind of pie."

I jotted my tutorial and lecture schedule in my planner while she chatted. Eliza's brain worked at lightning speed. If you didn't reply to Eliza, she would simply keep on talking. That had been my favourite thing about her when we'd all met in halls last year. I had been so nervous, but with Eliza, I didn't ever have to worry about what I was going to say: she always filled the silences.

"It's only Friday but I swear it feels like we've been back here more than a week. My deadlines are piling up faster than those dishes in our sink." I didn't highlight that they were mostly hers. "It's like every time we leave the uni bubble, we forget how much work there is to do while we're here." I leaned slightly in my chair, opening the fridge and grabbing the jam. "Thanks. It's against the law to eat peanut butter toast without jam. We're almost out of this by the way," she continued. I smiled and rearranged the magnetic letters on the front of the fridge to spell 'J A M'.

Eliza held out her toast for me to spread.

"You know I love a food shop," she said.

"Be my guest."

My phone buzzed and my little sister's face appeared, lighting up the screen. It was eight-thirty on a Friday morning. The time when Stella was usually zipping around the kitchen, annoying Dad with all the noise and hogging the shower. Friday morning FaceTime calls were unheard of, so I picked up.

"Hey Stel, what's up?"

My sister just blinked back, waiting for her microphone to connect. Eliza was leaning over, waving madly. Looking between the two of them, it was hard to believe that they weren't related. When I was younger I'd been afraid that I was the adopted child; dark hair and short legs where my sister and mother were blonde curls and willowy figures.

"Can you hear me?" Stella tapped her screen, and I heard Dad's voice from far away. "Not you Dad! I'm talking to Avery." She rolled her eyes. "So yeah, I need your advice."

"On what specifically?" I said. "If you're talking about your uniform, that's one too many buttons undone." Stella was the epitome of crossing the line.

"Don't let Dad hear you saying that. I got my ears double pierced yesterday and you'd think I'd tattooed a giant pair of wings across my back from the way he reacted."

"You haven't, have you?" Eliza piped up. Over the past year she'd become almost as close to Stella as me.

"I'm not dignifying that with a response, I thought you two were meant to be 'intellectually elite', or whatever that prospectus on the kitchen table says. This is a *boy dilemma.*"

"Eh oh." I was joking, but it was definitely new territory. At fifteen, Stella hadn't dated before, and although my own love life had never gone awry, I wasn't sure the boys of Westby High were ready for Stella's fire.

"So this guy, Elliott. He sits opposite me in Spanish – which I need your help with by the way, I can't seem to say anything other than 'I have blonde hair and enjoy the cinema' – and yesterday he liked my last three posts on Instagram. What do I do now? How do I follow that? I don't want to come on too strong."

Eliza was laughing behind her toast, and I wished I could've joined her. "Since when does liking an Instagram post mean that you're coming on too strong?"

"It doesn't. Keep up. But I can't just do the same thing back! I need to figure out a way of telling him I like him, without actually telling him I like him."

I tried to think back to being fifteen years old, but my romance had been much simpler. Luke had been my chemistry partner, and he'd accidentally set fire to his lab coat with the Bunsen burner whilst attempting to impress me. At a time of my life when nothing seemed funny, he'd made me laugh. And he'd been doing it every day since.

Eliza was the real player between us, with the ability to entice a man into asking her out every single week. I hadn't seen her remain interested with any one guy since I'd met her. I turned the screen in her direction, signalling that the ball was in her court.

"You have to lean over the table a bit, seem interested in what he's saying. Maybe even make a joke about him liking your Instagram, subtly let him know that you noticed, without putting yourself on the spot." She sat back, satisfied with herself. "Maybe even say something sexy in Spanish!"

I spat out my tea. "Tell me again how you came to be the maneater in this flat?"

"Avery's right. You're showing your age Liza,' laughed Stella. 'Maybe you're starting to lose your touch.' She paused, looking off screen for a minute then rolled her eyes again. 'Sorry. Dad wants me to do the dishwasher before school. Gotta go. Love ya!" She hung up before either of us could say goodbye.

"Elliott doesn't stand a chance."

Eliza burst out laughing.

There was a knock on the door and I banged my head against the table. "It's like the world doesn't want us to keep on schedule."

Eliza ran to get it, and I heard her murmuring with someone before walking back into the room. "Look what the cat dragged in."

Luke followed behind, smiling at me. "I was just on my way to work. Thought I'd come and wish you luck before that refresher test you have today." He dumped a little brown bag on the table. "Brought you a chocolate twist as well for ammunition."

Eliza's hand went to her chest. "You make me want to be in a relationship."

I smiled up at him as he rested his hands on the back of my chair. "Thank you. How're you feeling about how it went yesterday?"

"Same as last night,' he said. We'd had a long dissection session on the phone. "Dad emailed this morning to let me know that I need to up my game, though. It's only been a day. I'm not exactly sure what game I have to up yet."

I gave him a hug. Luke constantly felt the pressure from his dad. I'd spent the night before Luke's maths A-Level rubbing his back and stress-feeding him strawberries whilst he stared at the pages of his revision guide until his eyes were red. When Luke was stressed, he was cranky beyond belief. I was hoping for a smoother ride this time.

"You just missed Stel on the phone."

"My favourite substitute little sister. What's she up to?" Luke was an only child, and Stella was enough to handle for the both of us.

"Boy trouble."

Eliza interjected. "As in, she likes a boy for the first time and isn't sure how to tell him kind of trouble."

Luke shook his head. "I swear it was yesterday that I was taking her to the beach for ice cream, and she'd scrunch her nose up every time we even saw a boy. These years have gone quick." Although I missed the eleven-year-old Stella, I didn't miss that time. The years hadn't gone quick for me; every day without speaking to my mother had dragged by. I'd met Luke just after it had happened and even though he made me happy beyond belief, I hadn't been able to stop the anger towards her bubbling over the years.

I was still thinking about my mother when Luke kissed me goodbye and let himself out, Eliza staring at me with a cup of tea in her hand.

"I know that look. You're thinking about your family, aren't you?" My best friend was eccentric, and sometimes seemed like she was in her own world, but she was more observant than people gave her credit for.

"A little. It's hard to think of the past few years without thinking about *her*. She's hundreds of miles and years away and she's *still* disrupting my studies." If it wasn't GCSEs or A-Levels, it was the textbook in front of me now.

Eliza stayed quiet, obviously unsure what to say. It was awkward, Eliza being friends with both me and my sister, since our stance on our mother differed so starkly. I hadn't uttered a word to her since the day she'd abandoned our family for *Steve*, Dad's best friend of all people, going off with him to start a new life together with complete disregard for their old ones. Stella, after a year of clinging to my side wherever we went, had made up her own mind and visited Mum's new house every other weekend for a Sunday roast.

I wanted nothing to do with her.

I'd been fifteen when my life as Avery Emerson, formerly boring and typical, changed irrevocably. The house I lived in looked perfect from the outside; pots of geraniums covered the front porch of our detached home, and a welcome mat sat outside the door that sent the impression that everything on the inside was as peachy as it could possibly be. Unfortunately, first impressions are almost always a lie. I'd always wondered how differently we'd view the world if every house was made from glass.

I'd been at the library working on a history project when Stel had called me, sobbing. After the initial wave of panic that any big sister can relate to ("slow down and start again", "are you okay?", "I'm leaving school right this second") I listened to her describe between gasps that Dad had locked himself in their bedroom, and that Mum was in the driveway packing her things into the silver Ford Fiesta.

It turned out that Mum had walked in from work and announced that she was leaving. Stella had been in her bedroom, jumping on the bed even though she knew that she wasn't supposed to, when doors started slamming. Dad's best friend was waiting in his own getaway car outside his own home a few doors down, and I winced every time I thought about running down our street, waving when I saw him because I didn't understand, couldn't comprehend, what was going on. Overnight our house really had turned to glass: a window into the life you'd be thankful wasn't yours.

Thanks to the gossip of a small town, we became momentarily famous. Girls at school had giggled in the hallway when they pointed us out; the products of a messy dramatised affair. Stella should have loved it, ever the drama queen, but I could tell by the way she linked her arm through mine that it wasn't the kind of fame she craved. I'd stuck by her side, and Dad's, ever since, blocking my mother out with radio silence. She'd tried to contact me at first, but I wanted nothing to do with the woman who'd made my dad cry loud enough to be heard over the shower, and left Stella making her own jam sandwiches to take to school.

It had evolved over the years from tiaras and jam sandwiches to boys and high school drama, but I still felt the void where our mother should have been. I would never let Stella down like that.

Three

Even though Maia, Connie and I liked to study at the university library most days, or on the grass outside during the summer and the early days of autumn, my ideal spot for writing my stories had always been *The Hideaway*. The little café was aptly hidden on a side street, and was a refreshing change to the usual coffee chain queues. It also made (what I considered to be) the best hot chocolate in the whole city. Fairy lights and small reading nooks made the space the ideal location for a study escape. I hadn't told Eliza, or Luke, about my writing spot. It felt like a sacred space, where I lost myself in books and forgot about the outside world.

I smiled at the tell-tale chime that rang through the small room as I pushed on the door, alerting Emma to my arrival. She grinned at me and started frothing the milk for my hot chocolate, always one step ahead. Emma was a couple of years older, keeping the family business alive along with her parents. I would never tell the other baristas, but she was my favourite.

"So," she gestured over to my usual window spot with a tilt of her head. "Looks like you'll have to relocate today."

Sitting in my usual seat was a young man, his head bent over a notebook which he was scribbling in furiously. I raised my eyebrows at Emma, who laughed and used the sound of the milk steamer to muffle the noise. Although I knew that there was no sign on the table saying 'reserved for Avery, always', any of the other regulars knew that it was my favourite seat to write in, with its ideal location to watch passersby and imagine them all in their very own story. It was also the only table with a plug for laptop charging. Clearly, the man in my seat had had the same idea.

"He ordered a double espresso, and he's been writing like that for at least an hour now. I went over to take his mug and I swear the music coming through those headphones is loud enough to deafen."

"What do you think he's writing?"

Emma shrugged. "Be my guest and walk past his notebook. It's in hieroglyphics or something." She handed me the floral mug and reached under the counter, grabbing a slice of rocky road and plating it up. "Try this. It's Mum's new recipe and if someone else doesn't eat them, I will end up devouring the whole tray."

I faced the café, which was almost empty aside from the man and an elderly woman sat in the corner with a toasted teacake and her head buried in yesterday's newspaper. It was only eleven in the morning, what I considered to be my most productive writing timeslot, and I knew in an hour or so the lunch rush would appear. I walked over to find another empty table, watching the guy write intently from my new spot just one table over. I knew what it felt like to *need* to put everything down on paper. From the back I could only see a mop of brown curls, and a slightly Hawaiian looking overshirt. It was January.

I checked through my text messages, including a sneaky photo sent from Stella; a side profile of Elliott taken during what I assumed was Spanish class. She was a nightmare. Dad had been called in many times to retrieve her confiscated mobile phone. I fired back a response telling her to put her phone away and concentrate on conjugating verbs and pulled out my worn copy of *To Kill a Mockingbird*. I needed to find some inspiration somewhere to pull me out of the writing slump I was in, and I figured that the best place to start looking was inside my favourite books.

"That's a classic." Pause. "I mean obviously it's a classic. But like, a *classic*." When I looked up the man had swivelled in his seat and was facing me, gesturing to the book in my hands.

I smiled. "If I had a pound for every time I'd picked this up, I wouldn't need to go to uni."

He grinned back at me, revealing a small gap between his two front teeth. "You at York?"

"Do I scream student?" I picked up my mug.

"*To Kill a Mockingbird* screams English Lit."

"Well, aren't I predictable."

"If you are, so am I. I graduated two years ago." That would make him about twenty-three, which checked out. "Same degree too. You clearly have good taste in education.

And literature." He added the last part as an afterthought, his gaze wandering to the novel in my hand again.

"So, is post-grad life really as scary as I'm imagining it?"

"I wanted to write full-time so for me, post-grad life consists of a lot of instant noodles, wearing ten jumpers in the winter and agonising over a single sentence before sending off to submissions. I'm sure you have more steady plans." He took off his reading glasses and scrubbed his face with his hand, leaving it slightly red.

"I'm going to get my PGCE." He nodded. "What are you writing? I write a bit in my spare time." I thought back to the deadlines awaiting me. "Which admittedly, right now I don't have very much of."

"I'm battling second book syndrome. A lot of ideas are floating around in here," he pointed to his curls. "But I've discovered that at least eighty percent of them are utter rubbish. There aren't enough espresso shots in the world to drag a good storyline from me anymore."

He was being covert about it, but he'd let it slip about 'second book syndrome'. I crossed my legs and tried to play it cool. If I was talking to a published writer I might die on the spot. "Have you written anything I might know?"

He blushed suddenly. "I wrote a book called *Breaking the Surface*. Don't worry if you haven't heard of it." I didn't want to shake my head so I smiled instead because he was still *a real published writer*! "It came out last year and now I'm struggling a bit to get into my second. This seemed like the perfect cliché place to put pen to paper and try to do it again."

"I love it here," I said.

He nodded and gave me a warm smile. "I can see why. I'm Beckett by the way. Beckett Kearns." He held out his hand and I immediately took it, captivated by this exchange.

"Like the playwright?"

"Yes, clearly my parents knew that I was destined to be a struggling writer." I laughed at the look on his face, the embarrassment at having a name so true to his character.

This whole situation was surreal, particularly considering that I'd only walked in here with the intent of burying my nose within pages and barely speaking a word. I was trying not to freak out and ask too many questions about his book, or publishing, or what it was like to have someone *read your work*. I made a mental note to stop by Waterstones and see if they had his book.

"You know, I'm going to need you to keep writing in here so I can bring my copy of *Breaking the Surface* for you to sign."

Beckett grimaced. "The first time someone asked me to do that I completely panicked and accidently gave them my bank signature. I wasn't prepared! They're probably fleecing my bank account as we speak."

"I'll keep that in mind when you sign my copy."

"If you're going to rob me, at least leave me enough for heating. I got cocky when I got my advance and threw the pity party jumpers away and rented my own flat so it's all on me now! Enough about me though, what do you write?"

I looked up and my eyes locked on Emma, who was staring at me and mouthing 'interesting?' over the menu she had held up to her face. Beckett had used the brief interval to move from his table and sit opposite me in the armchair.

"Just some short stories, but I hope to branch out soon. I usually write there." I pointed to the chair that had his jacket on, and he batted me away.

"It's a dog eat dog world out here. Especially when it's clearly the best spot in the house for creativity." He looked at the blank page on his laptop that sat next to the notebook. "Although maybe not today."

"What a waste of the window seat!' And he laughed. "I'm starting to draft a full length contemporary at the moment. A last ditch attempt to get out of my Christmas writing slump."

He cocked his head. "Don't tell me, don't tell me. Tragic love story?"

I shook my head, a smile dancing on my lips.

"Family drama?"

Oh, how close he was to my own story. I waved him off again. "It's just a story about a girl. That's all you're getting right now."

"Who's being the mysterious writer now?" Beckett put his hands on his knees, starting to get up. "I absolutely cannot put off my adulting any longer. If I don't do some laundry, people are going to start thinking I'm the kind of person that wears Hawaiian shirts in January."

He paused. "You do realise you haven't even told me your name. Is it something horrendous?"

"Guess."

"Oh God I finally make a writing friend in this city and you're called Apple or something, aren't you?"

"Nope."

"Worse? Better?"

I paused, wanting to make sure that I ended this conversation on the right note. It wasn't every day that you met someone so likeminded. I loved Luke, but we tended to fall into less intense patterns of conversation. Writing wasn't his cup of tea. For me, it was the whole teapot. I stood too, holding out my hand for Beckett to take.

"I'm Avery. Avery Emerson."

I felt the spines, my hands skipping over familiar titles. I wasn't in here to browse; I was in here for a specific mission. Eliza always joked that if you let me into a bookshop alone, I'd come out having spent my entire student loan. There were stacks of books already piled around my room. The small bookshelf my dad had installed when I'd moved in, long overfilled. I'd spent my childhood sat on the beanbags in the children's fiction section of Waterstones, but I'd since broadened my horizons. Anything I could get my hands on, from chick lit to young adult historical fiction. I could lose myself within minutes. I had no idea what Beckett's novel was about, but I guessed I'd find out soon enough. And besides, I wasn't picky.

"Hi, I was wondering if you could locate a book for me?"

The shop assistant was a plump middle-aged woman, and she beamed at me, waving me closer.

"Of course dear, what can I find for you?" She had a handheld screen in her hand, fingers at the ready. I repeated Beckett's name, and she typed. "My twins, Joseph and Eve, LOVED that book when it came out. Eve even tweeted the author! He's local, I think…"

"Did he reply?"

"Almost straight away. She was made up. That book is really important to her, helped her with her anxiety."

I was surprised. I wasn't sure what I'd been expecting, but it wasn't mental health representation for teenagers. Somehow, that made me want to be friends with Beckett even more.

"Here you go. You're lucky that we have a copy left – all it takes is the internet to get talking and then everyone wants to read the same thing. Where did you hear about it?"

"Oh, someone was talking about it and I thought it might turn out to be quite interesting."

Four

I rearranged the shells on my window ledge; pink periwinkles and peach snail horns lined up as a reminder of home. Luke was lying on my bed, where he had been for the past hour, trying to solve a Rubik's cube.

"I can't get the yellows to align." He threw his head back against the headboard, hitting it a bit too hard. He was gripping the cube so hard I was scared it would break; stress brought out the worst in him.

"Are you sure this is about the cube?" I perched on the bed. "I haven't seen you this wound up in *months*. Is it work?"

"Avery, back off." A small smile let me know he was kidding. "I don't know, I just can't focus on anything with Dad breathing down my neck. Every day I get home to an email that digs me out. I swear the guy that's overseeing my progress is some kind of lapdog to him."

"Can you speak to him? Your dad that is."

"Have you met him?"

I had, and in the whole four years of our relationship, I'd avoided him as much as possible. Even though I knew what I wanted for my future and Luke was always telling me how much my aspirations to teach reminded him of his mother, his dad consistently managed to make me feel inadequate. My own dad might have had his moments post-affair where Stella and I hadn't felt like we were standing on the most secure foundation, but we'd never had to question his love.

Luke's hands had slowed on the Rubik's cube as he leaned his head on my shoulder. "Tell me something good. I want to talk about you."

It had been two days since I'd picked up *Breaking the Surface,* and I hadn't yet had time to return to The Hideaway and tell Beckett what I thought, as I'd been snowed under by coursework. "Well, I was reading in this café the other day…"

"No surprise there." A poke met my ribs.

"Do you want to hear something good or not?" A poke back. "I was reading and this guy started talking to me, and it turns out he's an author. Like, a real-life author."

Luke's expression was not one of excitement. "A guy? What guy?"

Jealousy had never been an issue between us. There'd been a minor wobble when I started at York in mixed dorms, but he'd visited two weeks into the term which had calmed his nerves. I was genuinely surprised at his response. "Don't be stupid, it doesn't matter that he's a *guy*. I already have my favourite guy right here."

His expression softened. "He's an author, huh?"

"Yes! I picked up his novel and it's good so far. I think I might ask him for writing advice if I ever see him again.

I mean, I might not see him – there's a good chance it was a fluke. But it would be great to have him take a look at something I've written."

"I think that's a great idea." Luke pressed his lips against mine. "That was a good 'something good'. You know what else is something good?"

"Hmmm?"

"One of those hot chocolates you make with all the cream on top. I'm sad and I need one." He nudged me off the bed, pouting.

He had me in the palm of his hand.

I'd put it off for three whole days, scared of looking like a stalker or even worse, a *groupie*. I stood outside The Hideaway, dawdling, checking my phone. Stella had posted a selfie on Instagram, licking an ice cream cone with raspberry dripping down the side, her hair flying everywhere and probably sticky from the sauce. My eyes narrowed as I leaned in closer, staring at the sliver of another person in the background of the photo. Dirty blonde hair, wavy just like Stella's. My sister had become protective over me in the past couple of years as she'd become closer to our mother. I knew she'd trimmed the photo because of me.

"Avery?" I jumped, almost dropping my phone. I was notorious for cracking the screen and having to sell clothes on eBay to get it fixed. Beckett was standing in front of me, grinning.

"I thought that was you! I was sat at my desk, writing," he gestured wildly towards the block of flats. "And I thought, 'that's definitely Emerson'."

I paused and tried not to sound like I wasn't ecstatic that I had a nickname.

"Well here I am!" I moved around on the balls of my feet, awkward. I hadn't even brought a book with me to pretend I had an ulterior motive for my visit.

"I haven't seen you here this week. I think the old lady with the newspaper thinks I've been coming in to see her. Yesterday she ordered me an espresso and winked when the barista brought it over to my table." He had a satchel thrown over his shoulder; brown leather and a gold buckle. His hair was messy, like the last time I'd seen him. Like he'd been running his hands through it in frustration.

"No Hawaiian shirt today?"

A grin. "It turns out that I actually *do* know how to work a washing machine. It was touch and go for a while, but here I am, in a boring white t-shirt."

I looked at his top. It was a little bit pink.

Beckett went to the bar, ordering what I assumed was his usual (a double espresso) and asking Emma what I usually had. Emma was already scooping chocolate powder into a mug, chatting with him. I assumed they'd been getting to know each other over the last few days. When I'd arrived in York and discovered the seat by the window, it had taken all of one week for Emma's chatty nature to draw me in. And it didn't seem like Beckett ever ran out of things to say.

"I don't understand how she doesn't get bored of me chatting away to her." Beckett sat down opposite, placing the mug in front of me and jerking his thumb back towards the bar. "I swear, living on my own forces me to build up a catalogue of things I want to talk about. I come in here and Emma just lets me rant. The day after I met you, I talked to her about books for, like, twenty minutes without taking a breath. She didn't even bat an eyelid. And mate, that girl can *read.*"

"Why don't you ask her out?" Call me nosy, but I kind of wanted to know if there was already a girlfriend on the scene.

"Hmm. Maybe." Beckett pulled some glasses out from his pocket and slid them on. He shrugged when he noticed me watching him. "I don't always need them, but I've just been sat in front of my laptop for six hours straight and you're looking a little blurry."

"Writing?"

"Always. I notice there's no Harper Lee today. Planning on writing something here yourself?"

I liked that he never failed to turn the conversation back around to whoever he was with. He probably had a lot he could tell me about his writing, but he preferred to chat about me instead. This was only the second time I'd met Beckett, but I already felt comfortable.

"Okay, so confession." Here it goes. "I might have been working up the courage to see if you were in here."

He flushed. "What? That's ridiculous! Am I that terrifying?"

'No!" I said quickly. "Look. I know you're probably super busy. And probably already have loads of published writer friends you hang out with and stuff. But I was actually going to ask you…" Why was this so hard? I swallowed. "If you might be up for a writing buddy."

Eliza was going to find this hilarious when I relayed it back to her. She was the smoothest person I knew, whether romantically or platonically. It didn't seem that I had the same knack for making friends. I noticed Emma watching us from the safety of the coffee machine and hoped she didn't think I was trying to seduce him. The old lady was also watching, probably wondering the same thing.

"Hmmm." Beckett pushed his glasses down his nose and looked through them, putting on a posh accent. "And what would I get out of this deal?"

"Erm, I–"

"Emerson, I'm kidding." He sat forward in his chair. "Okay, then. Let me see what you've got."

I pushed his shoulder. "Way to keep a girl waiting."

"Got to keep you on your toes." He reached down into his satchel, pulling out a notebook. "I can make some suggestions, although I can't promise they'll be any good."

Had my mouth dropped open? I snapped it shut. "Are you *sure* you're not too busy?"

"Avery." His face was serious. "I just moved back to York, all my friends have long gone from our university days, and I spend all day in my flat making up stories and eating pasta straight from the pan. I could do with a friend just as much as you could do with a writing mentor." I raised my eyebrows, and he flushed. "I didn't mean mentor. I definitely didn't mean that I think I'm good enough to be–"

I cut off his rambling. "I've been reading *Breaking the Surface* every night before I go to sleep this week. You're definitely good enough to help me out."

"You have?" He was suddenly doodling in his notebook, practically scratching through the pages, trying to bury himself into the ground. "Please don't tell me if you hate it. Second book syndrome is hard enough as it is without knowing that the first one was a fluke."

"It wasn't a fluke. You know it wasn't a fluke. The woman in Waterstones was falling over herself to recommend it to me."

Beckett was laughing now, clearly over the embarrassment he felt knowing that people had read his book. I'd expected someone of his success to be loud about it. "Okay, well that's definitely enough about my writing. Show me yours."

I froze, unsure whether to laugh or to interject with a comment about Luke. Beckett hadn't even noticed the innuendo, clearly innocent, so I ignored it and smiled as he talked animatedly.

"…I think the trick is to not plan. Sure, when you hit a bump in the road, you have to go back and look at what you're trying to say. For the main part though, I think you just have to follow where the characters take you."

I sipped my hot chocolate, getting the cream all over my nose and not even feeling a shred of self-consciousness.

University had brought me into contact with so many people; some of the best I'd ever met. But I'd never met anyone quite like Beckett before.

I was almost asleep – the first night all week that I hadn't shared my bed with Luke – drifting off and luxuriously hogging all of the space to myself when I heard a light knock on my door.

"Are you awake?" Eliza was trying to be quiet enough that she wouldn't wake me up if sleep had fully claimed me. Most of my friends got annoyed with their room-mates from time to time, but I struggled to find fault with mine. At my garbled attempts at a sleepy response, Eliza pushed the door open. She'd been out for a late-night library session with the people from her course, and she was clearly wide awake. The library on campus had a machine that sold takeaway coffee for a pound…

"I need to ask you something." She perched on the edge of my bed and I patted the spot right beside me. She climbed under the duvet, turning to face me with her head on her hand. She'd got back and changed into her pink pyjama set; wild hair tied in a matching scrunchie.

"Go on."

"How did you know you wanted a relationship?"

Not what I was expecting. "I don't know if I did, to be honest. The relationship kind of found me."

"Elaborate, please."

"I was probably at the lowest I've ever been." Thinking about that time of my life was always hard. "Mum had been gone for over a month at that point. Dad was a wreck and Stel was a limpet. Out of the blue this guy that I'd completely bypassed started making me laugh. I didn't stop to question a good thing."

Eliza nodded, not saying anything for a moment, which was rare. My best friend had never talked about relationships in the whole sixteen months that I'd known her. I was intrigued.

"Are we going to sit here in silence all night or are you going to enlighten me?" I was teasing, but I also craved the gossip.

"I met this guy."

"And?"

"I think I might like him. It's a weird feeling. He's in my trig tutorial and he always helps me out if I get stuck, or vice versa. It usually bugs me when people ask for help, but I *want* to help him. And like, when I stare at him, I'm not just thinking 'I want to rip your clothes off', but I'm sat there thinking 'I'd like to order a Chinese and binge watch reality TV with you all day'. What's happening to me?"

Eliza genuinely looked concerned. I knew her mum was a proper *Single Lady* through and through, and I imagined that the strong independent woman lifestyle had left Eliza with the desire to be just that. *Sans* man, and all of the things that came with it. I couldn't help but laugh at the terrified look on her face.

"What will my *mother* say if I bring home a nice boy?"

It amazed me how many of my peers and I lived our lives to please our parents. Luke was killing himself at his new job for a slice of approval, Eliza was afraid of relationships because her mother had always told her they were unnecessary, and I spent my days in constant fear that my dad felt I'd abandoned him too. You could separate yourself with distance, but family followed you wherever you went, wanted or not.

"No, I'm serious. I think I have to squash these feelings."

"Your tendency to be dramatic is showing. What's so scary about a date?"

"What *isn't* scary about a date?" She picked at a thread on my pillow. "I guess I'll just have to see where it goes. He might initiate it. I hope he initiates it. One night stands I can do. Relationships I cannot. Can I borrow that?" Her finger was pointing at a white slogan tee hanging over my wardrobe. Stella had sent it up in the post, and it had little strawberries across the front. A typical choice for my sister.

"Go for it. It's a petite though."

"Damn you for your tiny frame. Can I sleep in here tonight? My head is all over the place."

I turned off the bedside lamp with a click. She knew she always had a place here, whether she was thinking straight or otherwise.

Five

The click of the Polaroid went off and I stayed still for a second with my hands hugging my books, to make sure the picture didn't come out blurry.

"Taking these is so much pressure. This is why I stick to my phone." Connie was shaking the film, waiting for the picture to develop. "*Shake it like a Polaroid picture.*"

"That's a myth." Maia was sat at a table, pulling notes from a couple of books she wanted for our medieval literature assignment. "Shaking it does nothing."

"Alright killjoy." Connie stuck her finger out at Maia, who was already ignoring her. They had a whole sequence, but everyone on our course knew that they were thick as thieves. The most unlikely friends, the sci-fi obsessive and the drama queen, and yet it worked. I was somewhere in the middle, the mediator.

"I get the concept of capturing one specific moment, but like, look Avery. Your eyes aren't even open in this."

I took the picture and tucked it in my backpack. "Dad will love it regardless."

We were in the library, surrounded by the medieval literature section. The photo Connie had snapped revealed my figure dwarfed by the shelves, pages piled up in my arms. I planned to send the Polaroid home for Dad to stick on the fridge – he'd bought the cameras for Stella and I last Christmas, making us promise to provide him with enough memories for him to live vicariously through. I knew he'd love the photo from the library; my dad had a habit of telling everyone that he met that I was doing my degree. My A-Levels and all that surrounded them had been stressful, and he knew that. The weight of checking in on my dad, and the struggle I'd experienced when Stella let us know that she wanted to see Mum again had shaken me. Sticking biology spider diagrams on my wall and revising poetry had felt unimportant in comparison, but they'd both spurred me on, bringing me cups of tea to my desk and turning on the music for a dance party when stress drove me to tears. When we'd looked on UCAS the day that my results had been released, it had been the first time I'd seen Dad cry since the divorce. That time though, there had been no sad glint in his eyes.

"Any luck?" I gestured to Connie's phone, where she was swiping right on a dating app.

"So far, no good. If a boy is holding a huge fish in his profile photo, it's a nonstarter. If the only thing to show for himself is his golden retriever, he's probably hiding something."

"Golden retrievers can be nice!" I said hopefully.

Maia looked up and gave me a pointed look. "Avery. I'm not even remotely interested in dating and even I can tell you that a dog picture is a massive flaw."

"See?" Connie gestured to Maia proudly. "She does listen to me sometimes."

"I stand corrected. I will never date a guy with a dog again."

"You probably won't have to. Luke, that hot boyfriend of yours, remember?"

Maia put down her pen. "How's that going? Him being in York?"

"It comes with its own trials and tribulations. I keep having to tell him not to come over so I can get my work done. I know it's pissing him off a bit."

Maia raised her eyebrows. "What did he expect? We're at *university*."

It felt a bit weird badmouthing Luke. "He's just stressed I think. It takes some adjusting. For a year and a half we did distance, so this closeness wasn't an issue."

"What an amazing problem to have." Connie almost always sounded wistful when I talked about my relationship.

"Oh my God." We paused, turning to Maia, who was edging out of her seat. It could only have meant one thing. Maia had the ability to tune everything and everyone out when she was focusing on her studies, but there was one thing that disrupted everything.

"The auction is ending!"

"Weren't you just telling us to shush a minute ago?" I leaned in to view her screen. "We're in a *library* you know."

"You know all bets are off when these online auctions happen. I must have set the alarm on my phone wrong. I was banking on it being at six." Her fingers were darting across the screen, competing on the bidding of some unfathomable sci-fi memorabilia.

"For someone so serious all the time, this continually provides me with entertainment." Connie laughed, but I saw her open up the auction app on her phone. "Let me help you outbid."

We sat in silence, interrupted only by the occasional whoop from Maia as one of us got her back in the lead. "Vintagebuyer0356 is going *down*. I have been waiting far too long for this multi-positional Ripley to become available."

"If I win I might decide to keep it for myself." I was teasing, but the look Maia sent back could kill.

"You wouldn't dare." Pause. "Ha! You won't even get the option. Vintagebuyer0356 you have officially been outbid in this war."

Connie burst out laughing, but it was affectionate. We all had our quirks, and this one just made Maia, the untouchable coursework extraordinaire, more real. Besides, Connie had set up a specific group chat when the Boxing Day sales had started, desperate for aid in getting the deals she wanted. Last year when I'd had a writing meltdown, they'd both appeared in my accommodation with gummy bears and jam doughnuts. We were a team, and we had each other's back.

***

"I'm thinking we should go for hazelnut; I'm getting bored of soya." Eliza grabbed the carton and placed it in our overflowing trolley. I scanned our list for the next item, ticking milk off and sighing at the amount we still had to buy. When I was a lot younger, riding around in the shopping trolley and trying my luck for treats had been my favourite game. After Mum left, I spent too long doing it by myself that it had lost its charm. So while I pushed the trolley, book in hand, Eliza felt completely differently, still thriving off the fact that we were the masters of our own culinary destiny.

"We still haven't done veggies." Eliza clapped her hands together at the thought of such a mundane task. I returned to my Kindle and leant on the metal bar, immersing myself in the poetry we were reading in my seminar.

My phone buzzed. "Hi, what's up?" I smiled as I spoke, picturing Luke on his break at work.

"Just phoning to thank you for the note." He'd stayed over last night, and I'd put some leftover pasta salad into a box for his lunch, attaching a little love message. It was the kind of thing that would have made Stella gag. "So, I was thinking tonight, I'll cook for once. I'll light some candles, make it all romantic…"

I bit my lip, already feeling bad. "I thought I'd told you? Me and Eliza are watching that BBC drama tonight. We arranged it ages ago."

"You told me?"

I looked at Eliza, ticking things off the list at the other end of the aisle.

"Yeah. I'm sure I said something earlier this week."

"With Eliza. Again?"

"I've only spent one-on-one time with Eliza once since you arrived. Don't be so dramatic." I hoped he would hear the teasing in my voice.

"Yeah, I must have forgotten. Sorry babe, I want you to enjoy yourself. Just…" There was a pause. Luke sighed. "Just don't forget about me? I don't have friends here. I'm finding it a bit…"

I did feel guilty for having so many friends when I knew he'd left his own behind to live in the same city as me. Every time I went out for coffee or studied with the girls I pictured him on his own, and my heart cinched.

"Why don't you go out with some people from work? Or do something with Joe?" Joe, I'd learned from eating dinner in his new kitchen, was his flatmate. After two seconds in his company it was pretty clear he was career-driven. I couldn't imagine he would be much fun, but it was worth a try.

"I moved here to be with *you*."

"I know. I'm sorry. Can I see you on Wednesday?" Two days from now. "I have a lot of work to catch up on, and at least we saw each other last night."

There was another long pause. I didn't like upsetting him, but I really did need to start on my medieval literature essay.

"Sure. Have a nice time tonight A." His voice was softer, and we exchanged goodbyes as I hung up.

I could see Eliza dragging the trolley down the fruit aisle, picking up a mango and squeezing it, trying to find the perfect one. She'd invested in a blender last week and I'd since given up on my alarm clock; at eight on the dot I would wake naturally to the whirring from the kitchen down the corridor. It was driving Luke up the wall.

I lost myself in the haiku I was reading and felt a tap on my shoulder.

"Emerson!"

I jumped out of my skin, pressing my hand to my chest as my heart rate slowed. Beckett was stood in front of me, hair unruly as ever, beaming.

"Jesus! Beckett! You made me jump!"

"Yeah, I really snuck up there, didn't I?"

"Just a bit." I was pleased to see him. We hadn't arranged another writing session yet and last night I'd had my finger poised over the friend request button on Facebook, debating whether or not I had the guts to offer friendship so literally. I hadn't done it.

"You look like you're enjoying this supermarket experience." Beckett pointed to the Kindle.

"I look forward to it every week."

As he chatted on about his latest escapades with the elderly woman at The Hideaway, I peeked into his trolley, which didn't suggest anything out of the ordinary. None of the red flags you might look for: ten bottles of bleach or vodka.

"Are you judging my trolley?"

"Hey, if you leave it open for everyone to peek in…"

He laughed, reaching behind me to grab some raspberries. "I have a niece that adores raspberries."

"Cute. How old?"

"Three. If she had her way I'd be giving her sugar all the time, but I've been trying to introduce snacks that are less frenzy-inducing."

"My little sister used to beg me to get chocolate fingers. I only bought them when she promised she'd eat all her broccoli."

Beckett looked at me weirdly. "You were in charge of food shopping? God, no wonder you hate it now, the allure must have worn off."

"Yep. It got old extremely quickly."

"Avery?" Eliza was pushing our own trolley, clearly waiting for an introduction. I'd mentioned Beckett to her a few times, so I wondered if the description I'd given would be enough for it to click.

Beckett beat me to it. "I'm Beckett. Avery's friend."

Eliza raised her eyebrows at me.

"This is my flatmate, Eliza."

"Nice to meet you." Beckett gave an awkward little wave.

"So *you're* the man who has stolen my bestie. When she finally finished your book it took her a good few hours to return to reality."

"She paid you to say that didn't she?"

"What can I say?" I grinned at him.

Eliza was grinning too, already at ease. It took her so little time to adjust to someone new. "Avery has *not* been able to stop chatting about that writing session. She was up until two am the other night making some amendments to her chapters."

"Ah, I'm excited. She's going to be in Waterstones one day, mark my words."

I let out a squeak. Now *that* was a compliment.

"You alright there Stuart Little?" He pulled a face at me.

"Ha ha." I brushed off my blunder and he excused himself, needing to get back to his flat to prepare for his niece's drop off.

"You did not mention how attractive he is." Eliza had her hand on her hips. "Not my usual type, but still cute. In a creative way."

"He's just my friend."

"You've said."

I threw a clementine at her. "Because it's true. I like his mind and nothing else. Why don't *you* pursue it if you're that bothered?" It was a trick question. I hadn't heard her mention anyone else since she'd started talking to the guy from her seminar.

"If I wasn't broken," she was still referring to her budding feelings as a curse, "I probably would. But how weird would that be? Watching one of my flings sit on our sofa, coaching you. Hey, would you look at that. I'm not the only one who feels up my mangoes."

I followed her gaze to where Beckett was located, far enough down the aisle that he would never have heard our conversation. He handled three more before placing one in the trolley. As if his ears were burning, he looked up, and immediately flushed.

"There's always a perfect one, you know?"

Six

"Is that them?" Eliza's eyes were narrowed.

"Eliza, the car is blue."

"Oh right, maybe I need my glasses, I could have sworn that was blue."

"No, *that one* is blue." I clapped my hands and danced on the spot. Dad's Polo was pulling into the car park of our block of flats, and I could already see Stella's nose pressed against the window, pulling faces at us. My heart warmed instantly. She jumped out before Dad had even stopped the car.

"It's only been two weeks but I swear it has felt like ten years." Stel almost knocked me over, squeezing me. I coughed one of her curls out of my mouth. "I missed you to the moon and back, A."

"I can vouch for that." Dad locked the car, holding out his arm for me to step into a hug.

"How are you, Dad?"

"I'm fine Avery. How many times do you think I'll hear that today?" He winked. "Just so I'm prepared."

"Sorry." Clearly checking on Dad was a habit that I was finding hard to break. The Dad that had moped around the house, not speaking for days on end, was a different man to the one stood before me now. He rubbed his hands together.

"That drive gets me every time. Where are we going for lunch, girls? I'm starving."

"I spotted a little café on the way into uni yesterday." Eliza already had Instagram up, showing their page to Stella to see what she thought. "They have a little bit of everything."

"Sounds good to me. Luke meeting us there?"

"Of course."

"It's been weird not having him around when you're gone. Two of our favourite people–" he snapped his fingers "–poof."

I brushed off the guilt. "Well, I know he's excited to see you."

Despite the tension I'd felt over the phone in the supermarket, when I'd mentioned lunch with my family to Luke, he'd assured me he would be there. And Luke never let me down.

I stirred the soup in my bowl, waiting for it to cool. Stella was sat next to me, talking Luke's ear off about the guy in her Spanish class and asking his advice. He looked over her head for a moment, catching my eye and smiling.

"He asked me what I was doing this weekend. Do you think that meant he wanted to do something with me?" Her eyes looked up eagerly at him, trusting his opinion through and through. It was like she'd been cooped up with my dad for too long, whose advice when it came to boys was limited at best.

"I think it was probably just a question." Her face fell at Luke's response. "But if he's interested enough to ask, then that's a good sign. It took *weeks* for me to work up the courage to speak to Avery."

My dad laughed. "And once you started, you never stopped." He leaned into me. "She's gone boy crazy, Avery. I don't know what to tell her when she asks me which eyeshadow makes her eyes 'pop'."

I patted his hand. "I'm sure you're doing just fine, Dad."

"He told me to wear green eyeshadow."

"I thought it matched your eyes!" Stella put her tongue out at him and I felt warm and home.

"Anyway, how's the work going? Tough already?" The question from Dad was directed at both me and Eliza, who had tagged along like always to catch up with my family. Her mum was so busy working that she hardly ever had time to visit; I heard them on FaceTime every other night or so but had only met her once in passing. Dad, however, had taken Eliza under his wing, and she hadn't turned her nose up at the chance to be included.

"I have, like, four assignments. I think we've already been through a box of tea bags and it's only been two weeks since we moved back."

"Lucky for you, I brought a couple in the care package that Stella and I put together."

I leaned my head on his shoulder. "Thanks Dad."

"Dad *and* me, I'll have you know. I went trekking to the big supermarket to get the supersized bag of gummy bears."

"Don't listen to her. It was me that bought the pink tissue paper. And how's the job going Luke?" My dad was the type of man to ask everyone in the room about their own interests so that they never felt left out. It reminded me of a certain writer that I knew.

Luke waited until he'd finished chewing his sandwich to answer. "It's tough, I won't try and pretend otherwise. You might think I'd be in a better position knowing who my dad is, but I feel like they're putting me through it on purpose. Kind of like a punishment for getting ahead."

"Don't let it get you down. I bet your dad is proud regardless."

Dad had only met Luke's father once at my small eighteenth we'd had at our house. Clearly, Luke's father had been on his best behaviour.

"You'd think." I huffed into my lemonade, annoyed at the pressure Luke was under. I was feeling the pressure of coursework, but Luke seemed to have a permanent frown line between his eyebrows.

"I'm so excited for the ball. Look at these dresses I'm thinking of wearing." Stella showed her phone to Eliza. February brought with it the English Lit ball, and although it was an event you'd typically invite a date to, Stella had asked if she could come with me before I'd left Westby to start second year. Luke hadn't minded; everyone knew that if Stella wanted something, I'd try my hardest to make it happen. Plus, the idea of going with my feisty sidekick was not a bad one.

"I'm glad you're going instead of me Stel." Luke swigged his pint. "Avery gets in a right flap before those things, trying to get her eyeliner 'just right'." He mimed putting on some makeup and I shoved him, leaning over Stella's chair.

"I do not."

"Well…" Eliza grinned.

"Don't gang up on me!" Everyone laughed, and I couldn't help but join in, even though they were laughing at me. It was hard not to smile when Stella and my dad were beaming – a reminder that we didn't need my mother to bring the happiness she once had. We were fine without her, and we were doing better than ever.

Dad was in the kitchen fixing the extractor fan (the upside of having an electrician for a father), and I could hear Eliza chatting away to him as she opened the care package and boiled the kettle. Luke had had to go back to work, his lunch break only an hour.

"Luke seems like he's settling in here." Stella mused, fiddling with a frame on the wall and making sure it was straight. "Were you wearing a blindfold when you put this up?"

I threw a cushion at her. "You know you love my room."

"I see you put up the stars." The plastic shapes were stuck to my ceiling, lying in wait for darkness; their time to shine. I knew Stella's ceiling had the same ones stuck to it – I had helped her stick them up when Dad had been out at the pub with some friends. Our mother had loved astronomy; buying a telescope when we were really little and standing on the patio night after night, waiting for the lens to focus so she could see something beautiful. A few days after we'd moved into this flat earlier in the year, when Dad and Stel had long gone home with an empty car, a pink envelope had found its way through our letter box which I knew was probably the result of a leak of information from my sister. It was from Mum, practically bursting open with the weight of the plastic stars. I'd thrown them away at first, but it actually helped me feel close to Stella, so I'd rooted them out of the bin in the middle of the night, sticking them haphazardly on the ceiling above my bed.

"I think Mum would be really happy that you put them up. I think she thought you would throw them away."

"Stel…" It was a warning, and she knew it.

"I just think you should maybe–"

"I don't want to talk about her. We're having such a nice day, let's not ruin it." There were moments when Stella felt like my best friend, but there were also times she'd push all of my buttons and I'd be reminded of our blood relation. Talking about our mother was off limits, and she knew it.

"So…" she looked around for something to say, "since you're being as stubborn as always, help me change the subject."

I sighed. "I'm sorry, I don't want to argue with you. How are your friends?"

"*So good.* I went to Megan's for a sleepover last week and her mum made the best enchiladas, oh my gosh." She closed her eyes, remembering. "And we all got invited to a party next weekend, so that's cool. Meg has been teaching me to do a smoky eye."

"Elliott going?"

Stel wiggled her eyebrows. "I'm counting on it."

"Your first party though, that's huge." I hadn't been to that many when I was fifteen. They'd existed, but I was either too scared to leave my dad on his own, or I was spending time with Luke. On the odd occasion that we did go, I remembered a blur of Lambrini and sparklers on the beach. Parties in Westby tended to be tame, by most teenage standards.

"It's not that big of a deal," she bit her lip. "But I'm a bit worried about what to wear. The girls in my history lessons are a bit intimidating, and I know they're going."

As much as I hated that she felt self-conscious, it was refreshing to hear her worry about normal teenage things. Mean girls were a part of everyday life; runaway mothers were not.

"Don't worry about them. They're just insecure. Besides, jeans and a nice top will never fail you."

Stel smiled. "Jeans and a nice top. Got it."

"How is Dad, really?" I leant on my knees, anxious to hear her response.

"The same as usual. And by usual I mean absolutely fine. He's come a long way. Yesterday he took me shoe shopping."

"Wow, now that is progress."

"Yeah, he's doing really well. You know that spicy pasta he used to make for Mum?"

"No way."

"Yep. He made it for me. Last night he even dropped me off at her house. Sped away fast, but at least that's progress."

"You can say that again."

"And that woman that just moved in across the road keeps making funny eyes at him when he's in the driveway."

"She *does*?"

"I know, right. He just smiles back politely and gets in his car though. No conversation, no nothing. I brought it up with him on the drive here and he said he just isn't interested in dating."

"I wish he were," I said.

"I don't think he's fussed about sharing his life with anyone, to be honest."

"Well he was until she broke his heart." The thought of my father alone when we both finally flew the nest made my heart ache and anxiety curl in the pit of my stomach.

Stella shrugged. "I think he's made peace with it. You're going to have to someday, as well."

"Today is not that day."

Eliza called us into the kitchen for tea and I followed behind Stella, feeling strange. For once it wasn't like I was the older sister. I felt small.

Seven

I pushed the sugar on the table into the shape of a heart before running my fingers through the grains and starting over. Admittedly, I was always on time for things. Beckett however, was considerably late.

Luke: Sorry about last night, I wasn't thinking. Love you.

I ignored the message that popped up on my screen, closing my eyes and burying the hurt. After my family had left, taking with them a picnic that Eliza had made for their journey, Luke had dropped by after work.

"Stel seems to be smitten with that guy." Luke had walked out of my bathroom, towel around his waist and scrubbing at his hair with another. He always left them scattered over my floor, where they would never dry. In the past I'd found that endearing.

"Yeah, I think she really likes him." I'd been sat on my bed, legs crossed with my laptop balanced on my knees, writing some notes for Beckett before our meeting.

"Are you sure you need to keep meeting up with him? It seems a little over the top." I hadn't been able to see his face, but I knew it was a frown.

"I mean, he's my friend."

"You have lots of friends."

"Is that a bad thing?" We never fought, but something about the whole conversation had rubbed me the wrong way.

"I don't want to upset you." He'd put his head in his hands. "I'm just stressed. And I don't want to get left behind. I love you."

"I know." I'd paused, reaching out to him. "I'm sorry, come here." Laptop forgotten, I'd let him lay his head in my lap, stroking his hair despite the patch of damp it was leaving on my duvet.

"I bet Stella wants to spend every minute with Elliott. Remember that? Being fifteen and spending every day after school together?"

Sigh. "That was a different time. I hope she isn't spending every day with him. She needs her friends. And Dad needs us."

"Maybe dependence runs in the family."

"What does that mean?"

"Nothing." We'd sat in silence for a while, my head reeling from his comment.

"Do you think I depend on you for too much?" I asked.

"No. Of course I don't. We just make the perfect team."

Although he'd recovered it and spent the rest of the night stroking my hair in his lap whilst we watched TV, I couldn't shake the unease. He was completely right. I had depended on him a lot over the years, whether it was minor things like helping me with Stella's homework, or major events in my life, like the first time Stel had broken our pact and visited Mum, or letting me cry down the phone to him when I was lonely and homesick on my first night in York. He'd moved here to spend time with me. Maybe I was taking him for granted.

"Earth to Emerson." A hand waved in my face. "Where were you for a second then? I thought you were a goner."

Beckett sat down beside me, pouring some tap water from the carafe on the table and taking a slow sip, staring at me.

"Seriously, are you alright?"

It took me a moment to shake off the feeling of guilt. "Sorry, yeah. Lost myself for a second."

"If you don't feel in the right mindset to do this, we can reschedule..." Beckett still looked concerned, reaching out and touching my forehead which made me jump. "You okay?"

"I'm fine," I said, pushing thoughts of last night finally away. "I swear. Let's do this."

Beckett's story was a great escape from uni and my life. I felt privileged that not only was he giving me feedback on my own writing, but he was letting me read snippets of his second book. The first time he'd handed over the partially finished manuscript he'd had to leave the café for ten minutes whilst I read the first chapter, pacing around outside until he deemed it safe to come in again. Like most writers, he hated letting people read his stuff. I hadn't mentioned the thousands of copies of his first novel that sat on shelves all over the country for fear of freaking him out.

"Well, that's brilliant." Sometimes he sounded so English. "Problem?"

"I've left my notes at the flat. I can't do much without them to be honest, I'd made some very detailed notes about your protagonist. Do you mind if I run upstairs?"

"Not at all." I buried my head in his manuscript, picking up where I'd left off.

"Do you know what? I have much cheaper coffee. I'll give you a good deal."

"What?"

"If I remember right, my notes are somewhere on my coffee table. It would make more sense for you to run up with me for half an hour, so I can talk you through them before you have to leave for your tutorial." He misread my expression. "Not a serial killer, promise."

I'd actually been worrying about whether this was a betrayal. Luke had never made me question my boundaries with friends, but last night was still fresh in my mind.

"I promise, I don't bite." Beckett was edging towards the door, and as he began to suggest that he run up and be back down in five minutes' time, I batted his offer away.

"I really do have to be on time for my tutorial. This makes a lot more sense than sitting here like a lemon and waiting for you."

Two minutes later and we were outside the door to Beckett's flat. Number 23 in the block above the bakery across the road from the café. Beckett turned his key in the door and pushed it open. I could tell without putting either of my feet over the threshold that it was small, but it had a definite cosy charm.

"You have so many books." I'd thought my collection was elaborate, but Beckett had novels *everywhere*.

He shrugged. "It's a disease."

"Favourite author?"

"I like Amis, Hemmingway and Hunter S. Thompson is cool. But I think my favourite is Patricia Highsmith one hundred percent. Her sense of place is insane." I'd heard of her; she'd written the book behind one of Dad's favourite films and he'd been telling me to read her for ages.

"And yours?"

"Rosaline Green. No doubt about it." I'd been reading her books for years; contemporary thrillers that hooked you in until the final page. Nothing pleased me more than a plot twist.

"A respectable choice." Beckett hummed whilst I perched on the edge of the couch. He flicked on his coffee machine, moving fluidly around his kitchen and grabbing milk from the fridge.

"I don't have any of that hazelnut stuff that I saw in your trolley."

For someone that had chastised me for peeking in his own trolley, he was a hypocrite. "It's Eliza that buys that, don't worry."

It was surreal, sitting in his flat. It was one thing looking inside his supermarket trolley to gather information, but quite another to sit on this tattered sofa and be surrounded by him. This was without a doubt a writer's den; there were notes *everywhere*. Had I not looked before sitting down, I would have sat on a couple of A4 sheets that had the word 'Lola' scribbled on the top.

"Lola?"

He looked up, seeing the sheets and then pointing to a photo of a small blonde girl, about three years old, that was sitting on the desk facing the window. "My niece. I'm writing something for her birthday. Why? Did you think I had some kind of hot date?"

"Emma might be disappointed."

"I doubt she'd be interested in me. Every time I go into The Hideaway I'm cramped over my laptop, typing away and barely paying attention to anyone." He set the mugs down on the coffee table, which were also covered in pages of scribbles. "How about you? Any hot dates?"

I was surprised that I hadn't told him about Luke yet. Normally it came up in conversation pretty quickly, but Beckett was usually focused, getting to work as soon as we sat down. There hadn't been much time for small talk in the few times I'd seen him.

"I've been with my boyfriend, Luke, for a long time." I flashed my phone background at him before stuffing it back in my pocket.

"A long time as in?"

"Four years."

He whistled. "That *is* a long time. Practically married now." It was the usual reaction to any comment about my relationship. Was my life that predictable?

"I don't know about that," I laughed awkwardly. "But I can't imagine him not being in my life. I know who I am when I'm with him."

He mouthed my words back to himself, as if he couldn't quite understand what they meant. I was beginning to recognise his mannerisms, and I could tell there was something he wanted to say.

"What?" I played with the long wisps of hair falling over my shoulder, anticipating the next words to fall from his lips.

"It's just," Beckett hesitated before sitting down, and I caught a glimpse of a tattoo peeking out of his sleeve as he adjusted in his seat. "How can you only know who you are when you're with someone else?"

I shrugged, unwilling to say a bad word about Luke. "There have been times when I've really needed him."

"My sister's ex-boyfriend was kinda like that for her. Lucy was obsessed with Max until he broke her heart, and she seemed a bit lost for a long time after. Well, until Lola came along. She had to figure out her shit pretty quickly after that."

"How old is Lucy?" Beckett looked a little taken aback. "That was rude, wasn't it?"

"Nah, I like that you're straight to the point. Lola is three, and Lucy is twenty-two." He waited for it to sink in.

"That's…intense."

"She's the best mum I've ever seen. It's just been a difficult path."

I was the same age as Lucy was when she must've been pregnant with Lola. The thought of having a baby terrified me. I knew that Luke wanted kids, and he'd talked about it in passing a couple of times, but there were a million things I wanted to do before that.

"I can't imagine…" I started.

"She's tough," he said with a shrug. "Took it in her stride. Although I did change a fair number of nappies."

"Did you now?"

"Oh yes! Lucy knows how to keep us all in check."

"I think I'd like your sister." Beckett's answering grin was wider than I'd ever seen it.

"I already know she wants to meet my mysterious writing partner."

For some reason, the fact that he'd told his sister about me, paired with the fact that I was sat in his flat made me feel awkward. Luke felt uncomfortable enough as it was about this friendship.

"You know, I think I need to get to my tutorial." I started to pack up my things, leaving my mug untouched and almost knocking some of the papers off the couch in my haste.

"You can take these notes back with you if you want? It might help you make some tweaks." Beckett seemed unaware of my discomfort, one foot in the real world whilst the other dangled in make believe. "I think your protagonist is strong. There are just some things I wanted to mention about the side characters."

"Thanks." I grabbed the papers, turning to leave, but looking around at his flat one last time before I opened his front door. He was so welcoming – both literally into his flat, but also into his life – and I felt like I was abusing the kindness of both him and Luke. This was new territory.

"I guess I'll see you across the road." Beckett scratched his head, looking a little bewildered for the first time, perhaps sensing my unease. As I smiled and shut the door, I knew that one thing was certain; I had to keep this as low-key as possible. I didn't want Luke getting upset with me about this again.

Eight

When Stella was little, Mum and I would sneak off for little dates with each other to our local cinema. She would always sneak treats into the screen in her handbag to avoid paying the ridiculous inflated prices and somehow it had stuck. So as I waited for Eliza's dance recital to start in the university gymnasium, I reached down and pulled out some gummy bears. I'd invited Luke, but he had his limits, choosing to stay at home and play video games, trusting I'd come along after. The seat next to me wasn't taken, but that didn't stop me from rolling my eyes when a random guy sat gingerly down beside me. There were at least a hundred empty seats in this gymnasium, and now it looked like I was going to have to share my gummy bears.

"Avery, right?" I slowly swivelled my head around, completely taken aback. He was tall and lanky, but nothing about that or his light hair and high cheekbones seemed familiar to me. I was usually good with names, but this guy was not on my radar.

"Yeees," I said suspiciously.

He blushed, and for a second I felt remorse at not just pretending I knew who this boy was. Sometimes it was easier just to tell a white lie.

"I'm Jack. Eliza's friend?" It clicked. Eliza had shown me a blurry picture on his Instagram, but it hadn't been enough for me to remember her mystery man on impact.

"I do know who you are! You help each other in your tutorials?"

Jack looked put out that that's all I'd heard about him. He clearly wasn't aware of girl code – I could hardly sell Eliza down the river and confess her crush.

"Yeah, we've helped each other out a few times. She mentioned last week that she was going to be performing tonight, so I thought I'd come down and check it out. I've seen you tagged in her pictures…" He paused. "Does that sound weird?"

"In this day and age?"

"Exactly! So anyway, when I noticed you sitting here I thought I'd come over and see if you didn't mind a viewing buddy."

"As long as you don't talk through the show, I think we'll be good."

"Got it."

I looked at him out of the corner of my eye, his own wandering to the stage, probably trying to sneak a glimpse of my best friend. Fighting the urge to text her and alert her to his presence, I offered him some of my gummy bears.

He only took orange and yellow, which made me warm to him even more.

When you first met Eliza she could come across as quite chaotic, but once she started dancing, she was nothing but grace. It contrasted with the image of her I had, frowning over her equations, but I loved that she had the ability to surprise. She was currently on stage, twirling and floating in a sequined bodysuit that was beyond eye-catching. Jack was completely still beside me, and although he'd been checking his phone at regular intervals like a security blanket before the lights were dimmed, he'd kept it in his jeans pocket from the moment she stepped on stage. I could have moaned at how cliché this all was, but instead I just felt a pang of hope that maybe this time something might come of it. I'd been trying to get Eliza to take dating seriously the whole time I'd known her.

Luke was trying to get through to me. I could feel the vibration of my phone in my pocket but for once I ignored the call. He knew where I was, so I knew he wouldn't be annoyed when I didn't pick up straight away. There was something about the dancing that made it impossible to stop watching; I'd tried taking ballet classes when I was six years old, but apparently it's difficult to move to the music when you don't have a lot of height to carry around.

During the interval, Eliza waved over to me from the side of the stage, her eyes widening at the sight of Jack sitting beside me. Usually, if she saw one of her conquests on a night out, it took no time at all for her to run over and carry on where she left off. This, I could tell, was different. I willed her to walk over and join in the conversation, but she quickly avoided my eye contact and went back to stretching and laughing with a tall brunette. I wasn't used to seeing my best friend shy; if anyone was uncomfortable in a new situation, it tended to be me. Jack had stirred beside me, aware of her gaze, and his shoulders dropped when he realised that she wasn't making her way over. I patted his hand.

"Trust me, if she hangs back, it isn't because she doesn't like you."

"You think?"

"Definitely. After the show, she'll come over without a doubt."

As predicted, an hour later, she met us outside the union, where I'd texted her I would be. "What did you think A?" The question was directed at me, but she knew I'd enjoyed it without even having to ask.

"You were amazing, as always." I stepped back to let Jack into the conversation, who was hanging back, unsure. "Right, Jack?" Both of their heads whipped towards me, in a *"how could you do this to me?!"* manner, and if I hadn't been on the other end of their awkwardness, I would have laughed out loud.

"I loved it," he said.

Although she was mostly looking at the ground, I could tell Eliza was pleased with his response and saw her relax.

They were talking now, Eliza past her momentary lapse in confidence and gestured wildly, explaining the ins-and-outs of the dances. In her degree, where every aspect had to be just perfect and statistical, it was nice to see her looking so free. With her sequined leotard ensemble and her crazy blonde hair she looked like she belonged in the solar system. Jack must have paid her a compliment that I didn't catch, because her smile became brighter and she leaned in closer. I excused myself and tried to find my way through the crowd of people to the exit, pleased with a job well done.

Luke pressed the tea bag against his mug. "It's not a big deal. You just said you would be over by nine."

It was 9:15.

"Eliza got talking, you know how she is…" I left the sentence open for him to laugh. He didn't.

"How come you didn't call me back when I tried to call you?"

"You knew I was going to come and see you after." For once we were in his flat rather than mine, and although his flatmate was out, I could see traces of another man everywhere. The specs on the worktop weren't Luke's (who had always had 20/20 vision), and neither was the stack of *How To Get Ahead*-type management books on the coffee table.

"I just need to know that I can reach you when I want to."

I recoiled. "Do you not trust me?"

"You were with another guy." His voice was small, but the words packed a punch.

"I asked you if you wanted to come, and Jack is Eliza's friend, not mine."

"Avery, I love you, but the distance you're putting between us is stressing me out. Yet another friendship that I'm not a part of."

I saw Luke at least every other day, if not every day at some points, and whilst juggling a full-time degree, friends, and my writing, I didn't think that was too bad. I smoothed the frown lines on his forehead.

"I'm sorry. I didn't think."

He ducked his head into my palm. "That's okay. I know you're sorry. I'm just so *stressed* at the moment. Everything is making me paranoid."

"You have me, completely."

"I know." He smiled. "Let me just get some–"

As he moved to grab the sugar pot it slipped from his grasp, spilling thousands of grains over the floor. I put my hand to my mouth, a laugh escaping.

"It's not funny Avery!" He snapped at me and I jumped. His fist slammed on the worktop. "Just what I needed today."

I went into the cupboard, retrieving the vacuum, unable to speak. Luke never snapped at me. At other people sure, but never me.

"I'm sorry baby." He took the vacuum from me and pulled my head to his chest. "I'm just not in the mood for joking around. Someone at work had to tell me that Dad didn't want me on a project. He couldn't even be bothered enough to tell me himself."

So that explained the mood. "Luke…"

"I don't want to talk about it. Let's just get this cleaned up, okay?"

I did as he asked, unsure what I could say and what I couldn't. He was on edge, breathing heavily and shaking his head every now and then. When the sugar was almost all gone, I went into his living room again and found a movie to watch, hoping to smooth things over.

"Avery?"

"In here."

He stood in the doorway and smiled at me. "What a week, hey?"

"Yeah. I'm proud of you, though. You'll show them who's boss."

He leaned down to where I was sitting and kissed me. "The boss is the problem."

"Well," I made a mental note to be more of a support system for him. "You always have me."

"See?" He hugged me to his side. "It's you and me against the world."

Later, when I wandered into his bedroom brushing my teeth, I could see Luke lying on the bed with my phone in his hand, scrolling.

I took my toothbrush out. "What are you doing?"

Luke dropped the phone and patted the space beside him. "Nothing. Come here."

I indicated my toothbrush. "Just need to finish." On my way back to the bathroom, I paused. "Why did you need my phone?"

"I was looking at the time."

I didn't question why he hadn't used his own clearly-charged phone. I was still drained from our previous argument. What had he been looking for, or was I being too paranoid? I'd exchanged numbers with Jack at the recital so we could all go out for drinks sometime. I prepared to defend myself, but he didn't say anything, just switching off the lights and patting the spot next to him.

Luke quickly fell asleep, always one step ahead and losing consciousness as soon as his head hit the pillow. As I looked up at his ceiling, minus stars, I suddenly felt more alone than I had in a while. Eliza was probably still out for drinks with Jack, and I didn't resent her for it one bit. Stella was almost definitely watching football re-runs with my dad until he realised the time and sent her to bed, and Beckett…well, I had no idea what Beckett was doing. I was in two minds about our friendship, valuing the progress he was allowing me to make with my writing, and genuinely enjoying his company. I hadn't had a guy friend in a long time, so it was refreshing. I didn't want to give that up.

Beckett: Still on for tomorrow? I promise I won't wear the Hawaiian shirt.

As if he'd read my mind, the message came through on my phone. So I did know what he was doing. I looked at Luke, snoring despite our argument, and couldn't deny it was nice that Beckett had been thinking about me, too.

Nine

I read the words of Tennyson that were lit up on my laptop screen in time with the words coming from the lecturer's lips; my notebook beside me with the two lines written in blue gel pen. I was trying to focus on the poetry, which wasn't my strongest point, desperately attempting to make sense of the lecture notes so that when it came to writing my essay, the job would be marginally easier. My phone vibrated on the desk and I picked it up hurriedly, trying not to catch the attention of the other people sitting on my row.

> Beckett: *If I remember right, I'd say personification of the river.*
> Me: *Never thought befriending a literature graduate would come in so handy.*
> Beckett: *I feel used, dirty.*

I put my hand over my mouth to try to stifle the laughter, turning my attention back to the poem and adding Beckett's thoughts to the annotations. As it turned out, poetry was his forte. Stella was also messaging me, a constant stream of thoughts regarding her latest English assignment; it was like we had a cycle of literary aid in motion. She'd been trying to convince me to come and visit them in Westby, but it just didn't seem like the right time. Deadline week for essays was drawing closer with every passing day, and I was keen to keep an eye on the progress of Eliza's dating life, which was finally beginning to heat up after the dance recital. At least, they were the reasons I kept telling myself, a mantra of sorts. In truth I was anxious about Luke, knowing that I was standing on thin ice and needed to spend more time with him.

Beckett: Will you be frequenting our café today, Emerson?

Beckett and I were finally making some real progress with our projects, and I found myself picking his manuscript up from my bedside table instead of the actual novels I owned, keen to find out what happened to his characters. The ending of *Breaking the Surface* had made me cry; his main character finally opening up about his struggles with mental health to his friends and family. Beckett had a way with words – Eliza had found me under my duvet sniffling into my pillow. When I tried to tell him just how good he was, Beckett had brushed the compliments off and stared into his espresso. Beckett was not the type of person to brag.

And his writing wasn't the only thing that was inspiring me: even I'd switched to coffee in the last week or so. Coursework, writing, and my time with Luke was leaving me with very few hours to actually sleep. I looked at my screen again, smiling at Beckett's text. There was never any pressure to meet up – we usually just messaged back and forth until we found a time that would work.

Me: You can bet your bottom dollar.
Beckett: I'd bet all of them if it meant assuring your fine company.

I'd stopped talking about Beckett with Luke, afraid to upset him but also afraid to give up such a valuable aid for my manuscript. Besides, Luke was so stressed about his dad and work that he'd stopped asking how my writing was going. There was no need to inflame the situation, so peaceful omission was the way to go. I didn't think I had it in me to explain away my friendship with the boy in the window seat.

Luke: Want to come over after your lectures? I think I can get the afternoon off.

I bit my lip, unsure now what to do. The thought of lying in bed and watching movies with Luke was a welcome one, but I had a few specific questions I wanted to ask Beckett, and after that I'd planned to meet Eliza at the library for a study session to catch up with our seminar work. We were never able to help each other out – our courses being the exact opposite – but it was comforting to have someone to share the misery with. I made a promise to myself that next time I'd do what Luke wanted and spend my free time with him, but I had to prioritise my studying. I'd worked ridiculously hard to get where I was, and I couldn't let it slip. There was a fire inside of me lately to pursue other things in life, and I was so comfortable in our relationship that it felt like I could afford to. He may not have particularly understood my writing, but I was sure he would support it. And technically, Beckett *had* asked first.

Me: I'm so sorry! I promised Eliza we'd study ☹

A reply never came through, and although I put it down to a busy day at work, I knew he was mad.

When I walked through the front door he glanced up at the bell, smiling immediately and gesturing to the table where a French press stood waiting. I looked to Emma, who smiled at me and turned back to the milk frothing machine. I didn't know if it was in my head, but I was sure she was being a bit colder towards me these days. I made a mental note to keep a little more distance between Beckett and I whilst we worked. I dug around in the pocket of my jeans as I moved closer to the table.

"Don't worry about it." He spoke at the sight of me offering him money, and I stuck the change into the front of my bag.

"You spoil me. Next time it's mine." My offer was met with a shrug, but I was certain that I owed him one. It was one thing to meet with someone at a café, but entirely another to let them buy you a drink, and I wouldn't have blamed Luke for taking offence at that. Beckett was typing on his laptop, a crease in his forehead the only indication that something was up.

"Everything okay?" I slid my feet under the table, preparing myself that he might just tell me to mind my own business. I only had to mention work these days and Luke practically bit my head off.

"You're observant today."

"All days." I corrected him and he laughed, but I noticed that he didn't answer the question right away. His shirt was creased enough for me to wonder why and his hair, usually set into place, was slightly messier than usual.

"It's no big deal. Just my sister. She's dating someone new."

There was a moment of silence, because I was unsure as to how this was a bad thing. Moving on was a sign of growth, wasn't it?

"I know what you're thinking, and no, I don't mean I don't want her to date. She can do what she likes, I just get protective of Lola. I don't want her to get confused if Lucy starts bringing this man to their flat, and then he hurts her and suddenly the new guy is gone." He let out a breath, visibly frazzled. "Does that make any sense, or do I just sound like the annoying big brother?"

My heart clenched at the thought of him being so fiercely protective of his younger sister and her daughter.

"Honestly, I can't pretend to relate to that specific situation. But Stella, my little sister, just started to date. It would be a lie to say that I'm not feeling protective of her. I also worry that if she gets too involved with this guy, she won't spend enough time with my dad."

"Oh, I totally get that." He sipped his coffee. "Blech, that needs sugar. Anyway, I do understand. It's hard, when you have a tight-knit family, to not get over-invested in their lives. It's like you spent so much time trying to hold it all together, that it's scary to risk it falling apart."

We sat in silence, both a little bit in awe (I imagined) of how much the other could relate. I'd seen Beckett as a writing buddy, but never imagined that he could help me figure out so much more.

"After Max, the little shit who got her pregnant, ran off and left her to sort everything out herself, I put my guard up for her. She's unbelievably trusting – one of those *'everything will turn out alright, and if it's not alright, then it's not the end'* kind of people."

I raised my eyebrows.

"I know. I think she actually has that phrase hung up on her wall somewhere."

Who was I to judge? Beckett's sister had been through things that I could only imagine.

Beckett ran his fingers through his hair, clearly stressed, and took a sip of his coffee. "It'll be fine, I know it will.

He's going to have to work super hard to get my approval though."

It was a little unfair, considering that Lucy's new boyfriend probably hadn't done the things that her ex had, but I kept my mouth shut. I was a new friend, not someone that could input on drama that had been going on for years. Conversation clearly over, he pulled out his notebook. I mirrored his actions and we settled into our easy routine of running ideas past each other. It was the best part of my day – no one else in my life had such a careful eye when it came to critique. We had a system going where we'd switch a paragraph or two and sit in silence for a few minutes whilst we read each other's work, and then offer advice when we'd finished.

"I like what you wrote here." I pointed to a punchy conversation between two of his characters, their witty exchange making me smile. It was always a good sign, when you couldn't stop smiling at the words you were taking in. My dad told me that when I was younger, he could tell if I was liking a book by the expression on my face. If my face was blank, it wasn't to my taste, but if my expressions were clear, then it was a winner. It was how I'd judged pieces of work ever since. "Especially Sophia."

Beckett smirked. "She's great, isn't she?"

Beckett's love interest in the book was a young woman, short but sassy, and never afraid to speak her mind.

"Sophia is the woman we all hope we'd grow up to be. It's like, she's got a romantic interest, but she knows that she doesn't need it."

"I'm thinking that she gets this amazing job, and it intimidates Michael." Beckett was referring to his protagonist. "I wanted to tackle the expectations of relationships that are typically written within literature. Like, Sophia doesn't have to be this damsel in distress."

"Ew."

"Exactly, and Michael doesn't have to be her knight in shining armour. It's such an overused trope."

"I could not agree more." We chatted more about the way his plot was heading, and I added little details that I thought might bring the story to life.

"You know, you asked me to be your writing guide, but I think you might be helping me more than I'm helping you."

I pushed his shoulder, and then cursed myself in case Emma was watching.

"I'm serious! Your critique is flawless. Have you ever thought about editorial work?"

I hadn't. Luke had always said I'd make a great teacher, like his mum had been before she'd had him. I knew that I would love it – helping Stella with her homework every night had proved I had the patience for it – but it was books that had stolen my heart from a very early age. Looking into how they were produced, or edited, wasn't a bad idea. A classroom didn't scare me, but maybe that was the point. What about taking a risk?

"Maybe ask your tutor about editing opportunities. Didn't you say Alex Reynold is your tutor? I had him in my third year and he couldn't have been more supportive of my goals." Beckett wrote something down on a scrap of paper, sliding it over. "And I'm pretty sure my editor retweeted something about an editorial internship this summer. This is her Twitter handle. You should check it out."

"Now *this* is why I keep you around." I tucked the paper into my coat pocket.

"Glad to be of service. Now, where were we?" Beckett tucked his pen behind his ear and started to talk animatedly about my subplots, using his hands and waving them here, there and everywhere. This hadn't been what I'd expected when I came back to York after Christmas, but these moments in The Hideaway were like hidden gems, lying in wait for me to find them. I thought back to his sister's favourite quote. It definitely wasn't the end yet, but it was certainly alright.

Ten

"I'll get the carbonara, no bacon." Luke smiled at the waitress.

"I'll get—"

"And she'll have the arrabbiata."

I sat back, stumped. When the waitress left our table, Luke turned to me.

"On a scale of one to ten, how impressed are you that I knew your order?"

"How did you know I wasn't going to go for something different?"

I was met with a sceptical look. "Avery. You never change your mind."

"Hmm."

"Anyway, let's celebrate." He raised his beer. "To a day not spent cooped up indoors."

"We're still indoors." I was teasing, and he mimicked me.

"You know what I mean. It's nice to be out and about. I feel like I spend my life in that office."

"God it's so cold, even with this jumper on." I'd worn a knitted dress; we were seeing off the final days of January and it was still bitterly cold in the evenings. During the day, looking out of the window and seeing the sun peeking through the clouds, you could convince yourself that it was spring. One step outside and you were tightening your scarf.

The Italian we'd decided on was my favourite in York, with candles on every table and the lights dimmed low. I'd figured that we needed a night like this, to forget about work and the bickering we'd been doing. Luke had picked me up at seven with a bunch of yellow roses, which he knew were my favourite. They had pride of place next to my seashells.

"I've seen you a lot but I've been so stressed that I can't think of a single thing we've talked about." Luke rubbed his stubble. "Tell me about your week. It had to have been better than mine."

"I think I'm finally making some big changes to my manuscript. I'm really excited about it."

"Oh. With that guy?"

I hesitated for a moment. I'd consciously not been talking about him but Luke seemed so relaxed and in such a good mood. And I hated not being open. "Yeah," I said, lightly. "Beckett. He's got some great ideas for my story. I think his next novel might even be better than his first, you know the one I was reading a couple of weeks ago?"

Luke nodded, distracted. "Where do you meet him?"

"Oh, just a little café a few minutes walk from uni." I could tell by the look on Luke's face that perhaps I'd misjudged. "I've been trying to set him up with my favourite barista."

His facial expressions smoothed, and I let out the tension in my shoulders, smiling at the waiter as he placed the olives in the middle of the table.

"Thanks mate." Luke speared one with the toothpick, and I winced. I hated olives.

"Yeah, so Emma – the barista – likes him I think."

"Does he like her?"

A white lie was needed. I had no idea what Beckett was feeling; when it came to romance, he was a closed book. "I think so. We could double date!"

Luke's smile was tight. "I'm not sure I'd feel comfortable going out with the guy who seems to know so much more about you at the moment than me."

"I never said that." I was kind of shocked. It had never crossed my mind that Luke might have been jealous of the intellectual side of my friendship with Beckett.

"I know. It's just hard to admit that there's nothing I can give you when it comes to your book. I want to be everything you need." Another olive speared.

"Well that's why I'm the teacher…" I smirked, my last ditch attempt at distracting him.

"I'll be your student any day."

The mood calmed and lasted throughout dinner. When Luke was in the bathroom, I called aside one of the waiters and asked for the bill. He returned almost immediately.

"Hey. Do I recognise you?" he said. He was young, with slightly longer hair than Luke's and a lanky frame. I did recognise him.

"Oh my gosh this is going to annoy me. Where have I seen you?"

"I've got it!" The guy clapped his hands together. "James College, first year. I knew I'd seen you somewhere. Must have been the dining hall."

"Ah that's right! God, there were so many people having dinner in those halls, I'm sorry I didn't remember you." I couldn't remember his name, but I did at least genuinely remember seeing him whilst we'd all queued up during our allotted meal slots. Catered accommodation had been an easy solution to navigating first year, and it had been a running joke that the food was less than desirable.

"Honestly don't worry about it. Card machine?" I nodded and he went to go and get the machine from the host stand at the front of the restaurant. Luke sat down, raising his eyebrow.

"Did I interrupt something there?"

"No, he just recognised me from halls last year."

"A friend?"

"Not even that. I barely know him."

"I don't want to upset you, but…"

"What?"

"Were you flirting?"

I recoiled. "I definitely wasn't. Just being friendly."

Luke's expression was cynical, but he wiped it clean when the guy came over to the table again, card machine in hand.

"Just stick it all on one card mate. Can I add tip on there?" They chatted briefly for a minute until he walked away, clearly happy with the more than generous tip that he'd been given.

"What?" Luke reached across the table, taking my hand again. I resisted the urge to pull it back, completely and utterly confused at how quickly the conversation kept turning. I could barely keep my head above the water.

"I thought you said I was flirting?"

It clicked. "Yeah but it's not his fault is it?" He was laughing quietly, shaking his head.

"Can we go home now?" Again, the guilt sank its teeth into me. I had no idea how to be what Luke needed me to be lately. Living close to him was beginning to seem much more difficult than I'd originally thought.

For nine pm on a Thursday night, it was weirdly quiet. I'd been banking on the sounds of students and locals to soak up the silence that we'd fallen into. Luke seemed perfectly content to stroll along the streets, swinging my hand, but I felt awkward, unsure what to say. For the first time since he'd arrived in York, I ached to be alone. Snuggled under the covers with one of my favourite books or chatting with Eliza in the kitchen. I definitely didn't want to argue or feel guilty about offending Luke. I was counting down the days until February 12th, when I knew I'd be seeing my sister for the ball. There was nothing that time with my sister couldn't fix, and Eliza had a checklist on her phone of all the quaint coffee shops that she wanted Stella to see. I couldn't wait.

"You're a bit quiet."

"Just thinking." The swinging of our hands was slowing, and we'd turned onto a side street that was actually only a couple of minutes away from The Hideaway. I redirected us the long way back to his flat that passed the old city walls; The Hideaway was mine, and I didn't really feel like sharing it today.

"I don't want to keep arguing with you." The confession slipped out. "I'm still making you happy, aren't I?"

Luke pulled us to a stop, standing opposite with his hands grasping mine. "Of course you're making me happy. I just feel really paranoid at the moment. Like you're constantly flirting with other men and talking about it in front of me. It's not a nice feeling. After all we've been through, I feel like you're shoving everything back in my face."

"I don't think I was flirting in the restaurant, I—"

"You were twirling your hair." *Had I been?* "Every time we watch one of those reality shows and the girl twirls her hair, you tell me it's because she likes the guy. What am I meant to think?"

"I'm sorry that I did that. I honestly didn't intend to. I have all I want right here." I stood on my tiptoes and he reluctantly met me halfway, pressing his lips to mine.

"Do you love me?" He sounded unsure.

"Of course."

"I just need you to say it more." I thought back to all the times I said it; probably ten times a day. "I'm *really* stressed about disappointing my dad and getting everything just right at work. I don't want to be worrying about us as well. You're all I have here, Avery."

I hadn't realised that this was coming from a place of insecurity. It explained a lot.

"I promise, you never have to worry about disappointing me." There were times in our relationship when I'd been stressed about university applications, or my dad, and I was sure I'd been less than delightful to Luke. He'd taken it all, no questions asked. He'd been so good to me, and I at least owed it to him to accept that, right now, things were tough. It wasn't really about me, I knew that. "I've got your back, I promise." I said.

"I know you do." He touched the tip of his nose to mine. "I'm sorry. I'm being such a stress head. It's like everything at the moment is out of my control and I just–"

His breath hitched and he pinched the bridge of his nose.

"Hey, it's okay." I took his hand away. "We're a team, remember? Anything that's bothering you is my burden too. Let me in. Tell me."

"I keep disappointing him." Luke's eyes glistened with the promise of tears.

"Your dad doesn't deserve you."

"I keep doing things wrong. I don't know what I'm supposed to do." He began pacing.

"He doesn't deserve to be your dad." I meant it too. I'd never heard Raymond Calkins say a single nice thing to his son without needing something in return.

Luke sniffed. He looked as though he was steeling himself. Then he turned and smiled tightly at me. "Thanks," he said. "I'm okay now." He pulled me in. "I really appreciate that you understand what I need at the moment."

"Always. I would never intentionally upset you. And I promise that I'm just hanging out with Beckett because it's valuable to my career. I need to do this to know where I'm going wrong with my writing."

Luke stepped away from me, running his hands through his hair. "Will you *stop* mentioning him?! I swear you are trying to get a rise out of me Avery. I don't want to know about you 'hanging out' with another man. I mean. It's like you're actually *trying* to make me go crazy."

I stepped forward to wrap my arms around him and diffuse the situation, aware that this was the product of his stress, but his arms lashed out and he shoved me. I stumbled on a cobble and fell forward, landing on my knees while stopping my fall with my hands. Luke was suddenly panic stricken.

"That wasn't supposed to happen. Oh God." He had rushed forward, anger forgotten in his haste to pull me to my feet. We both stared at the small graze on the heel of my hand. I was so shocked and embarrassed that I was suddenly intensely grateful that it was a quiet night. I wanted to tuck this moment into the depths of my mind and leave it there.

"You pushed me." I knew my eyes were as wide as saucers.

"Listen, we've both had a drink, and I know that we were both upset. But you know I didn't actually push you, right?" He had gone from panic stricken to defensive in sixty seconds.

"But I fell." My voice was small.

"I'm sorry A. I'm so sorry." I was wrapped in his arms, and I tried to stop the tears that were forming. This wasn't Luke. I needed to ride this out until he was someone I recognised again. Someone I loved. "This was just a misunderstanding. Come on, it's been a long night. Let's just go home and forget about all of this. I would *never* hurt you; you know that." It wasn't phrased like a question, but it sounded like one.

I nodded and he breathed out a sigh.

"Let's get that cleaned up as well. I'm sure Mum gave me a first aid kit when I moved in." Luke took my hand, inspecting the blood. "We'll need to use my tweezers to get that piece of grit out. God, you're clumsy. Let's get you home."

I let him whisk me away, in too much of a daze to properly process the last few minutes. I *had* had a couple of glasses of wine. I *was* clumsy. I knew my Luke, and he wouldn't have deliberately pushed me over. I knew that.

"I love you." He kissed my forehead.

I also knew it was probably best not to tell anyone else about this.

Eleven

"I think I saw that internship." My tutor, Alex, started typing away, the light on his monitor blinking.

"I mean it's not set in stone. I was just thinking I might explore what else there is on offer."

"Look." He cut me off. "Teaching is an extremely respectable profession. My wife teaches primary and God only knows she must have the patience of a saint. And it's also great that you want to pursue the career of a writer. From your work, I can tell that you'd make a great one." I could sense a 'but' was coming, so I waited. My conversation with Beckett had been playing on my mind over the past couple of days and the idea of editing other people's writing was tempting enough for me to arrange a meeting with my tutor. Alex wore a trendy bow tie over a white button down, and I would have placed him in his mid-forties. I was lucky that I'd been assigned to his tutorials; everyone knew he was the best in English Lit. If you needed some advice there was no one better to give it to you. I saw Maia coming out of his office at least once a week, her confused expression going in replaced by one of clarity, happy to continue with her coursework.

"Earth to Avery." Alex was smiling at my blank expression.

"Sorry. I can sense there's a 'but' coming?"

"But," he grinned, "I've read your work, and I think you'd be an excellent addition in the editorial profession." When Beckett had said it, I was sure it might have been a case of a friend trying to boost me up. I was surprised that Alex thought I was capable of it too. And after the other night with Luke, it was comforting to think that in at least one area of my life, mistakes were rare.

"Here are a list of internships over the summer." He sent a wry smile my way. "Luckily, our connections here at the English department go far and beyond." Flicking through the list, I recognised a couple of publishing houses that I'd read on the spines of my bookshelf.

It was hard to imagine letting go of my teaching goals. For years, when we discussed the future, that had seemed to be my calling. After doing some research on English Lit alumni, Dad had suggested other careers in passing but I'd been confident in mine and Luke's plans. Besides, the thought of teaching children to love books as much as I did was a welcome one. Between my teaching and Luke training to be an accountant, the future looked bright. Now though, as I sat facing Alex questioning what I thought had been my life plans, I felt strangely okay at the thought of letting them go. Editing sounded like a great fit for me, and was something I could easily pursue in London, as planned. Luke could still train for accountancy – a path his dad had favoured over traditional methods of getting a degree – and I would definitely have opportunities, going by the list Alex had given me. Nothing major had to change for Luke. Just me.

"Reading stories all day everyday doesn't sound like a bad deal." I said, and Alex chuckled, reaching behind him to grab a notebook.

"Your first step towards achieving that is to apply for the internship you mentioned, and as many others on this list that you fit the criteria for. Maybe you could trial edit some work, offer a free service and see how it goes until you find your feet. We actually have a few alumni authors…" He trailed off, looking through a list of contacts, and I saw where it was going. I hadn't mentioned who had led me down the editing trail in the first place.

"I had the pleasure of tutoring one of them myself. Beckett Kearns." Alex stood up and went through his shelves for a moment before snatching out a copy of *Breaking the Surface*. "He sent me a signed copy when he got published last year. A really lovely guy." How had everything managed to come full circle? I'd left it too late to mention that I knew Beckett, so I let Alex chatter on in blissful ignorance. "I think I have a contact number here somewhere. Fantastic student, and an even better writer."

"I think I've seen his book in Waterstones. I'll get in contact with him." I decided to have a little fun. "Who knows, maybe he's writing a new manuscript that he'd like some help with."

"Can't wait to see what that young man does next. One to watch."

I tried to picture Beckett sitting in this same seat three years ago, getting career advice. The thought made me smile.

It wasn't until I'd arrived in York that I'd learned to appreciate a roast dinner in its best form.

"I swear my mouth is watering." Connie looked longingly at the contents behind the glass as we queued up in The York Roast Co. It was our midweek tradition, after catching the 66 bus from campus to the centre of town, stuffing our faces with the Yorkshire pudding wraps before melting into a food coma and spending the rest of the afternoon at either mine or Connie's. Maia's housemates kept to themselves, so we rarely went to hers.

"Veggie?" Connie nudged me pointedly to wake me up from my daydream, moving her eyes from me to the guy standing behind the counter. I blushed and nodded, confirming my order before he passed me and moved onto the rest of my friends. He lingered on Maia's dark eyes and wild black curls a little longer than he had on the rest of us, but she remained oblivious, tapping her meal plan into her smart phone. I'd met Connie and Maia during the first week of university, when we were so terrified by the thought of sitting on our own in the lecture theatre that quite frankly, it would have taken something dramatic for us to reject one another's company; luckily, we'd remained a three ever since.

"Apple sauce or cranberry, apple sauce or cranberry." Connie weighed up the decision with her hands. "You know what, let's live life on the edge. Both."

"That's…interesting." Maia pointed to the fluffy stuffing behind the counter. "As long as there's extra of that in mine, I'm golden."

"Okay, so Maia wants stuffing and I want double sauce. Any special requests Avery?"

"I hold a place in my heart for double helpings of potato."

Maia grinned. "Now *that* is something I can get behind."

We paid and walked up the narrow stairs with trays in hand, the smell of the roast dinner wraps engulfing us.

"I've been dreaming of this since ten am. Was it just me, or was that last lecture about three years long?" Connie spoke through a mouthful.

I settled in beside Maia and unwrapped my lunch. I had forgotten just how much I enjoyed these afternoons with them. It was getting harder to balance seeing my friends on top of seeing Luke as much as he seemed to need.

"Speaking of those poetry lectures, how are you both doing with the three-thousand word count on Tennyson?" Maia was easily the smartest of us, her mind always on some assignment or another. She was also effortlessly cool, even though we made fun of her sci-fi obsession. We'd made predictions over what she might become in the future; Connie had gone bold with the Prime Minister, whilst I had the sneaking suspicion that she would one day take over the position here at York for Head of English. Before Beckett, she'd been my go-to for any queries.

"Ugh. I don't even want to think about that assignment." I pinched the bridge of my nose.

"Yeah you're putting me off my Yorkshire pudding."

"I'll happily have it."

"I know your game Maia," Connie wrapped her hands around her food protectively. "Scare me into giving you the holy grail."

"Seriously though, have you guys even started? It's due in less than two weeks. I've finished drafting, just need to pull my argument together..."

"I think I've written less than a hundred words." As much as I loved Maia, she was a constant reminder of how behind I was falling.

"It's hard to juggle time when you have a Luke." Connie was joking, but it hit home.

"I'm really sorry for bailing on you last week. Life is a bit hectic."

"Honestly," Maia wiped her mouth with a napkin, "don't worry. Connie helped me out designing my outfit for London ComiCon this year. I'm going as Black Widow."

"Yeah, you really missed out there." Connie was deadpan.

"Oh shut up, Con. If I have to listen to you drone on about Dave from the pub, you can help take my measurements for a costume from time to time." Dave was Connie's latest dating attempt; a bartender who had poured her a free pint on her a cappella society bar crawl.

"Anyway, point is, don't stress about missing it. How was your Italian dinner date?"

I looked at Maia, her face open and bright, and hesitated. It would be so easy to vent and get their opinions on what had happened, but I didn't want Luke's name dragged through the mud. "It was great. A perfect evening."

"I think I might ask Dave to take me there."

"How is that going?" If the conversation wasn't on my relationship, I might be able to relax and finish off my lunch.

"I think it's going well, but I say that every time." Connie's laugh wasn't sincere, and I felt a pang of sympathy.

"I'm sure this one will stick."

Maia looked up from her Scrabble app that she'd loaded whilst she waited for us to finish eating. "And if it doesn't, who cares? Any guy would be lucky to have you, and if he doesn't see that then he wasn't worth it in the first place."

We both stared for a minute, stunned.

"What? I may not care about dating personally, but it doesn't mean I don't pay attention."

My phone buzzed on the table, and after seeing the name on my screen, I turned it over, ignoring it. I'd told Luke that this afternoon I had to prioritise my friends.

"You can get that you know." Connie gestured with her wrap to my phone. "It's really buzzing."

Persistently ringing me until I caved in and picked up was an odd quirk that Luke had picked up since he'd moved here. I didn't want to enable it.

"It's nothing."

"Doesn't sound like nothing." Maia had put down her phone and seemed focused on watching mine vibrate on the table.

"Well it is, okay?" My voice was sharper than I intended, and they visibly flinched before swiftly changing the subject to Connie's upcoming date with Dave. I turned over my phone.

12 missed calls. I gritted my teeth.

"Hi everyone."

I jumped, turning around in my seat to see Luke at the top of the stairs.

"Oh." Maia looked at me, clearly trying to see if this was something I'd been expecting. "I didn't know you were joining us."

He scratched his head. "Avery mentioned it earlier, and I've had an awful morning at work. I thought I'd pop by on my lunch break to see if you were here, but if you want me to leave…" Luke wasn't even paying attention to me, instead waiting to see my friends' reaction.

"Go down and get yourself a wrap. We'll wait for you." Connie smiled. "And if you're feeling generous I'd love a Sprite."

He grinned, more comfortable now that he'd been welcomed in. I felt guilty for the anger that was rising in my chest – if he'd had a rough morning, I didn't want to lay it on him as well – but he'd known that today was important. I'd ditched my friends last week for our date and balancing everything was something that mattered to me.

"Yeah, I'll go get one." He wandered off downstairs to order and I smiled weakly at my friends.

"Sorry about this."

"It doesn't matter. Besides, now I get a Sprite without actually having to walk anywhere."

I tried to laugh along with Connie, but my skin still prickled with irritation at the intrusion.

"I think I'm going to go." My friends tried to protest, but I waved them off. "We were almost finished anyway, right? See you tomorrow for our 9am." Connie groaned but Maia smiled, not fazed at the thought of an early seminar.

'If you insist.' Connie smiled and gathered up the rubbish from the table, dumping it in the bin as she grabbed her bag. "Want to go shopping?" she said to Maia.

"Sure." Maia began to collect her things.

Luke was starting to come up the stairs when he saw us coming down. "Let's go," I said.

"But I just bought my food…"

"We can sit outside."

He nodded, handing the can of Sprite to Connie.

"You're a lifesaver, I'm parched. See you guys later."

I followed Luke to the bench by the gardens, watching them wander off without me, Connie animated, Maia listening whilst turning her hair around a finger. When they were out of earshot, I turned to Luke.

"How did you know where to find me?" I played it as lightly as I could, like it was no big deal.

"That new feature on our phones." He spoke through a mouthful of food, and I wished it had been enough for me to question whether I'd heard him right. He'd *tracked my phone?*

"What?" He shrugged. "It's a cool feature. Plus, you weren't picking up your phone again."

"I was out!"

"So?" He was so naturally oblivious about the fact that he'd intruded on my date with my friends that I couldn't hide my irritation. 'Come and sit with me?"

"I don't want to sit with you."

"What?" His words were garbled, mouth full, but his eyes narrowed. "I just wanted to spend time with you. Don't be ridiculous."

"I'm serious. I want to catch up with them and go shopping."

"Avery." He grabbed my arm. "You promised you wouldn't make me feel like the last priority again."

"I feel like I haven't seen my friends enough lately. I had to cancel on them last week when we went out to dinner…"

"Wait. You didn't say anything to them did you? About your fall?"

"Of course not. Do you know how bad that makes us look?"

The grip on my arm tightened. "I know, and I'm sorry. Please come and eat with me. I'm lonely and I walked all the way here on my lunch break to be with you."

I looked up at him. His cheeks were red; from the cold, or anger, I couldn't tell.

"Luke…"

"*Please.* I've been there for you so many times. Please be there for me now. I have no one else." He sensed my indecision. "It's him isn't it? That's why you don't want to spend time with me."

I left it a moment too long to reply, weary from the constant reassurance I was expected to provide. Beckett had nothing to do with what was going on here.

"Oh God. Do you know how hard it is for me to watch you slip away, too preoccupied with other people to pay attention to me?"

"I thought you liked my friends!"

"They're okay."

My head whipped back, hurt that he would insult my friends like that.

"I feel like they're encouraging you to spend less time with me." It was literally the opposite, but I held my tongue. My friends were one of the best parts of living here, and he wanted to take them away? I gritted my teeth.

"I think maybe we need to spend a few days apart." *Had I just said that out loud?* "We need to get used to our new living arrangements, and I don't think spending every day together is working. I don't want to upset you, but I feel like I can't do anything right at the moment."

Luke looked panicked. "Babe, you don't mean that. You can't leave me alone right now. I'm trying to fit into this new city. The same city I moved to in order to be with *you*, remember?"

"I know you did. I love you for that. But I'm stressed at the moment, and I don't think this is healthy–"

"Why are you saying things that I know you don't mean?" He was twisting my arm, but I wasn't sure he even realised he was doing it.

"Would you stop?" I looked down at my arm. "That hurts."

"Sorry, sorry." His eyes welled up. "*Please* come and eat lunch with me. I'll worry otherwise and mess things up this afternoon at work; get in even more shit than I'm already in."

I looked at him, so desperate to spend time with me. Lonely in this life he'd chosen to live for me. My heart broke at the thought of walking away from him.

"Okay."

Twelve

I'd been cleaning the kitchen for about four hours, and it had reached spotless status at about the two-hour mark. I'd made the flat smell like a hospital ward, but I couldn't let my mind drift from the task at hand, so I kept my rubber gloves on and continued to scrub the surfaces. It was surprising that I hadn't yet worn the worktops down to nothing. Eliza was out with some friends so I couldn't pester her, and it was only early afternoon so Stella would be at school. Beckett had been off the radar for the past couple of days, probably stressed about his sister. I couldn't sit on my bed replaying what had just happened with Luke in town one more time because it was starting to drive me crazy. I was stuck; so, I cleaned.

"I'm back!" Eliza's voice chimed through to the kitchen even though it was the last room on the corridor, and I put on what I assumed would look like a normal facial expression. I knew I was overreacting about what had happened, but I was still shaken.

"Hey!" I didn't turn around, but heard her footsteps come to an abrupt stop as she entered the room.

"Where did you hide the body?" At that, I did turn. And for the first time since the episode with Luke in town, I burst out laughing. Cleaning products covered the surfaces and the floor was still wet; it looked exactly like a clean-up act. "You did wipe the door handles didn't you? That always catches people out." Her face was completely serious until she burst out laughing too, and I resisted the urge to reach out and hug her. I didn't want her to know I was upset.

"I just thought the place was starting to get a bit on the dirty side." I shrugged, pulling the gloves off and putting the mop back into the bucket.

"Whatever you say." She tiptoed past the damp spots, making her way to the fridge and grabbing an apple. I was so on edge I could practically feel the tension keeping my neck rigid. *Was it obvious?* I smoothed my hair down.

"How was your lunch?"

She chewed. "It was good, we ended up at that cute café you write at actually. I was hoping I'd catch a glimpse of Beckett writing away, but I didn't. How was yours?"

"Good." I didn't elaborate, and because she was quite content to relay the contents of her panini, she didn't push.

"Are you seeing Luke tonight?" She was sorting through her shopping bags on the table. I was glad she was occupied, because I was unsure how to respond.

"No." I busied myself with the cloth in my hand; anything to keep from looking over. I felt my shoulders relax as Eliza kept talking, the knot in my neck smoothing until there was no tension remaining. I desperately wanted

Eliza and Luke to be as close to each other as I was to each of them; what had been going on lately might put a spanner in the works. As long as I didn't let it slip, I could fix things with Luke and everything could go back to normal.

But in the meantime, I needed something different. Separate. I needed to be away from everything that reminded me of the tangles that was rapidly becoming my relationship.

The front door was cold against my knuckles as I debated whether or not to actually go through with this. Would Beckett think it was weird to show up unannounced? His presence in my life was calming and, right now, I needed some of that. So I knocked. And held my breath. About ten seconds passed and I felt my skin flush with embarrassment at the thought that he might have seen me outside and decided not to answer. The floor creaked from just inside the flat and I waited a couple of seconds before turning to go. There was even an old school peephole on the door – there was no doubt in my mind that he'd seen me.

"Let me, let me!" The voice was small and muffled, but it was obviously coming from the other side of the door. It opened slowly, like the person on the other side was struggling underneath its weight, and just like magic, a little girl stood in front of me. Her face peered from behind the door, and I recognised her instantly. Beckett was babysitting.

"My name is Lola." She was wearing a t-shirt with a unicorn emblazoned on it, with a matching tulle skirt. I could imagine that this was an outfit she'd picked out herself, but the half-hearted attempt at braiding her blonde curls made me smile. That was all him. I bent down to her level.

"My name is Avery." Lola reached out a finger to touch the long braid running over my shoulder.

"Rapunzel." She said it under her breath, but it was audible enough that I heard someone stand up from further inside the flat.

"I thought Rapunzel had blonde hair," I said.

Lola put her hands on her hips. "But it was *looooong* hair. Like yours." She let out a breathy sigh. "Rapunzel."

"And all this time you've been telling me that your name is Avery." Beckett pulled the door open further and smiled wide at me, glancing down to see what his niece was doing. She was staring right back up at him, and it made me want to grab a camera.

"I was just passing through." My gaze went to the window, as if to suggest that I'd been on my way to the café. "And wanted to check that you were still alive." Beckett smiled at that, like the thought of my detour pleased him.

"Well, do come in Emerson, we're about to have a tea party." He gave a grand gesture towards the living room, where I could see the table was laden with treats and a teapot – a stark contrast to the layers of A4 that I'd seen covering it last. His laptop was open on the kitchen counter, and I could see some notes on the screen, but clearly other priorities had taken precedence. "Aren't you going to invite our guest inside Lola?"

Despite not knowing me in the slightest, Lola grinned. "Come in, Rapunzel." She skipped over to the table and extended her tiny hands into a toy box, pulling out a plastic tiara, which she offered to me as I stepped inside. This wasn't what I'd been expecting when I'd made the spontaneous plan to visit Beckett, but it suddenly felt like exactly what I needed. Pink paper plates were set at each seat (there were way more seats than humans, but I'd clocked the teddies that had been set up alongside the feast). Sandwiches had been cut into heart shapes with a cookie cutter that was still lying on the counter, and cookies from the bakery downstairs were set neatly on a plate placed in the centre. I noted that they were the cookies with rainbow smarties dotted throughout, and I couldn't imagine they had been Beckett's choice. Lola guided me to a seat next to Beckett and started pouring from the teapot into small plastic cups. I stifled a smile when I saw that it was blackcurrant juice instead of tea, but Beckett caught on and winked at me.

"I don't think Lucy would have thanked me for loading a three-year-old up on caffeine." The way he acted towards his niece was endearing; his nature was gentle, and he had a way of talking to her that was tactical, and yet didn't patronise her.

"Don't you think you should introduce our other guests?"

Lola looked up at him with wide eyes and then pointed to a big fluffy bear that was sat in the seat next to her.

"This is Steve." I laughed out loud at the thought of the man who broke my family as an overweight, over-fluffy bear but Lola frowned slightly before turning back to her tea and I bit my lip.

"Never question Steve." Beckett's expression was faux-serious, and I was again so happy to be there – it was a much better alternative to scrubbing the kitchen floor.

"Hi Steve." I shook his paw to try and reconcile my new friendship with a three-year-old, and she smiled, pleased.

"I know your name is Avery." She tilted her head. "But you do have long hair like Rapunzel." We both laughed at that, and I picked up a cookie, grinning at Lola and chatting to her about her other bears. This family had a way of making me feel just right. And when I looked at the table laden with sugary goodies, and then at Beckett making sure my plate was constantly full, I couldn't help but smile.

Lola was sat in the corner of the room practicing her 'finger painting', a concept I had long forgotten since the days of nursery and pinning pieces of artwork on the washing line in our back garden. Beckett was sitting at the kitchen counter, trying to go over some notes with me whilst she was preoccupied. It was obvious that babysitting duty offered no mercy when it came to work.

"How long do you have her for?" I traced my fingers through some sugar that remained on the table from our tea party, which had come to an abrupt end once Lola spilt blackcurrant down her unicorn t-shirt. There'd been a moment of chin-wobbling that suggested a full-on meltdown, but Beckett had jumped into action and changed the outcome before the tears actually began to fall. Apparently finger painting and a cuddle from Steve was all you really needed to counteract sadness. I wished it was that easy.

"Lucy dropped her off yesterday so she could spend a few days with her new boyfriend." I waited whilst he paused. "I've just got my fingers crossed that it all works out. I want her to be happy, but I'm always concerned about this little pixie." He pointed to Lola, who was singing to herself. Behind the façade he was putting on, I could tell he was stressed out, maybe for his sister, maybe partially due to the upcoming deadline for his manuscript. There was no way he'd have been able to wear a tiara like mine; he was running his hands through his hair too often. I'd assured him that he could take a break from helping me in order to focus on his own work, but he had waved me off, telling me he was too invested in my story to abandon it now.

"Anyway. What *does* bring you here?" He hadn't really looked up from his screen, but when he asked the question his eyes flicked upwards to meet mine. I'd been afraid that eventually he was going to ask this; I was probably outstaying my welcome by this point. Just for a couple more hours I wanted to pretend I didn't have anything to sort out in my mind.

"Nothing really. I just wondered how you were doing." He smiled.

There was a feeling in my stomach that wouldn't go away, no matter how many cookies I ate or how many bears I was introduced to. I'd looked down at the floor without realising, and my answer couldn't have been convincing enough, because Beckett reached out and gently touched my arm. I flinched without thinking. Beckett moved his hand back like a shot, and I could see confusion settling in his eyes, along with a hint of anger. His touch had been nothing but gentle, but it had unsettled me.

"I'm sorry…I…"

"Has something happened Avery?" Gone was the usual joking demeanor, or my nickname, and I couldn't believe I'd been so transparent. I had thought that after passing the Eliza inspection I was golden.

"I'm fine, promise." I sent him what I was sure would look like a convincing smile, and turned away, ending the conversation and going to look at Lola's finger painting creation. It was a little shaky, four stick people sat around a square (the fourth I assumed to be Steve). An imaginative depiction of a teapot was sat between us, and a rainbow perched above our heads.

"Steve wanted to be a person today." She said it matter-of-factly whilst tucking an escaping tendril of hair behind her ear. I smiled at Beckett, who was close enough to hear her comments, but he was staring at me, as if for the first time, he couldn't figure me out.

Thirteen

After a tense week, it was a relief to be gossiping and drinking wine with my best friend. Eliza had been busy lately too, between dance practice and time with Jack, so even if I'd wanted to talk to her about Luke, there wouldn't have been time. That was what I kept telling myself anyway.

"Less than two weeks until the ball." Eliza used her straw to stab the glacier cherry. "Stella called me yesterday to show me three different pairs of shoes."

"She keeps texting me photos of dresses." I got out my phone, showing Eliza.

"I like that yellow one," she said. "Have you got a dress yet? My ball is a couple of days after yours and I still need to find something. Hmm... I know!" She wiggled her eyebrows.

"You are so predictable."

"Shopping trip?"

Eliza's favourite thing in the world was a shopping trip. It didn't matter whether it was the food shop or dress shopping, she could psych herself up for it and be hyper the entire time.

"Am I subjecting myself to hours of dresses?"

"Yes. And you don't have a choice."

"Great."

We settled into easy conversation, like always. It was refreshing to be out with my best friend, away from the stresses that Luke was bringing to my life.

"Did I tell you I met Lola, Beckett's niece?" Even though Eliza had only met Beckett once, she constantly asked about him and the progress we were making, both in our writing and our blossoming friendship. I wasn't the only one intrigued by him.

"Was she cute?"

I sipped my wine. "The cutest. It was so nice to see that side of Beckett. I mean, he's nice to everyone that he meets, but with her he's so gentle. And he speaks to her like an adult, not like the three-year-old that he's babysitting."

"I want to meet her. In fact, I want to meet *him* again. I don't like you having a secret life from me." She waggled her finger at me. "Kidding. But he was kind of cute, in a Brainiac sort of way."

"I thought you were smitten with Jack?" She'd been talking about him non-stop, and I knew she'd met him on campus a couple of times. On the one occasion they'd ventured out of the university, he'd taken her roller skating, and when she'd shown me a video clip of him falling all over the place I knew he'd done it to satisfy her athletic side. It didn't take a genius to realise that Eliza couldn't sit still for long, and it was nice that he'd clearly considered it. I approved.

"I *am* a bit smitten." She bit her lip. "I've never felt like this before. Mum rang me yesterday to check in and I couldn't bear to tell her that I was dating seriously. You know what she'd say." An eye roll ensued, before she paid attention to her cocktail again.

"Well I like him. He only took the yellow gummy bears."

"A glowing recommendation. I was thinking about inviting him round and cooking dinner, but I just know I'll be a bundle of nerves. Can you invite Luke over, for an impromptu double date? I'll owe you one for the rest of time."

"That's a long time."

"Imagine how many breakfasts in bed you could get in that amount of time. I'll bring one piece of toast with marmalade, one with jam, just how you like it." She knew that she was offering up something I'd find hard to refuse. "Plus, I want to see Luke more. You're always in your bedroom. I feel like he's shy, maybe this will bring him out of his shell."

She probably couldn't understand why I was hesitating. I was wary of his unpredictability lately, but although she didn't quite know the truth, she was onto something. Maybe a dinner date would ease his worries.

"Come on, you know you want to. Jack loves economics, and you know Luke loves to talk money. They're a match made in bromance heaven."

She was pulling a puppy dog face, willing me to say yes. The only thing holding me back was the fear that he might behave irrationally. I didn't want Eliza to think anything was wrong, but the longer I took to reply, the more her face fell.

"Is it Jack? Please tell me you like him."

"Of course it isn't Jack."

She blinked slowly.

"Fine, I'm sold. Tell me the night and I'll be there. I'm holding you to the toast deliveries though."

"Toast for the rest of the *year* I promise. You're the best. Can you help me figure out what to cook? You know you're better at it. My attempts at cooking are way too unpredictable."

"How about something simple? A pasta? You might need to make a separate one for yourself, I know Luke isn't vegan, and I imagine Jack isn't either."

"You're so right! He won't want to eat courgetti, he hates veggies. See? What would I do without you?"

I rolled my eyes. "He clearly fancies you so much I imagine it wouldn't matter if you served him canned soup. When are we having this dinner party?"

"Hmm, I need a couple of days to get the ingredients together and figure out something to wear. The day after tomorrow? Friday?"

"That's perfect. Luke will have finished work for the week."

As we chatted, ordering more drinks, I hoped that meant he would be in a better mood than he had been in lately. I had no idea what we'd do on a double date if he wasn't.

***

I kicked my shoes off, falling onto my bed and pulling up the internship application. There were about ten questions of varying length, and I figured it would take me most of the morning to answer them to my best ability. The dinner date was tomorrow and I still hadn't asked Luke, putting off the inevitable when we had arrived back at our flat last night and instead staying up with Eliza, eating cheese toasties and watching *Friends* until we fell asleep. Now, I couldn't really put it off any longer. I opened my phone to type out the text, and weirdly, it started ringing.

"Hello?"

"Hi honey! I wasn't sure if you'd answer. I live in permanent fear that I might call you in the middle of a lecture." Dad was clearly doing something in the kitchen at the same time as holding the phone up to his ear. I could hear clattering in the background, and the kettle was on.

"Hey! Haven't spoken to you in a while, how are things?"

"Stella is counting down the days until she comes up to visit. Promise you'll meet her straight off the train? I don't want her wandering around on her own."

I stifled a laugh. "She's fifteen."

"Fifteen is still too young to feel disconcerted in a new city." Stel had visited lots of times, but it was Dad's prerogative to be overprotective. I think he was making up for the fact that when I was fifteen, he was too busy mending his broken heart to be overbearing with me.

"She tells me you're applying for an internship? Well, she mentioned it briefly before she ran off for school this morning. That girl is never on time for anything."

"That's so weird, I was literally just sitting down to start my application."

The kettle had stopped boiling now, and I imagined him pouring the water into his mug. "Don't let me interrupt you if you're busy. I was just in between jobs and thought I'd check in on you."

"It's okay, I hadn't got stuck into anything. It's an internship for a publishing house. I've been writing with this local author, and he thinks I'd be good at editing. Alex – my tutor – says the same."

"You know –" There was a crunch, which I presumed was his custard creams. "– I saw that a York alumni had gone on to do that. I'm so proud of you, whether you get it or not. It's important to explore your opportunities. Tell me about the writer! Stel hasn't really mentioned that to me."

I hadn't told Stella too much about Beckett, instead waiting until she came up. "His name is Beckett Kearns. I can send a copy of his book to the house if you fancy reading it."

"You know it might take me the rest of the year to get through it but send it over. Anything one of your friends has written is interesting to me. Did he go to York?"

I smiled, knowing that what I was about to say would make my dad excited. "Yep."

"*How* did I miss that during my searches? Milk him for all he's worth, Avery – you never know what doors he might be able to open for you." For someone that, until Mum had left, had never been the one going to parents' evenings or reading over essays, Dad had really risen to the occasion. I never detected a hint of frustration when he couldn't understand my university essays. During Christmas, when I'd had three due, he'd sat in his armchair and read every single one. The dictionary was always on the table beside him, just in case, and he quietly got on with it, sometimes reading sections four times until he understood what I was talking about.

"So, Stella tells me that the neighbour keeps flirting with you Dad." It was probably off limits, but I was intrigued.

"I swear your sister keeps trying to play cupid. The woman is lovely, but I'm just not interested. I've grown to like my own company, you know that."

"I do but–"

"I'm quite content with my beans on toast and *Match of the Day*. You're starting to sound like Stella."

There was a tone in his voice that suggested he was tired of having his private life poked around in. Dad had gotten over my mother, that was clear, but I think his experience with her had wearied him for life.

"I get it Dad. I'll try and come home sometime in the next month or so. You better have plenty of custard creams in the cupboard when I do."

"You betcha kiddo. I'll let you get back to your application. Feel free to send me a copy to read over before you send it off. I know I'm only an electrician, but I did get some qualifications back in my day."

I wanted so badly to reach through the phone and give him a hug. "You know I value your opinion more than anyone else's, Dad." We said goodbye and hung up, the smile still on my face when I pulled the papers onto my lap, opening my laptop screen. Dad never failed to remind me how far we'd come; him more than anyone.

Luke: Why aren't you answering? I'm trying to get through to you.

The smile was wiped clean from my face. I'd been about to text him about tomorrow night, but seeing his possessive text, I hesitated. I'd caught him looking over my shoulder to read my texts a few times now, and the paranoia was eroding my sympathy for the stress he said he was under.

Eliza poked her head into my room. "Was that your dad on the phone?"

"Yup."

"Aw I'm sorry I missed saying 'hi'. Quick question."

I looked up at her. She had an apron on, and flour all over her face. "If my cake had turned out like a flatbread, you know, hypothetically."

I raised my eyebrows. "You might have used the wrong flour."

"Oh shit, you're right." She stamped her foot lightly against the wooden floor. "I mean, you *would* have been right, had I made that mistake. See ya." She skipped back down the hall. I looked back at my phone, fingers poised over the keys to invite Luke to the dinner party. As if he could read my mind, my phone rang.

"Hello?"

"Baby, hi. Who were you on the phone to just now?"

"My dad." I was being blunt, and Luke could sense it.

"Hey, don't be short with me like that. I just like to know why I can't get through to you. It panics me when you don't answer."

"If I can't speak to my dad for ten minutes, what am I supposed to do?"

"I mean, if you know I'm about to finish work, just tell me you're too busy to call. I always try and call you on my way home from work."

My head was in my hands as I hung up, ending the conversation as quickly as I could. I felt like I was on a leash.

Tomorrow, for one night, I just wanted to have a laugh with some friends. I tapped back onto my home screen and opened up a different chat.

Me: Eliza is having a dinner party for her new beau and needs moral support. You in?

There was a reply almost instantly. I imagined him sat at his desk by the window, surrounded by dirty mugs and handwritten notes. It was practically a favour to get him out of his writing space for one night.

Beckett: A meal that doesn't involve a microwave? Do you really need to ask?

I put the phone down and got back to my application, ignoring the sinking feeling in my stomach that I'd let Luke down. Maybe I'd suggest going out for coffee with him later in the week, when we'd both had time to miss each other. Right now, it felt smothering, but in a few days, I knew I'd want to see Luke again.

Fourteen

Eliza was bouncing on her tiptoes, unable to sit still even though *Countdown* was on; her guilty pleasure. She'd disappeared a few hours earlier for an 'emergency' shopping trip, and from a glance in her doorway, it looked like her entire wardrobe had been emptied onto her pink, fluffy rug. It was amusing to see her this nervous to have a boy over.

"Sit down would you? We still have ten minutes before they're even supposed to be here."

"I can't. Does my hair look okay?" She smoothed it over for at least the tenth time, and I held back from saying that it wouldn't matter if she'd dragged herself through a hedge backwards, Jack would still be interested. She'd been messaging him all day, even when we'd been sat in the library, supposedly working. Beckett hadn't texted, but I knew he would show up. He was so far into his manuscript that writing anything else, even a text, probably freaked him out. Luke had been messaging constantly, even dropping by this morning when I was on my way out to uni. We were on good terms again, like I knew we would be, but I was still glad that I'd invited Beckett. Eliza needed stable moral support, and with Beckett around, I knew we could provide it.

"Your hair looks beautiful. Now would you come and watch this? I don't put it on for the good of my health."

"How can you be so *calm*?"

"Because it's just dinner. Pasta, some conversation, maybe…" I paused dramatically, "even some music."

I hadn't been banking on anything else.

Jack had brought a bunch of red roses, which I'd taken from Eliza and put in water, immediately clocking onto how much my best friend's hands were shaking. Once the initial introductions were over she'd fallen back into her usual constant chattering, and was now busying herself at the hob. Jack was standing beside her with his arms crossed over the front of his smart white shirt, clearly nervous himself.

When Beckett arrived and was introduced, he quickly picked up on the vibe too; so, to give them some space, we'd moved to sit next to each other at the table and started talking about Lola.

"She's coming to stay again next week and she's been pestering over FaceTime for another tea party with you. It seems that you made quite the impression."

"A three-year-old who loves bears and cupcakes? It was hardly mission impossible."

"I don't think you realise how quickly Lola can decide that she doesn't like someone's company. One wrong move and you're out." He mimed cutting his own throat.

"That is so gruesome."

"What can I say? It isn't all tiaras in Lola-land." Beckett gestured to the kitchen, where we could hear Eliza laughing as she plated up the pasta dish she'd been stressing over all day. "I thought Eliza was a commitment-phobe."

"She is." I leaned in so that there was no chance I would be overheard. "This is a first."

"Wow, and we have front row seats? I knew this was a better plan than sitting at my desk and pulling my hair out."

"Tough chapter?"

"Tough *book*. Anyway, I need a night off from it. I can't stop looking at that stack over there. Impressive." He'd been staring at all the books on our living room floor. I knew that feeling, to want so desperately to run your fingers over the loved spines of favourite books. All of my favourite characters were kept close to me, easily accessible if I ever had a quiet afternoon. It had been extremely difficult to transfer the number of books I wanted to take with me from Westby to York, but Dad had been convinced that it was doable, and it had been.

Beckett was crouched in front of the stack now and I waited for his verdict. If he was about to bash one of my favourites, I'd axe him quicker than Lola would.

"There are darknesses in life and there are lights, and you are one of the lights, the light of all lights."

I met his gaze, shocked at the way his voice stirred something up in the pit of my stomach. Beckett remained oblivious to my emotions; he smiled and held up his book of choice. "*Dracula*. When I was a kid this scared the living crap out of me." I burst out laughing and he shook his head. "No seriously, I couldn't keep my head outside the bedcovers." I did *not* want to think about Beckett and bedcovers. I did not, I did not, I did not.

"I can't imagine you being frightened of a book."

"Ah yes, because I am so macho now." He laughed at his own joke. "Believe me, ten-year-old Beckett had to sleep with the light on for weeks." Aside from the fact that it was extremely impressive to read at that level at ten years old, it was also so endearing to hear him admit to it. It was refreshing. I tried to picture the man in front of me at that small age, a little boy surrounded by too many words to know what to do with. I'd been terrified of *Dracula* too, and I'd had to sleep in my parents' bed for a couple of nights, tucked up in my safe place. It fascinated me; the effect that printed pages bound together could have on our day-to-day lives.

"Is this?" Beckett squinted. "Oh my God it is." He picked up *Breaking the Surface* from the stack. "You definitely planted this here to flatter me."

"I did not." We were both laughing now.

"You're telling me, that these both belong in the same book stack?" He held up his book next to my battered copy of *To Kill a Mockingbird* that I'd been reading at The Hideaway when we first met.

"They're special to me." I shrugged, but Beckett turned away, smiling.

"You believe in my writing a lot more than I do."

"That's what friends are for."

"It is." He looked back at me and in that moment, I was suddenly aware of something different. His eyes seemed darker, glinting with warmth and delight in the candlelight.

"Dinner is served!" We both jumped at Eliza's voice as she strode in carrying the biggest bowl of pasta I'd ever seen. I felt a shot of guilt. As though I'd been caught in the act of something very, very wrong. I leapt up and started to move things out of the way on the table to make space for the pasta bowl. "I tried to make a garlic bread as well but it's a bit burnt…wait. Are you two alright? You both look like you've seen a ghost."

Beckett said "No ghosts," just as I said "We're fine!" and Beckett's laugh was so relaxed that I wondered if I'd imagined it. That all those accusations from Luke had made me start to think things that weren't real.

"This is really good." Beckett had flown through the dish Eliza had put together, and Jack didn't seem to be too far behind. My guest seemed to bring an element of serenity to the double 'date' (if Luke found out that Eliza was calling it that, he'd flip). Beckett had a stream of conversation topics and, despite being a bookworm, tried to talk about things he knew would draw everyone in. I could tell Eliza was grateful for the effort.

"So, who wants more?" She tucked her hair behind her ears and picked up the serving spoon, passing more to Jack, who had his plate held out.

"If I eat any more I might explode." I patted my stomach.

"Wimp." Beckett grinned and held out his plate to Eliza as well.

A knock at our door startled me enough to drop my fork. I leant down to get it at the same time as Beckett, and we bumped heads.

"You know, that was very cliché." Beckett grinned at me, but I couldn't smile back. The second knock at our door in as many seconds confirmed what I'd been thinking. I knew I should have invited him to the dinner party. Of course he would show up unannounced.

"Who is it?" Eliza popped her head back in from the kitchen where she'd gone to get more beer.

"I'll be right back." I headed down the hallway trying to think of scenarios but he was going to know as soon as he saw my red dress that I was doing something worth barging in on. I peered through the frosted glass to see Luke's face on the other side. I hadn't been wrong. This was about to become a nightmare of epic proportions.

"Are you going to stand there forever." Luke poked the glass. "Or let me in?"

Down the hall, Eliza called out. "Is that Luke? I'll grab an extra plate!"

I'd make up an excuse to Eliza about why Luke hadn't been able to come; a games night with his flatmate, even though I knew they'd barely spoken ten words to each other in the entire month they'd lived together. Now I was facing the moment that Eliza realised I'd made it all up, when I'd have to think of another lie to get myself out of the first one.

"Hi! What are you doing here?" I opened the door and let Luke in, and he kissed me slowly.

"Just thought I'd drop in and see my girl. I brought you these to say sorry for how annoying I've been lately." In his hand was a box of truffles. I instantly felt shame for being so irritated with his behaviour. He was trying his best.

"Thank you." I touched my nose to his and he grabbed my waist.

"Wait, why are you so dressed up?" I felt like I might burst into tears.

"Eliza decided to cook dinner for a few friends tonight. She's going to grab a plate for you to join in." Hopefully, this would lessen the blow that he hadn't been invited in the first place. I'd been waiting for a good opportunity for Luke and Beckett to meet, but this really wasn't shaping up to be a great one.

"Cool, is her new boyfriend here?" He was trying to look into the kitchen.

"If you call him that in front of them both, they'll die on the spot."

"Noted. Shall we go in?"

I hesitated.

"What's wrong with you?" Luke shook his head at me and led the way to the table where Jack was sat, oblivious, and Beckett was bolt upright, sensing my unease already.

And there it was.

Luke's eyes were straight on Beckett. There was a moment. He looked at me and then he looked back at Beckett but when he spoke his voice gave nothing away. "You must be the writer."

He'd covered up his reaction so perfectly that only I had noticed, I was sure. I resented the fact that he hadn't used the name that I knew I'd told him, but at least he hadn't just punched him. Silver linings.

"It's Beckett. Nice to meet you." Beckett had stood up to shake Luke's hand and kept trying to meet my eyes, but I couldn't do it. All I'd wanted was to have a night away from the unpredictability of Luke, but now he was here, it looked as though I'd had different motives. But if Luke thought that, he wasn't letting it be public knowledge. As he said hello to Eliza and was introduced to Jack, he smiled and joked. I'd expected fireworks, but he was eerily calm. Happy even.

"What are we eating?" Luke grabbed one of the stools from the kitchen and sat between me and Beckett, "This smells amazing." He took the plate from Eliza. "I really appreciate you feeding me. If I'd known I'd be interrupting—" He looked at me and my stomach sank.

"No worries mate." Jack passed him a beer. "I've been waiting to meet you anyway. All Avery does is harp on about you."

Thank God for Jack. I threw him a 'thank you' glance across the table as Luke squeezed my leg gently beneath the table.

"This is delicious," he said tucking into his pasta and I watched him with all my fingers crossed that he would behave himself.

My bedroom door slammed behind me.

For the first half an hour since Luke had arrived the evening had carried on without any issues. Luke being his usual fun self, holding my hand underneath the table and stroking it gently like he used to when we were out together in groups. It was like nothing had ever happened and so I relaxed. Maybe I'd imagined those looks when he'd arrived. Maybe he'd understood that I hadn't meant to hurt him tonight.

"So, Beckett" Luke had said to him almost as soon as he'd sat down. "I hear you've been helping Avery with her writing. It's great isn't it?"

Every time I'd offered up my work for some beta reading, Luke had promised that he would do it later. He'd never got around to it, as far as I was aware.

"Yeah, it's great. I think she'll do amazing things with her writing."

Luke frowned. "As a teacher, right," he said with a definite edge to his voice.

Beckett quickly looked at me, knowing not to mention the internship if I hadn't yet.

"Avery will make a great teacher. Anyway, I don't want to speak about her when she's sitting next to me."

Luke laughed. "You're right. Sorry, babe." And he'd squeezed my hand again.

It was only when Eliza had stood, Jack following behind with a stack of empty plates in his hands, to start dessert, and Beckett, Luke and I had been left in awkward silence, that I realised how wrong I'd been.

"Can I steal her for a few minutes," he'd said to Beckett, his grasp of my hand tightening.

"Of course." Beckett had been awkward, staring at the tea lights in the centre of the table.

And then, as soon as he shut the door to my room, the truth was out.

"Why didn't you say anything about tonight?" Luke stood right in front of me so I had to look him in the eyes. My red dress made me feel too exposed; like I *had* been hiding a secret within this dinner party, and my skin prickled with guilt. I was aware of how it must look to him, from the outside. *From the outside.* When had he stopped being on the *in*side?

"I'm so sorry. Eliza decided to have dinner with Jack and she needed moral support, and things have been tense between us recently…" I trailed off, flustered.

"I don't understand why you would rather have him here than me." The word '*him*' curled on his lips like an insult. "What is that guy's deal anyway?"

"His deal?" I was genuinely perplexed. Beckett had been nothing but civil the entire time.

"That cringey 'artist' look. Messy hair, creased shirt. Does he think he's some sort of artsy heart-throb?" Luke's laugh was dripping with malice.

"I don't think he means it like that." I crossed my arms. "It's just how he is."

"Defending him now are we?"

"Well he's hardly here to do it himself! He's my friend, and I don't want to be rude. I'm sorry I offended you, but I really just wanted a night with friends." I moved to walk to the door but Luke's arm hooked around my waist, pulling me back.

"Luke, let me leave." His grip on my waist tightened, and I gasped. "Seriously, that hurts."

"We're in the middle of a conversation."

"Can we just go back out? This doesn't need to be a big deal. Let's just go back and eat dessert."

"How can you even say that?" He eyes begged me to understand. "Avery you're leaving me behind."

"I'm not Luke. I'm trying to build a life in York with my friends, *and* you."

"Why am I not your first choice? You will always be mine."

"Don't make this into something it isn't."

"You still invited him to a dinner party over me."

He had me in a loophole. It was cruel of me to leave him out and choose my new friend over someone that had been my everything for so many years. I knew that, and yet... Did I deserve this?

"I know how it looks. I should've thought." I sought out his eyes. "I'm sorry, Luke."

"God, that's beginning to sound very inadequate. I've turned my whole life upside down for you and you're *sorry?*" He laughed, incredulously, shaking his head at me. "I need your help, Avery. You looked after your sister and your dad when they needed you. Now it's my turn. This is *my* turn to need *you.*"

I swallowed. He had me. When he leaned down to kiss me, I didn't refuse him.

The first time Luke had ever kissed me, it had felt like fireworks. He'd brought a blanket to the beach and we'd sat on the sand, ignoring the cold, excited to be in the moment. I didn't feel fireworks like that right now. All I felt was that something bad was about to happen.

"How can I go back out there now? Everyone knowing you didn't want me here." He shook his head and I couldn't help but reach out for him. "I didn't move to York to look like a fool."

"You don't look like a fool," I said, trying to placate him.

"We both know that isn't true. You exclude me from your life, you spend time with everyone but me. It's embarrassing. Do you think I'm always going to hang around, waiting?"

My throat tightened. I knew we were struggling, but had I pushed him away *that* much?

A tear ran down my cheek and before I had the chance to hide it, I saw him soften. "I'm sorry. Of course, I won't leave. I've got you. You can trust me. It's these people trying to split us apart. They're getting into your head, and you're letting it happen."

I felt my heart break. Looking into those eyes that were so familiar but hearing things that I couldn't understand. Didn't *want* to understand. If I could just see beyond them, to the man who was my best friend. He was angry and upset. This wasn't him. He didn't talk like this. I wanted the chance to get back to what we'd had in the past.

"Avery?" His hand gripped my arm. "Talk to me. Tell me what's wrong." When I looked away, he caught my chin, holding it firm, almost daring me to move. For the first time in our relationship I suddenly felt trapped and a bubble of panic began to rise in my throat. "We can't leave each other now, you hear me? We need to stick together, like always."

A knock on my bedroom door. "Everything okay in there? Dessert is ready!" Eliza's voice was bright, none the wiser.

"All's fine!" Luke's voice was so upbeat that I did a double take. "We'll be out in a second."

Maybe, if I acknowledged our problems, we could work on them. Work on us.

"We're not fine." It came out almost as a whisper, and a part of me wished that I could immediately snap my fingers and take the words back, coax them between my lips like the confession had never occurred. We weren't fine, and I could tell by the flicker of fear that crossed his eyes that he knew I meant it.

"Don't be stupid." He paced, running his hands through hair that I realised so badly needed a cut. "We're fine. It's your new," he made quotation marks in the air, "*friend* that isn't."

"Beckett has done nothing wrong. *I've* done nothing wrong."

Luke spun around and pointed his finger at me. "You invited him, when you should have invited me."

"I invited a *friend* Luke." He grabbed my arm again, this time hard enough to make my eyes water. This wasn't my boyfriend of four years. This wasn't us.

"I love you. Do you hear me?" His hair had fallen over one of his eyes, but the other was enough for me to see his anger as well as feel it.

"I hear you." I hated how fragile I sounded as I twisted to try and free myself from his grasp.

"Good," he said. He looked at me for a moment longer and then dropped my arm. "They'll be getting suspicious," he said before snatching a cardigan from the back of my door. "Put this on. That dress is inappropriate."

I wrapped myself in the wool, my arm stinging, glad to cover the marks I could feel blooming.

"Sorry, Eliza!" he said, as he walked out of my room. "Hope we didn't ruin dessert."

I was a couple of seconds behind, staying to glance in the mirror and wipe away the mascara tracks.

"I tried to make chocolate melts. Like a cake, pudding, hybrid kind of thing?" Eliza cocked her head at the attempt. "It will be a miracle if there is actually anything remotely melty in the middle of these."

"Looks good to me regardless." Luke smiled wide, grabbing a scoop from the middle of the table. "Ice cream anyone?"

I had moved seats, putting some distance between me and Beckett. Beckett was watching Luke, his eyes flickering back to my face.

"It's not a problem, me being here tonight?" He leaned over when Luke had left the table to get more beers.

"He's just stressed." When I smiled back, it was the first genuine expression I'd worn since stepping out of my bedroom.

"Work?"

I nodded, and Beckett turned back to the dessert, seemingly satisfied knowing that he hadn't caused any conflict. Luke might have wanted me to tell him the truth, make him uncomfortable enough to leave, but I didn't want that. He brought more calm to an atmosphere than anyone I'd met.

As everyone chattered on through the night, going through the wine and beers we had in our fridge, I smiled in all the right places, trying to ignore the ringing in my ears. I felt an overpowering sense of discomfort, like I had no idea what to do. I hadn't felt this way since the day Mum had left, standing on the doorstep watching her car drive off. Rubbing my eyes like it might have been a dream, or a nightmare, like she might run in and tell us that it was all a joke. She hadn't, and I'd walked back inside to face a hysterical Stella and a deadly silent father that I didn't recognise. I'd felt so lost, and despite everything, all I'd wanted was my mum.

Time passed and I vowed to never think those thoughts again, but here I was, four years later. Sat at a dinner table with a boyfriend that I couldn't do right by, and despite my best interests, was starting to scare me. Sitting next to a new friend that was starting to blur the lines. And all I wanted, all I needed, was a hug from my mum.

Fifteen

"We both know it's your best colour. Try it on, would you?" Eliza wasn't looking directly at me, just holding the hanger adamantly in one hand whilst she perused the rest of the rack, attempting to find a perfect dress for me to wear to the ball. When I didn't reach to take the long, red dress from her she finally glanced up and tried to shove it into my hands. "Luke practically bugged out when he saw you in red the other night. It's your colour, I promise." My eyes closed for a second, as the memory of Luke calling my red dress *'inappropriate'* welled up. Bugged out? Well, he might have been. But it hadn't been a good thing. I had shoved the dress deep inside my wardrobe, even the thought of it making me feel sick. I'd been replaying his grip on my arm hundreds of times, unable to sleep through the night without waking up in a sweat. The whole night had been surreal.

"I don't want to wear it, okay? Red and green don't go together," I pointed at my eyes. "I'll look like a Christmas ornament." Eliza shrugged and shifted the dress to sit over her arm.

"I'll try it on then, since you're being such a drama queen. Try this one." She'd plucked a short, sparkly green number from seemingly nowhere – the girl had a knack for last minute shopping.

"At least *this one* will match your eyes." I knew I sounded pedantic, but I worried what would happen if Luke saw photos of me wearing another red dress. Even if I knew that it probably *was* my best colour.

I had to admit Eliza knew what she was talking about when it came to clothes. The dress was ideal; the deep emerald green working well with my pale skin tone and black hair. I shimmied out of the changing room to pose for her, and she feigned light-headedness.

"If being a mathematician doesn't work out, I definitely have a future somewhere as a personal shopper. A fashion advisor for the stars. A runway designer."

I laughed, shaking my head. "You didn't *make* the dress."

"A minor detail I can ignore for the fantasy."

I clocked that she'd put on the red dress she'd originally picked out for me. It hugged her curves in all the right places. "And that dress will make *Jack* bug out. See? Win-win situation."

She blushed and flipped me the finger, still wary of flaunting her relationship. "I'm only wearing this because it could hear you rejecting it." She patted the dress sympathetically.

"You're a weirdo."

"A well-dressed weirdo."

Eliza was happier than I'd ever seen her. She'd been so carefree the past few days, high on the success of our dinner. Although it had been full of angst for me, I could hear her and Jack giggling behind her door late into the night. She was so happy now that it had felt cruel to burden her with anything that had been happening to me. Or at least that's how I justified the secrecy. The moment I admitted that Luke wasn't the perfect boyfriend I'd made him out to be, was the moment I couldn't take any of it back. As long as I contained the damage, everything had the potential to return to normalcy.

"Avery." I spun round to see Maia waving at me from the other side of the shop, ducking between people's arms to get to us. She had a short white dress slung over her arm.

"Jeez that's bold. A white dress? If I wore that I'd look like an accidental bride." Eliza turned back to her mirror.

"It's Maia. She might not care about it, but she can pull off anything." At that moment she bounded into the changing rooms. "Hey!" I said, pulling her into a hug.

"God, am I glad to see you!" She'd definitely been dragged here against her will. "Don't let Connie loose on me. There's safety in numbers."

"Where is she?" I ignored the envy I felt that they were doing yet another activity as a twosome. But I'd been declining so many invitations, and after the weirdness in town last week, what did I expect?

"Somewhere over there, looking at dresses that show an alarmingly large amount of skin."

"Well it's nice to see you, anyway," said Eliza. "It's been ages."

"If I could have chosen somewhere to catch up, it would not have been here."

"You aren't the only one dragging your heels. Avery is being a right killjoy." I stuck out my tongue and she smirked. "Apparently red isn't her colour anymore."

"Red has always been your go-to!" We all turned to see Connie appearing beside us. "What do we think of this?" She was holding up a pale pink two piece, with plenty of glitter.

"It's…bold."

"Avery is being polite." Maia poked the dress. "That looks itchy. Very itchy."

"No pain, no gain. I'm going to go and try this on." She headed into a changing room and Maia shook her head, smiling.

"I'm sorry we didn't ask you to come with us. It was so last minute. I was watching *The Martian* and Connie appeared at my door. She's very persistent when she wants to be."

"It's fine. We're all here now anyway."

"I haven't even seen you to ask you yet. Who are you taking to the ball? Luke?"

I wrung out my hands. "No actually. Stella has wanted to be my date from day one." I couldn't believe how grateful

I felt for my persistent little sister now. The thought of bringing Luke stirred anxiety in the pit of my stomach.

"I can't wait to see her again. We're going to need some girl power. Did you hear Connie say that she's bringing Dave?"

"Dave?" Eliza finally joined in again, interest piqued.

I raised my eyebrows at her. "Her new boyfriend."

Maia laughed. "Let's hope this one lasts longer than the ball, eh?" She hung the white dress onto the returns rail and looked at me. "Did you get my texts? I was worried about you after we left you at the restaurant. Luke looked pretty pissed off. Did you make up?"

Eliza was paying even more attention now. I wished the ground would swallow me up.

"Eh, it was pretty annoying for him to show up, but it was fine. He'd just had a rough morning, you know."

Eliza smiled but Maia didn't look convinced.

"I mean, I guess it's nice that he wants to see you," she said. "But are you sure you're okay? It looked like he had your arm pretty tight."

Damn it Maia, just leave it alone.

"I honestly don't know what you mean," I said. "Everything's fine." Eliza's eyes were switching quickly between us, and the energy in the room felt charged. Luckily, Connie came out of her changing room at the exact moment that Maia looked like she was about to open her mouth again.

"Connie! How was the dress?"

She grinned, pleased to be the centre of attention. "Scandalous. Shall we go Maia? I have that nail appointment booked for four."

"If you insist. Bye you two." They walked off, shoulder to shoulder.

"I haven't seen those guys in a while. They seem good." Eliza was fishing, and I didn't look her in the eye.

"Yeah. They're good."

"Have you ever wondered if Maia might, you know, *like* Connie?"

"As weird as the contrast between them is, it has crossed my mind." I thanked the lord that Eliza had decided on this topic rather than one about me. I'd asked Maia about her feelings for Connie once, but she'd insisted that it was just a soft spot, nothing more, nothing less. I had my doubts.

"They'd make a cute couple. Anyway, what was Maia on about? Did something happen with Luke?" There it was. I turned away, putting one of my reject dresses back on the rack.

"It was literally nothing, just a little fight. They happen."

"She said something about him holding your arm?"

"Shall we pay? I like this one enough to just go for it."

"I mean, you know I love Luke. But you looked kind of upset the other night too. I never would have mentioned it if I thought the incident was isolated but..."

Shit.

"I love that you're concerned but it's just been a tough week for us. You know, bickering over the tiniest things. We've been together ages – it happens from time to time."

"Not to you and Luke, though." Eliza caught my hand in hers, stopping me from running off. I'd never given her any reason to doubt my boyfriend before; when it came to romance, I was the steady one.

"We're sorting through it. It's no big deal."

"There's no shame in admitting that you're having–"

"Eliza!" I lowered my voice when she stepped back and several people around us turned to stare. "It's called a *relationship*. People argue. It's normal."

Her face fell. "Avery, I didn't mean to offend you. I know I don't know that much about love and stuff…"

I'd messed this up as well. I considered throwing my dress down and legging it out of the shop.

"I'm sorry," I started, but she squeezed my hand.

"We don't have to talk about it. I just wanted you to know that you could, if you wanted to. You can talk to me about an argument, and I won't judge either of you. I can be very neutral when I need to be."

This was the point. I could break down and tell her everything, even if she was only expecting me to rant about a few inconsequential bickers. I could relieve the weight on my shoulders, cry to my best friend about how insecure I was feeling. But then I pictured Luke's face, telling me that he needed me. That he'd moved to York to be with me, to make our relationship smoother. I couldn't sell him out like that. Besides, we could sort it out on our own. I was sure.

"I know I can talk to you." I smiled, hoping it seemed genuine, and not like there were millions of secrets left unsaid behind my lips. "Shall we go and pay?"

I looked at the application one last time before sliding it into the envelope.

The questions hadn't been too difficult; previous writing experience, previous editing experience. I didn't have much evidence of either. I'd been too freaked out at the thought of making roots somewhere other than Westby during Freshers' Week to join the student newspaper, instead preferring to sit in my room and FaceTime Stella until the night Eliza stumbled past my door, half drunk and intent on dragging me out on a bar crawl. The rest was history, as well as the brief idea of writing for the paper. I'd ended up emailing my tutor for a reference and putting down my sessions with Beckett as editorial experience. I was sure he'd laugh when he heard that. The application had said that they were considering people with no experience whatsoever, but a little bit of a white lie was better than nothing at all.

"Whatcha doing?" Eliza was leaning against my doorframe, a hot chocolate piled high with cream and marshmallows in one hand, and her laptop in the other. "Peace offering?"

"You didn't need to do that." I accepted it, taking a sip and getting cream on my nose. "But I'll never refuse a hot chocolate."

"I feel like I got all up in your business. Luke's a good guy, I know you love him. Let's label this afternoon a shopping success, regardless of my nosy moment?"

"I'd like that."

"So," she perched on the edge of my bed. "Can I sit here and do my seminar notes? Misery adores company. Is that your internship application?"

I looked down at the envelope again. "Sure is."

"What did Luke say? I bet he's so excited for you."

"I haven't even got an interview yet. I'm going to wait until I hear back I think, so he doesn't get his hopes up for me." That wasn't the truth; I just wanted to keep something for myself. But I didn't need to tell anyone else that.

"I have every faith you'll do it. My notes on differential equations, however…" she pointed to the notes on her lap, "…less faith."

I got out my own coursework, and we settled into comfortable silence. My application was on the edge of my desk, waiting for a stamp. It was nice to feel like my future was in my own hands.

Sixteen

Looking at us in the mirror, it was difficult to believe that Stella was four years younger. Or, when you took into account her long legs and blonde hair, that we were even sisters at all. In typical Stella style she was still applying liner to her eyes, catching up with Eliza who was sat on my bed flipping through a magazine.

"All I'm saying is that I would be *forever* in your debt if you did it. I'm not a cheat."

In the reflection of my full length mirror I saw Eliza roll her eyes. "Stel, it's cheating."

Like always, my sister's overnight bag had come prepared – her maths homework sitting on top of the suitcase to try and tempt Eliza, who said no every time at first, but would be seen sitting at our kitchen table late into the night puzzling over the GCSE sample questions. It was a predictable turn of events, and Stella knew it. I could already see Eliza looking over at the page of problems wistfully. Done with her liner, my sister turned around to face Eliza, who whistled. She'd opted for a long yellow dress, calling me ten times whilst she was in the department store to make sure that I wasn't going to ruin our look by wearing red and showing up like the Mcdonald's sign. I'd shown the text to Eliza in victory; the red dress had been a bad idea after all. I smoothed my hands over the dark green material I'd opted for, the sequins on the bodice sparkling in the reflection of the mirror. For a moment I regretted that Luke wouldn't be standing by my side tonight. We hadn't spoken much over the past few days, just checking in now and again whilst I waited for him to cool down. I'd expected him to come over and see us off; compliment our dresses and catch up with his substitute little sister, but there had been no sign of him. I drowned out the worry that I'd pushed him too far, turning up the music we had on in my bedroom. Tonight was about my sister, not him.

"How's Elliott?" I turned my attention to Stella, who'd arrived three hours earlier, whining about the long train journey; Westby wasn't exactly easy to get to and from via public transport. She'd been dating her Spanish lesson lover for just under a month now, and at this point, I had to admit that I was intrigued. Dad had called about a week ago to say that he'd finally been introduced, and that he was less of the nightmare he'd been expecting. I took that as a positive sign. Not many boys made as good an impression as Luke when it came to parents; some people just knew all the right things to say.

"Good. He asked me to be his girlfriend last week." Eliza squealed and sat bolt upright, clapping her hands. "And obviously I said yes." In a lot of ways, I saw similarities between my best friend and my little sister.

Eliza had fallen onto her back dramatically, staring up at my stars and sighing. "I'm hoping Jack does that soon to be honest. I'm tired of pretending I don't fancy the pants off him."

"Wow." Stella raised her eyebrows at me. "Do we need to check her temperature?"

"I've been thinking that ever since she first mentioned him. Our girl is *smitten*."

"Shut up. I am not. I'm just happy."

Stella jumped on the bed, and I winced at the thought of her dress ripping before we'd even had our photos taken. "If you're happy, so are we." She may have been fifteen, but she was one of us, through and through.

"Doesn't it just feel like everything is falling into place?" Stella flopped back onto the bed to lay next to Eliza, her hands on her stomach, staring up at the ceiling.

Looking at the pair of them, I had to hold back from stamping my foot and saying that, on the contrary, it felt like a lot of things were falling apart.

"Mum likes Elliott. She's invited him over for Sunday dinner."

Stel was never afraid to test my boundaries and see if I'd decided to breach the impasse by bringing up our mother at every given opportunity. She was studying my face, daring me to bend.

Eliza sensed the tension. "That's so nice. My mum would freak if I turned up with Jack."

I turned back to the mirror under the pretense of touching up my eye makeup. I didn't want them to see the sudden tears welling in my eyes; if there was someone best to talk to when you felt like you'd lost control, it was classically your mother. And I'd alienated mine. Only Stella was able to remind me of the barriers I'd erected. Too much time had passed to even think about changing it.

My sister took my silence as permission to carry on. "You should call her. I know she'd be happy to hear your voice." She'd been eleven when Mum had walked out – young enough to easily repair a relationship, to create new patterns and forget old ones. I'd been fifteen and the loss of the most important relationship in my life at that age was pretty impossible to forget.

"I can arrange a date if you want." I saw Eliza's eyes flick up to meet mine in the mirror, willing me not to blow.

"Stel, stop," I said. "I have absolutely no interest in pretending to be her daughter." I hoped it sounded final enough to shut my sister up.

"Okay so this is officially my favourite night."

"You're easily pleased." I nudged Stella, argument forgotten as we took in our surroundings. It was the one evening of the academic year that people shed their usual joggers and hoodies and dressed to the nines. We were sat at a circular table on the edge of the dancefloor with Connie, Maia, and Dave; Dave floundering under Maia's intellectual microscope while our starter of soup grew cold.

"You know, I'm not sure I'd pass Maia's intelligence test." Stella whispered in my ear, not yet performing her classic party trick of talking way too loud after just a few sips of wine.

"She seems hard to please, but she's a softie." Maia used intellect as her suit of armour in social situations, but it was only a front. I could see her hands knotted on top of her knee, her tell-tale sign that she was feeling socially awkward.

I patted her hand. "You okay?"

"Never better. Am I speaking too much?"

"Nah. You're doing just fine."

"So, Stella, what are you thinking of taking next year for your A-Levels?" Connie leaned on her elbow, slightly tipsy too.

"Eugh, don't mention that in front of Avery. She won't stop pestering me about it."

"It's important!"

"They were more important to you than they are to me." Stella would forever be the rebel in our family. She'd never planned more than a day in advance.

The lights suddenly dimmed as the DJ resumed his place at the front booth, gesturing for the Head of English to come and give a speech. Around us students groaned, consuming enough alcohol to be bold. As she started to speak I looked at Stella, who was listening with wide eyes, possibly the only person in the room paying more attention to the speech than their phones. It was a constant worry, Stella's motivation. From an early age, after reading approximately five bedtime stories, I'd known my place. Mum had introduced me at family gatherings as the future writer, even though I was six years old and had only got as far as telling my stories out loud. Stella was more of a wild card, and I vividly remembered all of the times (back when we were still a complete family set) that we'd sat around and guessed where my sister would end up. On my thirteenth birthday, whilst we had braved the May showers and toasted marshmallows in the back garden, she'd announced that she wanted to be a veterinary nurse. For a while, watching her play animal hospital through the crack in her door, I'd been convinced. Mum never was though; she called Stel a free spirit, and throughout all the guessing games had maintained that Stella would have multiple different passions. Watching her now, looking entirely overwhelmed, I had to agree.

A tap on my shoulder startled me from my thoughts, and I turned to Stella, assuming that she wanted my attention, poking me like she used to when we were younger. She looked just as startled as I was, staring up at a figure in a tuxedo, who I quickly recognised as Beckett.

"Hi." He didn't elaborate on why he was here.

"Of all the people I was expecting to tap me on the shoulder…"

"I thought I'd surprise you."

Under the table, Stel kicked my ankle, wanting an introduction.

"This is Beckett. Beckett, Stella. Stella, Beckett." I signalled between them. "Seriously though. Why are you here?"

Beckett slapped a hand over his chest. "You mean, when you mentioned the ball–" He made a grand gesture around the room, picking the exact moment that a drunken third year tripped over the slight incline on the dancefloor, "–you weren't asking me to be your date?"

Stella subconsciously lifted a hand to her mouth, panic stricken. For a moment, it felt like our roles had been reversed. I poked Beckett.

"Ha ha. What are you really doing here?" He had now crouched down a bit, his hands resting on the back of my chair. "And I'm really not that small." He laughed, realising what he'd done.

"You're small, deal with it Emerson. And as for you," he held out his hand, "I've heard more about you than you could ever imagine." Stella took his extended hand, and I received another swift kick underneath the tablecloth. I willed her to accidentally catch Maia's ankle and have to deal with the repercussions.

Beckett was all smiles, none the wiser. "I got invited last minute as part of an alumni thing. Let me tell you, the company is not nearly as good as over here at table seven." This all made sense, considering the gushing Alex had done when I'd sat opposite him in his office. Beckett would always be a crowd favourite without even trying. He could make friends anywhere. With anyone. Like Luke, but in a completely different way. Luke grabbed hold of the crowd's attention, whereas Beckett slowly drew you in. When I glanced around the table, Maia was still in conversation with Dave, oblivious to the intrusion. Connie however, had put down her soup spoon and was watching the exchange slightly too intently. I looked at Beckett as an outsider might; just over six foot, with dimples and curls. He was cute, in an alumni kind of way. But still. Dave was sitting right next to her. She really was shameless.

"So, as I was saying," he sent a pointed look my way, letting me know he'd seen my mind wander, "it's really just a matter of figuring out your best pose." Stella was nodding along, and I tried to figure out what they were talking about.

"I've always considered myself to be the traditional hand on heart, act shocked kind of girl." My sister posed as she described, and Beckett mimed a click of a camera.

"Classic. Although not as much so, as this." He pursed his lips together and held up a peace sign, at which she threw her head back in laughter. "I imagine Avery to be kind of like this." He placed his hands in his lap and faked an angelic expression. "We're discussing the merits of finding your signature pose for the photo booth." His finger pointed to the foyer, which had a sign for the booth.

When it came to the details of the event, clearly no expense had been spared. Walking away with a physical memory of a wonderful night, a fleeting moment caught on camera, was a definite winner when it came to students.

Student walls were always *covered* in snapshots of drunken nights out.

"Trust you to encourage Stel to want to wait in that line all night." I narrowed my eyes at Beckett, and he mimicked me.

"Well I wasn't about to do it on my own, now was I?" He grabbed my hand, pulling me out of my seat just as they started to collect the bowls of soup.

"But what about the main course?" I said.

"Really?"

I laughed and let him pull me away knowing the actual meal tended to be the least glamourous part of the night, and the veggie option was usually borderline inedible. Stella was looking at Beckett like he was talking pure magic. As we made our way to the back of the line, I caught Maia staring at us. We locked eyes, and instead of looking away, she just raised her eyebrows. I shook it off; I didn't want to think about what that expression might have meant. Or what the comfort I felt in Beckett's presence meant. Or that the idea of sitting in a room with my actual boyfriend caused my chest to tighten.

Seventeen

"He just waltzed up behind us!" Stella was recounting the previous night's events to Eliza, who was scrambling some eggs on the hob whilst I poured orange juice into three glasses. We had arrived back at the flat in the early hours of the morning, waking Eliza up and collapsing into bed after a long haul in heels.

"He's really something, isn't he?" I turned at that, wondering where this glowing review of Beckett was coming from. Eliza was smiling to herself as she tipped the eggs onto buttery white toast and carried a plate over to Stel, who put down the strip from the booth she'd been holding onto for long enough to pick up a fork and dig in. In the end, we'd all opted to look as goofy as humanly possible – Beckett with bunny ears, Stella a hot pink feather boa, and me finally settling on a huge pair of red glasses. The shots had been a series of the comedic poses that Beckett and Stella had devised in the queue (twenty minutes, as predicted) and when they'd printed, I couldn't help but agree that it had been a good move. Back inside the ballroom my friends were picking at dry pieces of meat and craning their heads to see if someone, *anyone,* could get them some more gravy, but out in the foyer we had been in fits of laughter. And now, with a strip of photos tucked safely in my purse, there was no chance of my ever forgetting.

"I just don't know why you've never elaborated on this Avery. Beckett was telling me about your writing and how good it is, and I'm not going to lie I'm kind of mad that he got to read it first."

This wasn't the first time that Stel had interrogated me in the last twelve hours, and there wasn't a reasonable answer that I could offer up. I *wasn't* sure why I'd kept him mostly to myself; maybe out of loyalty to Luke, or possibly because I liked the idea of Beckett being partially a secret, partially mine. I could be anxious about my relationship, waiting and hoping for the pattern to change, but then I would sit with Beckett over coffee and the anxieties would melt away. Stella knew the darkest parts of me, even more so than Luke. If I'd opened up to her about my friendship with Beckett, I worried what she'd see.

"Mentioning him slipped my mind. I'll send you a couple of chapters to read on the train home."

"You better." Stella reached for the salt and pepper containers – two little cats that we'd been given by Dad when we'd moved in. It was already midday and we were still in our pyjamas (even Eliza, who had been sat at the table surrounded by Stel's homework when we'd padded down the hall in our slipper socks half an hour earlier), which left a fraction of time until my sister had to leave.

Stella's train was at two thirty, so I focused on making the most of having her here. Every time I went a while without seeing her, I forgot how much I liked being in her company. Not a lot of sisters we knew got along like we did, but with our past behind us we just operated more like a team. Even the smaller things, like knowing that at least for a while, we had to be each other's greeting when we walked through the front door. Instead of sitting with Mum at the kitchen table with a hot chocolate after school, we sat with each other. And whilst it may have looked flawed on the inside, when you were part of the duo, it worked.

I knew that my leaving to go to university had taken its toll on Stella. Even though Dad had slowly become the man we knew before the affair, our team of two had split. Besides, there was some advice that you just couldn't get from your dad. Seeing her there at our kitchen table, hair piled up in a messy bun and looking as young as I remembered, made my heart a little happier. I ruffled her head and got up to get a glass of water, leaving her momentarily to chat about factorising with Eliza, who always purposely left one or two mistakes in the homework to avoid raising suspicion. Like my sister and me, they had also formed a system.

"What would I do without you?"

Eliza looked up from her toast at Stella. "Get an F."

"Pffft. That's rich coming from you." I turned to Stella. "You should have seen Eliza trying to make a cake the other day."

"I have absolutely no problems admitting that without Avery, I'd be failing beyond recognition."

Stella spoke through a mouthful. "See? We all need each other. A well-oiled machine."

"God knows I prayed for sisters during my childhood of boredom." Eliza blew a kiss at me. "Wait. Can you hear something?"

I winced at the squeak of the chair legs moving backwards as Stella tilted her chair, leaning in the direction of the noise. "Yeah. There's definitely someone knocking at your door."

Eliza lifted up the spoon from her coffee in an obvious panic to check her reflection. "It's probably Jack. We're going walking along the river this afternoon."

"Hurry up with my homework then." Stel's smile was like butter wouldn't melt.

"Good work takes *time*. Be right back." Eliza skipped down the hallway to the front door, but the voice that echoed through the flat wasn't Jack's. It was deep, and familiar. I rushed back to the table and snatched the strip of photos from Stella, shaking my head as a signal to her to keep quiet about them whilst I shoved them in the first drawer that I laid eyes on, underneath a white and blue checked tea towel. I ignored her stare, instead focusing on adjusting my ponytail so that it looked somewhat decent.

"Hey babe." He strode into the kitchen, swinging his car keys around his fingertip and leaning in to kiss me before grabbing my chair and sitting next to Stel. "I thought I'd drop round and see the nightmare child before she left."

Stella to her credit seemed to have recovered from my freak out, poking Luke on the shoulder whilst she ate the rest of her breakfast.

"How was the ball?" He seemed in good spirits, so I released the tension in my chest. I could never predict these days what might set him off. To see him in such a good mood, freshly showered and pleased to see me, reminded me of all the things I loved about him. Before I could answer his question, Stel stepped in. I crossed my fingers behind my back that she wouldn't mention the third member of our party. There would be no way for me to explain myself out of that one; regardless of how innocent the night had been. Beckett had gone from my quiet companion to a ticking time bomb.

"It was amazing Luke. Look."

I went back to the sink and turned my back to the conversation as Stella pulled out her phone to show him some photos. She'd looked up quickly in the interim to meet my eyes, so I was confident she'd received the message loud and clear. Stella might have been fifteen, but she wasn't stupid. I concentrated on getting the glass of water I'd originally gone for, trying not to think about the dress I'd worn, and what he might think.

"You both look beautiful." A hand on my waist made me jump, and I spun round, seeing he'd crept up behind me whilst my thoughts had wandered. "*You* looked beautiful." He kissed my cheek. "Hi, I love you." I melted at the words as he nipped my neck, pressing his lips to the point that always tickled me.

"Love you more." I smiled up at him, and Stel cleared her throat.

"You know, I am eating."

Luke laughed, holding his hands up. "I can't be held responsible for my actions with Avery, you know that." He meant it as a harmless comment, but the irony was there.

"Well, try. I want this toast to stay down." That was the relationship she had with him; a sarcastic brother-sister balance. I'd never forget all the times that I'd relied on him to pick her up from various appointments and sleepovers when I was just too busy – or couldn't figure out a route on the bus to get there. I realised I was subconsciously leaning into him, feeling the warmth and gratitude that I associated with the memory. He put his hands on my shoulders, massaging them whilst spurring off a retort to my sister, catching up with what had happened in her life in the short while that we'd all been apart. It was reminiscent of so many afternoons in Westby, the three of us hanging out before Dad got home and three became four again. I watched the water in my glass ripple as I spun it. That was the beauty, and the chaos, that came with routine. With habit. It was built into you, hard to change. Or even, to get out of at all.

Stella had been quiet whilst we sat on a bench outside the station, waiting for her train to arrive. I had a feeling I knew why, but I was keeping my thoughts to myself, hoping she might do as well. Unfortunately, I knew my sister.

"That was weird, right?" I didn't have to check to know that she was referring to the photos that I'd snatched from her, which were still concealed in the drawer. There were some people you could hide things from, no matter how close you were, and there were some that you never could. My eyes were watering from the intensity with which I was staring at a crack on the ground.

"You know Luke. Best not to cause drama over nothing." I laughed it off, but despite my best efforts it fell flat.

"You aren't cheating on him, are you?"

"*What?!* No, Beckett is just a friend. Luke gets touchy about it, but it really is nothing. Just no point in stirring it."

I wanted to vent to Stella. To tell her about misplaced jealousy and spats, leaving out all of the other stuff, like my grazed hand, or his grip on my chin when I'd tried to get away from him at the dinner party. But I couldn't tarnish Luke's reputation like that; there was no point in destroying four years of good family relations. If it was the opposite way around, I would have liked to think that Stella might confide in me the way that she'd done in the past if girls at school were being mean to her. Depending on me to make things right. But it wasn't that way around. I was the oldest Emerson girl we had left. And now was not the time to start escalating what I had convinced myself were tiny moments of stress. Stella had her GCSEs coming up; enough to deal with without my issues.

She still looked sceptical. "As long as you're sure."

"I am. Have you started revision yet? You said over Christmas that you'd start in February."

"Yes Mum. I have some Chemistry in my bag to read on the train. Don't forget to send me your writing though, I can't work well without some form of available procrastination."

"You're a nightmare."

"A dream, and you know it." She wiggled her eyebrows devilishly. "Come home soon, okay? Dad is getting restless without seeing you. Plus, I think he enjoys having you around to take the pressure off him being cook all the time. That's definitely the one responsibility he's still bitter about."

"As long as that's the only thing."

"Indeed. Now pinky promise that you'll visit me soon. I'm going to need all the help with poetry that I can get." She held out her little finger and I shook it.

"I promise."

The train pulled in and I lifted the case, hugging my sister tight before the doors shut and she sped off. Gone again. It was consistently difficult to say goodbye. Especially now. It had been a nice break from the whirl of my own thoughts to be surrounded by Stella, who wouldn't leave you alone long enough to have a single thought that didn't involve her.

My phone buzzed, bringing me back to the reality.

Beckett: Do the words 'we're going on a field trip' excite you as much as they excite me?

I burst out laughing, alone on the train platform. Beckett's texts always came at the right time to bring me back from sad trains of thought – no pun intended.

Me: Depends where we are going?

I didn't want to do anything to antagonise Luke if I could avoid it.

Beckett: No telling, but I will reveal that it is strictly writing related.
Luke can rest easy.

I winced. So he had noticed that Luke was wary of him. This was all becoming very awkward, but the sound of a writing field trip did sound like the perfect way to battle the loneliness I felt whenever Stella or Dad left to go back to Westby. York was not my own little seaside town, but I did need to make it my home, at least for now.

Me: Time/Place?

Eighteen

"Give me two seconds!" From behind the door I could hear a lot of fumbling around; typical Beckett. I was learning to not be ready at the time he said he would be. I hadn't been given any pointers; just that I needed to be at his flat within half an hour.

I jumped back a little when the door swung open. "Sorry, sorry." He was hopping on one foot, trying to put a sock onto the other. His haste to be ready, darting around the kitchen to grab his wallet and keys, was endearing. There was a flicker in the back of my mind that questioned what Luke might say if he could see me now, but I shoved it down. I had to at least try and reclaim some of my choices. Even if the thought of the repercussions kept me up at night.

"I'll literally be one minute."

I stepped inside, making myself comfortable on the sofa knowing that it was going to take him longer than sixty seconds.

"It really doesn't matter, take your time." I got up to get some water, and he sprung across the room and intercepted my movement. He seemed to notice how close he'd accidentally moved to me, and took a small step back, still blocking my walk to the tap.

"Being a bit tight with your water supply aren't you? I promise, I'll only have a bit."

"What would I do without your wit? You can't get a drink because we aren't staying here."

"We aren't?" By this point he was already on the way back to his room. I'd never been in there before, but through the slight opening I could see it was anything but immaculate, unlike Luke's had always been. If you left any trace of your belongings lying around Luke pounced on the opportunity to lecture you about "his space". I'd assumed that was just a male thing, although now it was evident that it was just a Luke thing. I wasn't sure whether I preferred his immaculate bedroom, or this glimpse of a messy alternative. You could tell a lot about a person from their bedroom.

"I know, don't faint from shock now Avery." His voice sounded muffled from behind the door, and when it opened fully I saw he'd grabbed a jacket. I tried not to seem like I was trying to look past him into the bedroom, but I imagined it was a fruitless and completely transparent effort. My eyes tracked his movement across the floor in an attempt to deduce the location of our destination. If there were any clues to be found, he wasn't telling. As he bent down to grab his wallet my eyes were once again drawn to the ink on his bicep, and I made a mental reminder to ask him about it sometime. It looked like some sort of object, but I couldn't be sure.

"Any clues?" Beckett smiled whilst he thought I couldn't see, and he lightly touched the front of a novel that was on his worktop.

"We aren't straying too far from the usual agenda."

As soon as we turned onto Sloane Street, I clocked onto the final destination. I couldn't put my finger on what I'd been expecting, but this was perfect. He glanced at me sideways, like he didn't want me to notice where he was looking, and I saw him catch sight of my fingertips resting against my leg as we walked. I curled them instinctively.

"The Little Library. Good choice." That earned a warm smile that reached all the way to his dimples.

The Little Library was a tiny independent bookshop on the edge of the city centre, crammed so full of potential purchases that you could grab an iced latte from the drinks bar and spend hours perusing the stock. Jed, the owner, was always on hand for recommendations, delighted to share his passion with anyone that might listen. I hadn't been here in a while, so I was excited to check out their new releases: The Little Library was impressive in its obvious adoration of authors you hadn't discovered yet. Impressive but unassuming; kind of like Beckett.

"An ideal field trip, am I right?" We stepped through the doorway and I took in a deep breath. There was nothing quite like the first inhale when you entered a bookshop; the scent of new pages and crisp covers.

"You're definitely right. Look!" I pointed to a copy of *Breaking the Surface,* stacked up beside a sign that read 'Local Author'.

Jed leaped out from behind the counter, his red hair all over the place and his glasses pushed up onto his head. "Beckett! I have some new stock…" He pulled a fineliner from his shirt pocket and Beckett blushed.

"I didn't plan this." He said before leaning onto the table to sign the copies.

"I can confirm. Total surprise attack, he didn't stand a chance." Jed grinned at me. "Anything I can help you with today?"

Beckett clipped the lid on the fineliner and handed it back to Jed. "Just going to browse I think."

"Perfect. I'll pour you both some coffee."

"Any chance of a hot chocolate for Emerson?" Beckett pointed to me.

"A pretty high chance I'd say. Go and have fun kids."

We headed for the first bookshelf, ready to peruse the displays.

We were book drunk.

If you spent enough time reading excerpts of books, barely keeping your head above the water and trying not to get caught in the tides of the stories, you found yourself a little delirious from the *potential.* Beckett and I had been sitting in a corner of the shop for at least an hour, pulling books from the shelves and flipping to a random page, reading a paragraph or two and then letting our imaginations fill in the blanks. There was a perfectly good sofa on the other side of the shop, but we'd been so excited that we'd just sat on the rug by the Young Adult section, pulling out chapters and mulling over the stories. We'd been reading the first few chapters of Rosaline Green's new book, and I clutched it to my chest, certain of my purchase.

"One day, someone will be sat here reading your new book. Reading about Sophia and trying to figure out her story." I smiled to myself as I imagined a customer picking up a hardback and falling in love right away with the characters he'd written. Maybe I was a little bit biased, but it didn't take much work to imagine the scene.

"And your book too. I refuse to release my new book without you sending yours off to some agents."

"What a beautiful dream."

Beckett looked at me sideways. "Avery?"

"Hmm?"

"What's your biggest fear?"

That threw me off. We had a rhythm nowadays, a pattern of conversation that was neutral, allowed. Meaningful conversations about our deepest fears might have been pushing that boundary.

He took my silence as hesitation and sat up a little straighter. "When I was seven, we went to the seaside." Beckett slid the book he was holding back onto the shelf. "How I went seven years without experiencing the seaside I do not know, but anyway, not the point. Lucy was five, and she loved every second. We got these huge ice creams with raspberry sauce that dripped down our chins, and Mum spent the entire time running after us with a wet wipe." His eyes crinkled at the edges, like I always noticed that they did when he talked about his family. I could picture the scene almost perfectly, coming from a seaside town myself. Stella and I had posed for many photos with that same raspberry sauce smeared over our faces.

"And I decided that it would be phenomenal to play a game of hide and seek on the beach. Imagine the potential, right?" I couldn't help but smile. I was a big believer in potential, and clearly Beckett was the same. "So much sand. It stretched out for *miles*. And I don't know if you've been to the beach…" He trailed off and looked at me expectantly, and I realised that actually, I'd never disclosed that much information about myself.

"I grew up by the sea." I laughed at his mouth falling open in surprise.

"You kept that one quiet, Emerson." I waved him off and rested my chin on my hand; enthralled with this seaside story despite the fact that I could close my eyes and see the real thing in my memory, time and time again. There was no doubt about it, Beckett was an excellent storyteller. "So anyway, since you *live there,*" he shook his head, still chuckling, "you'll know that it's actually pretty darn cold most of the time."

"Damn that sea breeze." I chimed in, way more invested in this story now that he knew I had experienced the trials and tribulations.

"So, I thought running around looking for each other might warm us up a bit. The slight problem was that as soon as I uncovered my eyes, I'm seven years old, and alone on a wide stretch of sand." My heart clenched at the thought of a younger Beckett, alone. Not a lot of feelings struck a chord with me as much as being lost. I knew that one like the back of my hand.

"It took barely a minute to find Mum, crouched – a bit pathetically, I might add here for comedic value – behind a rock. Lucy was nowhere. I mean literally, nowhere. We weren't worried at first; she had those stupid kiddy armbands on and she'd taken lessons." I knew where this was going now, and all of a sudden it became a little less comedic. "We found the armbands abandoned by the edge of the water. Lucy was always intent on moving faster than the other kids her age. And then Mum screamed, and we saw her, and she was far out Avery. Far out. She was panicking in the water, you know that moment that you realise that you're in over your head?" I nodded slowly. "She was only five, but she knew what was happening. We managed to get her back to shore, and she coughed up what must have been a litre of water."

My hands gravitated to cover my mouth. Stella and I were beach babies, and we had always known when it was time to put our armbands on. "Was she alright?"

"Yeah, she was fine. Five minutes later she demanded another ice cream and off she trotted to the truck. But I have never stepped in the sea since." It was only then that I remembered the original question.

"Never?" My whole childhood had consisted of sand between my toes and the smell of salt lingering in the strands of my hair. We hadn't been on many holidays as a family. Everything we wanted, we already had.

"Never." He sighed, letting his finger skip along the spines of the bookshelf he was leaning against. "Your turn."

It had been a while since I'd actually thought about what I was afraid of. What immediately came to mind was the usual assortment of trivial fears – I'd never once seen a spider and not called for Dad's help, and Eliza thought it was hilarious to send me links to snake videos. That wasn't however, the exact truth.

"I think my biggest fear is being alone." Beckett nodded, which I saw even though my eyes were barely open in anticipation of his response. He didn't suck in a breath and tell me I needed to stop being so melancholy, like Luke probably would have done, or reassure me that there was no way I could ever feel alone, like I knew Stella would. He hadn't even spoken yet, despite the thirty second pause.

"That doesn't surprise me."

I wasn't sure whether that was a compliment or an insult, although I was safe in the knowledge that he'd probably intended it to come across as neither. There was palpable energy between us, like there had been at the dinner party. Maybe it was being in an environment surrounded by books that brought out this honesty between us, although I had my doubts. I had a feeling it was just us.

"Why does it not surprise you?"

"Four years." He didn't have to look at me for it to hit home, but he did, and I felt it even more. There was no way that this one was a compliment. I hadn't mentioned anything about the troubles I was having, but maybe I didn't need to. Maybe the things that were left unsaid were the most powerful. "It's not a bad thing necessarily." That was the thing about Beckett; it was almost as if he could sense discomfort. "I just think that you'd be okay on your own too."

I was suddenly aware that it wasn't just the two of us in the bookshop – we were tucked away, sure, but I could hear steady chatter behind us, and around the corner I caught a glimpse of wheels touching the ground as two new mothers congregated around the soft play children's books. Jed was frothing milk at the front of the shop, laughing with a man and offering up a new book that he'd just received in a stock delivery.

I had turned away from Beckett, but it felt like his eyes were burning a hole in my head. What had I expected him to say, honestly, when I'd confessed that my most prominent fear was being on my own? That was the thing about honest people. They tended to draw out the truth from everyone else, too.

"When my mum left…"

Beckett raised his eyebrows in surprise, like he couldn't believe I wasn't choosing to change the subject. I knew that he would have let me, wouldn't have held it against me. But for some reason, I wanted to explain myself.

"When she left, it was like she took Dad as well, even though he was physically present. He wouldn't come out of his room for *weeks*. Stella and I ate enough spaghetti hoops to feed an army." I smiled at the memory, even though in truth, it was a bad one. How we played rock-paper-scissors at the bottom of the stairs, desperate to avoid entering Dad's room, waiting for him to snap out of the darkness. "For our whole childhood, he was happy. I remember piggybacks on the sand dunes, and the time that he set up mini golf on our front lawn. And then all of a sudden, he wasn't." There were a lot of people in my life who would have interrupted at this point, desperate to spare me from talking about this. Even though Luke had stepped into my life shortly after it had happened, we'd never directly spoken about it. He'd just walked in and stayed. No nonsense, just a neat little safety net. Beckett wasn't the same kind of safety, but I was slowly realising that feeling safe didn't necessarily mean that you were. "For the first time in my life, I saw someone feeling completely alone. I'd do anything not to feel like that."

Now Beckett looked directly at me, sensing I was done. Instead of reaching out for me, or trying to pretend that those memories weren't tainted, he just smiled.

"You know, loneliness doesn't have to be forever. It's temporary, necessary." I wasn't sure where he was going with this. "And for what it's worth, I think that loneliness is where you really find yourself."

Nineteen

Luke appeared from around the corner, not spotting me. He looked calm today; peaceful in a way I couldn't always count on. It was Saturday, he had the whole weekend ahead of him before he had to go to work again, and we were meeting in a public place. I had nothing to worry about.

"Hey babe." He finally noticed me leaning against the wall and strode over, planting a kiss on the top of my head. "I am *starving*. Where's that place again? The one with those chocolate orange brownies?"

I knew what he was talking about. "And the raspberry and white chocolate blondies?"

"Yes, wow, I need that."

I led him to Cakes & Coffee, the cute café a few minutes away from the River Ouse. We pointed to some of the desserts lined up on the counter, grabbing a corner table, Luke talking my ear off about the aspects of work that weren't stressing him out. It seemed that he'd finally cracked his flatmate, getting him to go out for a pint last night, and his father had called him to thank him for the progress he was making. It appeared that things were looking up, and I couldn't have been more grateful. Anything that was good for Luke, was good for me.

"So I might have got you something." He looked embarrassed for a moment, and then reached into his back pocket. "I know I've been a massive loser lately, but I promise that's in the past now."

I raised my eyebrows.

"I was looking for the perfect thing to give you to tell you that I'm sorry." He pulled a slender velvet box out from his pocket.

"You're lucky that didn't fall out on the way here!"

"I know, I'm lucky. In more ways than one." He kissed me again before pushing the box to my side of the table. I was almost scared to look inside. Didn't he know that all I wanted from him was compassion, and that the rest didn't matter? I opened the box anyway.

"It's beautiful." Nestled into the velvet was a silver bracelet, simple and elegant. I never wore extravagant jewellery, and he'd clearly been paying attention. The thought made my heart beat a little bit faster, solid proof that he wasn't hellbent on breaking it. "Where did you find this?"

"I got it at that vintage store you like. You know, the one with the fairy lights on the ceiling?"

"You're the sweetest."

Luke's expression was one of satisfaction. "No one knows my girl like I do."

I ignored the possessive statement. This was going to be a nice day, and I wasn't going to let anything get in the way of that.

Luke held the umbrella high enough for him to stay under it as well as me, and we hurried along the road to my flat. We'd had a few days of English February sunshine, and now it was back to normal, constant rain. I unlocked the front door as quickly as I could, Luke poking me in the back to hurry me up.

"Is that you Avery?" Eliza's voice was coming from the kitchen, so I walked towards it, shaking the rain out of my ponytail. "How was town? Buy me anything nice?"

I gestured to the oven she was standing by. "Cook me anything nice?"

"Touché. Hey, Luke." Eliza waved at him before leaning down and getting her vegan mac and cheese out of the oven. "Are you guys staying here tonight?"

"Probably." Luke looked at her meal longingly.

"I can make you some of that for dinner if you want."

He pulled me to his chest. "Hey Eliza. Did I ever tell you that I have the best girlfriend on the planet?"

Eliza rolled her eyes. "Once or twice you massive goon. Anyway, I'm going out for a bit after I've eaten, just to see Jack and go over some of our notes for the seminar on Monday. When I get back we should watch a movie or something." She took her food to her room and Luke flopped onto the couch, sighing.

"Today has been a really good day."

"Yeah?" I hated how hopeful my voice sounded.

"Yeah. I feel like everything is right with the world again. Dad is finally off my back. I can't tell you how nice that feels. Yesterday, there was a sticky note on my desk letting me know that I'm invited to a team bowling outing next week."

"I wonder if you'll be invited to the one after that once they realise you suck at it." I tickled him and he tickled me right back.

"Still good enough to beat you on our first date." It was true; for our first date he'd taken me to the local Westby bowling alley. It was a little cliché, but we'd been fifteen. I still had the little pink bunny he'd won for me on the claw machine after we'd finished our bowling match, and the photo we'd taken, our tongues bright blue from the slush puppies we drank on the beach after it got dark.

"That was a perfect first date." I smiled at him, the nostalgia overwhelming me.

"I wouldn't dream of providing anything less. Now how about that mac and cheese?"

Luke was three beers in, which was definitely why he'd let me put Coronation Street on. It reminded me of home; something that all three of us always agreed on, when we got tired of Dad's football or Stella's reality TV.

"Do you even know what's going on?"

"Nope, haven't watched it in weeks." I basked happily in the fact that I didn't need to know what was going on to feel close to my family. They were probably sat on our small couch in Westby doing the same thing.

Me: Coronation Street?

She texted back within the minute.

Stella: Are you stalking us?

"You're all nuts." Luke looked at the texts and then at me.

"I love you too." I sipped my wine, although I was still only on my first glass. I had work I wanted to get done tomorrow, and if I drank as much as Luke, I wouldn't even be able to open up the Word document. I watched the characters on the TV, but mostly Luke in my peripheral vision. He was so relaxed tonight, different. I leaned my head on his shoulder. We were going to a house party on Monday and I'd been anxious about it all week. Maia for one, clearly had her doubts about Luke and I didn't want to make things worse, especially since he'd revealed that my course friends weren't his favourite people in the world, either. All it seemed to take was one wrong move and a day could be turned on its head. Tonight though, held good omens for Monday.

"You're affectionate tonight."

My phone pinged at the same time as his observation. I read the email quickly, eyes passing over the first sentence.

Dear Miss Emerson, we are pleased to inform you…

Oh my God. I'd got an interview for the editorial internship. I jumped up, squealing.

"Oh my God!"

Luke looked at me warily. "What is it?"

"I didn't want to tell you until I knew if I'd made it past the first stage. I definitely didn't think I would, I mean, I have next to no experience, the only thing I have is my reference from Alex and…"

"Avery." Luke stood, putting his hands on my shoulders. "You're babbling. What's going on?"

"I got an interview at a publishing house. For an editing internship. Isn't that *great*?!"

Luke was silent, chewing his lip and clenching his fist around the bottle of beer. I felt my face fall.

"I thought it was great."

"You did this without even telling me? I thought we were meant to be a team."

"I only didn't mention it because it was a shot in the dark." I hadn't thought he would see it this way. I gulped back the fear that was rising in my chest. The fear that I'd done something very wrong. "I didn't mean to make you feel like that. As soon as I heard back I was going to tell you. It's a good thing." I grabbed his arm but he shook me off.

"Oh, so teaching is out the window now is it? Our carefully thought out plans, just scrapped over one email?"

"Well no, but–"

"God Avery. Why do you have to ruin a good day?"

"I just thought that…" I trailed off, nothing springing to mind.

"Thought what?" I felt a creeping up my spine; the horrible feeling that I'd messed up.

I tried to backtrack, plastering a smile on my face and starting to get up off the couch. "It doesn't matter. It's nothing, really."

He pulled me back down, winding me. "Avery." It was a warning. The back of my neck prickled. "Look at me!"

I jumped, reactively looking him in the eye. I tried to remember that he loved me, and I was being paranoid.

"Why would you want to abandon the plans we'd made?" His voice quieted. "Those plans are the only thing getting me through this year. This job."

"I'd never thought of this option before. It doesn't change anything. We can still go to London. I wouldn't make a decision like this if I didn't think it was right for us."

"You shouldn't be making a decision like this on your own at all! What if you do this internship and then you get some big break in *editing*," he sneered at the word, "and it isn't in London? What then? What am I supposed to do?"

"I didn't think of that." It was true, I hadn't. I'd been so caught up in the idea that I hadn't been thinking about London. Or Luke. I'd just been carried away in the thrill of the moment.

"I love you, but you make it so damn hard." His voice broke on the last word as he scrubbed at his eyes, swaying a little. "You don't keep your promises anymore Avery."

I didn't dare argue.

"We had it all planned *out*. Our future, your future." I felt myself physically recoil, and I wanted to retaliate, but something inside me warned against it. This didn't feel like any of our fights in the past.

"Damn it!" He raised his arm, throwing his beer across the room.

"*Ow!*" He'd clipped my jaw with the bottle. I clasped my hand to the spot near my chin that throbbed.

"Oh my God." Luke's eyes were wide. "Let me see."

I had recoiled, moving away from him, but he stepped forward, gingerly taking my hand away from my jaw. I stared at the ground, where the bottle had smashed, fizzy liquid seeping into our rug. Thank goodness it wasn't Eliza's red wine. I recited the method to get beer out of a carpet in my head. *White vinegar, detergent, warm water. White vinegar, detergent, warm water.*

Luke put his hands on my face, bringing me back.

"Avery. I'm so sorry." He clasped his hands behind his neck and started pacing. "I wasn't thinking! I just got so angry. I just wanted to smash something. I didn't mean to…" Luke's breathing hitched, and I put my hand on his chest, steadying him.

"It was an accident." My voice rose at the end. It wasn't a question. And yet.

"Of course it was an accident." Luke pulled me toward him. "I must be drunker than I thought. I had no idea you were that close."

I exhaled, closing my eyes. It had been an accident. I'd seen it. I ignored the feeling in the pit of my stomach that screamed this was the second accident we'd had in a very short space of time.

"Luke, I–" Part of me wanted to tell him to leave. Wanted to tell him to leave me for good.

"Avery, I know that you're sorry for applying without telling me." He held my chin. "It's okay, we'll just tell Eliza that we were drinking and messing around and you slipped. No big deal."

I stopped.

"What if it is a big deal?"

"No. It's not." He kissed me gently. When he kissed me like this, like I was something precious, I crumbled. My jaw ached as I pressed my fingers to it and I knew I would have a mark in the morning. Was that a small price to pay for the days like the one we'd had today? Where we laughed about nothing and I was reminded of who we used to be?

"Avery?"

"Hmm?" I was calmer now, my heart beating slower in my chest. I ignored the sting of my jaw. Ignored the sting of my broken heart.

"Delete the email."

I'd wanted to celebrate, pour myself another glass of wine and snuggle up with my boyfriend, basking in the success of both our weeks. But it had been me who had kept this from him. Maybe I deserved to be in the wrong. I opened up my phone and did as he'd asked.

"I feel better now. Like I can see our future again." He smiled at me. "I've got to go."

"Where?"

"Home. I need to cool off, and I don't want Eliza to see us upset."

"I'm sorry about the application."

Luke stroked my hair. "I know. I'm sorry about the bottle. I really am. I shouldn't drink this much, no matter how tough the week has been. I know that."

"It's fine." I bit back everything else as he gathered his things and turned to leave.

He looked closely at my chin. "You'll be able to cover it up with makeup, right?"

I paused. If it was really an accident, why did I need to hide it?

"Yeah. Yeah I can cover it."

The door shut, and after a few seconds my body started moving like clockwork, taking the shards of glass in the kitchen over to the recycling bin. I watched my hands move to the cupboard like they weren't even mine, picking up the bottle of white vinegar to remove all evidence of the beer. *White vinegar, detergent, warm water.* I changed into a pair of pyjamas, desperate to shed the feeling of unease. The whole time I wandered around the lounge in a daze, cleaning up after my mess, the same thought circled my brain. *People that love you aren't supposed to hurt you.*

So what were you supposed to do when you couldn't seem to stop loving them?

Twenty

It had taken two applications of concealer, but I'd managed to cover the bruise on my jaw. Covering my shame however, was proving to be a bit more difficult. It licked at my skin and raced through my veins. I was dripping with it. I was spending the day in The Hideaway, skipping my coursework to write stories and take my mind, well, anywhere but York.

"Try this." Emma slid a plate in front of me, with two small pieces of cake on it. "One is mandarin and dark chocolate, the other is pistachio and vanilla. Mum is thinking of extending our business to cater for weddings and she needs feedback."

"Wow," I said. "Thank you!"

But Emma lingered, clearly after something else. "Spoken to Beckett lately?"

Ah. We hadn't met here for a while and clearly she'd noticed.

"We went to The Little Library last week. I'm sure he'll be in soon." I added the last bit on a whim when her face fell. I had no idea where he was and today of all days, I just wanted to be alone.

"Well if you see him, tell him I said 'hi'." Emma smiled, a bit sadly. "It'd be nice to see him again."

Hearing Emma talk about Beckett stirred something inside me that I couldn't identify, and considering how muddled my brain already felt, wasn't something I wanted to explore.

"I know, I know. It's a phase I think. Maybe try chicken nuggets? Works every time for me."

I looked up from where I'd been focused on my writing. A woman a couple of years older than me had sat down at the next table along, and was carrying a cappuccino in one hand with her phone pressed to her ear with the other. "Mum, I get that. But we can't have her not eating anything. Try chicken nuggets, I promise it'll work." A pause. "Love you too."

She had her hair up in a high ponytail and was wearing workout clothes. She sighed heavily when she hung up, pinching the bridge of her nose. I turned away so she wouldn't see me staring and got back to my manuscript, figuring I'd work on another chapter before switching over to the section I'd promised Beckett I'd look over for him before Tuesday. The cake testers were still in front of me, untouched: every time my thoughts wandered to last night, my stomach turned.

"Avery?"

I jumped, almost knocking over my hot chocolate. Had the woman sat next to me just said my name? I went back to my writing, figuring I must have heard her wrong. I was pretty sure I didn't know her.

"Avery?" There it was again. I flicked my eyes up.

"Yes?"

Her eyes lit up. "That could have been embarrassing. I thought it was you. Then again, long black hair and green eyes isn't the clearest description in the world."

Was I supposed to know her?

"He did say though that you always sat by the window. When I noticed you sat there, it clicked." Finally, she registered what must have been a clueless expression on my face and started to laugh, her cheeks flushing. "I'm Lucy. Beckett's sister?"

Of course. Now I considered it, she looked pretty much like an older version of Lola.

"Yep, it's me. I'm surprised he's mentioned me enough for you to recognise me!" My voice sounded false to my own ears, but Lucy bought the happy pretense.

"Are you kidding? He talks about you all the time."

I felt my own cheeks redden but brushed it away. "I take it he's also mentioned this place."

"All. The. Time. I was curious. He tells me he's found a lot of inspiration within these four walls." It might have been a figment of my imagination, but it seemed like she paused to look at me knowingly. "How lucky that you'd be in here at the same time!"

I was very aware of the fact that I had hardly brushed my hair this morning. I probably looked like a yeti. Lucy was more put together than me by a long shot, and she had a *child*.

"Now that I've bumped into you, I might as well take this cosmic coincidence as a chance to say thank you." She must have picked up on my confusion because she went on "I know that sounds weird, since we've only just met. I kind of want to thank you for giving Beckett something to concentrate on mainly, other than me." The more that she spoke, the more she surprised me. The way Beckett had described her, she'd seemed a lot more fragile. It could have been a façade, but it didn't seem like it. This girl had strength. In abundance.

"I mean, I get that it's going to be stressful for Lola to acclimatise to a new man, but I really like him. Beckett has been overprotective since like, forever. It's nice for his attention to be drawn elsewhere."

I sipped from my mug; my hot chocolate had cooled in the time it had taken me to get to it.

"I get where he's coming from. I have a little sister that I would do anything for, but I also understand why it could get annoying. If you want me to say anything to him…"

Lucy waved me away, beaming. "He was right, you're kind."

My heart swelled a tiny bit.

"Believe me, you're already doing enough. I thought I knew what the concerned version of Beckett looked like back when Max left me to be a single mum, but for some reason he seems even more stressed now that me and Lola are completely fine. Like, he doesn't want anything to ruin it, you know? You take him someplace else for a while, and that makes me worry less."

Now I was definitely confused.

"Worried about him?" As far as I knew, Beckett was in his prime. Yeah, he was worried about his niece, but it hadn't seemed to be a cause for concern. I anxiously ran over my conversations with Beckett from the past few weeks, wondering if he'd let onto something that I, wrapped up in all my own drama, might have missed.

"I worry because *he* worries." She rolled her eyes, and I felt something click. She had always seemed so strong in the stories Beckett told me, but meeting her in real life I realised how much spirit she had. She may have been only a year or so older than me, but she felt so much wiser. "He worries way too much. He's trying to fill the void that Dad left when he died. Me and Mum don't need that – we love goofy Beckett - but it doesn't stop him from trying."

I barely heard the last few words, my mind too caught up in the revelation before them. My heart ached for Beckett.

"I didn't know that. About your dad." I wouldn't even have known what signs to look for if he'd been hiding it from me. My heart ached for him, the man that seemed to be full of concern for other people, but rarely for himself.

Lucy sighed. "He didn't mention it, did he?" When I shook my head, she glanced across the road towards his flat. I almost expected to see him looking back at us from the window.

"He died of a heart attack when we were in primary school. Mum and I both see it." I looked back at her. "We see how Beckett feels lesser because of it, I mean."

I tried to sift through my memories, searching for any indication that he'd ever tried to bring it up. Of course it had happened a long time ago but I was painfully aware that it took a long time for some wounds to heal. Especially when it came to family.

"He's trying to fill that void. He always has. But we're okay – it took a while, but we got there. I don't need a replacement father. I just need my big brother." She cocked her head. "And a babysitter once in a while."

I thought of the similarities between Beckett and me, and all the steps I'd taken over the years to try and stretch myself further than a single person: to be the person in our family that Mum had been. To fill our own void.

"You okay? You look really pale."

"I just relate a lot to Beckett. He's doing his best."

"I know. But I'm thankful that he has a friend here now, at least. I hate to think of him holed up in that flat twenty-four seven. His stories take his mind away from that space, but I still worry."

I never thought about what I gave to Beckett, only the friendship and writing experience that he provided to me. I didn't know that much about him, not really.

"Anyway, enough of that talk. It's all very morbid. What do you think of his new story? He's hardly told me anything about it."

"It's brilliant. Would we expect anything less?" It felt good to be part of a team; part of Beckett's team. "Sophia, one of the characters in the book, is especially inspiring. I like her a lot."

"Oh? He did mention her." She took a sip of her coffee and smiled over the cup. "I think she might be based on you."

I almost spat out my hot chocolate. "I don't think so!" I said, coughing.

"Why not?" Lucy shrugged. "I know that he always draws his inspiration from real people. It isn't too far out of the realms of probability that he would base a character on you."

"She's nothing like me."

"From what I've heard, my brother thinks quite highly of you. Probably more than you think."

Beckett's protagonist was strong in all the ways I wish I could have been in those past few weeks; all the ways I was not. The thought of being his muse however, even if he never revealed it to me, made me flush. I knew what Luke would think of it, and for that reason he could never know.

"Oh God," Lucy put her hands to her mouth. "I always do this. When I feel comfortable with someone, I overspill. Please don't say anything. He'd die if he knew I'd said any of this."

She looked so concerned that I rushed to provide reassurance. "Don't worry, I won't tell."

She squeezed my hand. "Thank you. I'm really sorry." Her phone buzzed. "Ugh. I'd better go. Lola's been staying at my mum's for a few days and she's having a food crisis. She won't eat anything but junk at the moment. Typical three-year-old."

I smiled, suddenly reminded of the beans on toast teas in Westby.

"I can see why you and Beckett love coming here, it's like a bubble away from the rest of the world. What a nice place to work." Lucy seemed wistful for a second. "Every time I visit Beckett here in York, I wonder what it would have been like to go to university. Must be nice. I took a gap year that turned into the longest of gap years."

She was talking about her pregnancy.

"I think you got a pretty good deal."

"You can say that, you're Lola's new favourite! I've heard all about the tiaras and tea parties." Lucy grinned. "Try telling me I got a good deal when you see us attempting to feed her anything green." She gathered her things together. "It was nice to meet you, Avery. I hope I see you again sometime."

She walked out of The Hideaway, already dialing another number on her phone. I couldn't help but feel ashamed that I was so broken when she, of all people, was clearly not.

Twenty One

"Tell me when to stop." Connie poured the gin into my cup, splashing in a bit extra after I said the magic word. "It's a *party* Avery. Come on." She linked her arm through mine and we moved from the kitchen into the hallway, looking for Maia. Connie had intended on bringing Dave along but he'd cancelled on her last minute (the beginning of the end, Con predicted), so she had come solo. Maia had tagged along to make her feel better, despite the fact that she'd been saying all week that she wasn't going to come because of her deadlines.

"There you two are." She found us at the same time as we clocked her. "I just got caught in a conversation about threesomes with some guys that I don't even know." She pointed to her *Star Trek* t-shirt. "What about me suggests that I would be interested in that?"

"Your obvious sexual magnetism." Connie swerved Maia's swipe, laughing. "Hey Avery, where's Eliza?"

"She's prepping for her seminar. And she was at her ball last night, so she's already feeling a bit fragile."

Luke was here somewhere, but I'd lost track of him as soon as he'd stepped into the house. He'd shown up late, waving off my complaints with a comment about work, and then gone in search of beer. Never mind the etiquette of bringing something of your own to drink before you started searching through the host's cupboards. I craned my head around, looking for him.

"Luke gone AWOL?" Maia twisted her head, clearly on my wavelength.

"I think he had a bad day at work. He'll reappear soon I'm sure." I thought back to the beginning of second term, over six weeks ago now, when my friends had been jealous of mine and Luke's relationship. Now, I was struggling to cover up all of the cracks.

"There he is." Connie pointed him out, standing in the kitchen talking to Roxie, the host of the party. "I'd claim him back if I were you, she's known for getting frisky at parties."

"*Connie.* She doesn't know what she's saying Avery. We all know he wouldn't do that."

"I trust him. Let's go find somewhere to sit." I felt happier now that I knew he was still in the vicinity. Especially if his attention was directed away from me for a few minutes. Plus, it was always nice to know that your boyfriend was a catch. Judging by Roxie's persistent hair flicks, she clearly thought he was.

"I'm just going to go and find Lewis from our poetry seminar. He mentioned he'd be here." Connie waltzed off and I sat down on the couch beside Maia, who was staring at the space that Connie had just vacated.

"You okay?"

She sighed. "Yeah. Don't worry about it."

I waited. To get Maia to open up, you just had to be patient.

"It's just, I'm kind of sick of watching her trail after guys who let her down. And it *sucks* that she'd never trail after me."

I tried not to overreact.

Maia's had told us how she felt about both men and women during Freshers' Week but I'd never heard her say anything more about it. How had I missed this? Had I been so wrapped up in myself?

"Connie loves you Maia," I said.

"I know she does. That wasn't quite what I meant."

"I know," I said. "How long have you…"

But she waved her hand dismissively. "It's never going to happen," she said but her smile was sad. "It's a classic tale of unrequited love. The libraries are full of them. It's fine. I made my peace with it. Just sometimes…"

I impulsively hugged her. "I'm glad you told me."

"So am I." Maia leaned her head on my shoulder, and I stayed silent, knowing that there was nothing I could say to make this any better. I just had to be there for her to help her ride it out. She took a long gulp from the mug of wine she was holding.

"Don't say anything, though,"

"Pinky promise," I said, and we looped our little fingers together.

"Heyyy, Avery!" Lewis, the boy Connie had disappeared to search for, sat down next to us and wrapped me in a drunken embrace. Maia immediately clammed up.

"I didn't see you at the pub quiz last week. Where've you been?" He leaned in again, probably thinking that I couldn't hear him over the music.

"Loads of work on!"

"Promise you'll be at the next one?"

A white lie. "Promise."

"Hey Maia." Lewis noticed Maia sat next to me and waved. "Have you seen Connie? She said she'd be here."

I squeezed Maia's hand and answered for her.

"I think she's in the kitchen maybe?"

He smiled. "Perfect. See you guys later?" He walked off without waiting for a reply. Maia beside me was quiet.

"You okay?"

"I'm beginning to think this party was a tragic idea on my part."

I poked her. "Hey. We wouldn't get to hang out if you hadn't come."

"A silver lining to every great tragedy." She paused. "You know, it really *has* been a while since we saw Luke. Maybe you should rescue him."

Maia was right, but I was glad he'd given me the space to be a friend to her when she needed me. It made me feel better to know that occasionally, I could still be there for my friends as well as Luke.

The room was getting crowded and I couldn't see him.

"I'll text him to meet us in the garden."

"Yeah, good idea. My signal is rubbish in here anyway, and one of my auctions starts in ten minutes."

Me: Where are you? Meet in garden?

I smiled once I'd sent the text. See? We could be like the old Luke and Avery. I hadn't received any of his usual text messages hunting me down. Maybe we were turning a corner and going back to the time when we could spend all night apart at parties and come back together happily on the way home.

"Okay." I put my phone back in the pocket of my jeans. "Garden?"

We made our way through the crowd of people in the kitchen, and when I saw Connie pressed up against Lewis, I sped up, not wanting Maia to see.

"God, that was a mission." Maia sounded upbeat again. "How on earth do you unlock this door?"

I rolled my eyes. "I thought you were the clever one. Hang on, let me just–"

I flipped the latch and the door swung open.

Maia gasped, and my mouth dropped.

There was hardly anyone in the garden. Hardly anyone but Luke, who was kissing Roxie, pressed up against the garden wall.

"Do you…" Maia had her hands over her mouth. "I mean, he might not know we're here. Do you want to leave?"

I didn't speak, in shock, but shook my head. If we left, who knew what would happen.

"Luke?"

Roxie sprang out from against the wall, her lips smudged from kissing my boyfriend. "Shit." She looked to Luke to fill the silence with an apology, but he was just staring at me.

I slammed the door shut. It was only the four of us out here. The smokers were clearly out front.

"I'm…" Roxie edged towards the back door.

I broke out of my horror, able to speak again. I turned to her "Don't tell anyone." Roxie's mouth opened. "You owe me." I narrowed my eyes at her and she nodded, clearly grateful that I was giving her the chance to get off scot free. She dashed inside, leaving me with Maia and Luke.

I turned to Maia. "I don't want anyone to find out about this."

Luke still hadn't spoken.

"But Avery…" Maia looked unsure.

"*Please* Maia. Give me time to sort this out. I have no idea what I'm dealing with. I'll come and find you."

She nodded. "If you're sure. Text me when you're done here." She shut the door quietly behind her, but I could still see her shadow through the glass, guarding us.

I looked to Luke. He had stepped into the light and I could see his cheeks were red. I hoped that was shame.

"How – " I spoke slowly, furious, " – could you do this to me?"

"It was only a kiss Avery."

"*Only a kiss*?!" I couldn't believe how cool he was playing it.

"We were talking. She got close and next thing I knew…"

"How would you have felt, if you'd walked out here and seen me *kissing* another man?"

He snorted. "I saw you with that guy downstairs, all over each other."

"What guy?" I thought back to the past half an hour. "Wait. You mean *Lewis*? He was asking me where he could find Connie."

"Sure. He was all over you. I saw it, don't lie."

I thought back. Oh God. The sloppy drunken hug.

"Did I hug him back?"

"I—" Luke looked panicked now. "I don't know, I didn't think…"

I'd been trying to hold back my tears, but suddenly the sobs broke free. "I feel sick." I sat down on a half-broken garden chair. I felt him come close but shook him off when he tried to touch me. "I would never do this to you. Never. I love you."

"I love *you*. That's what I'm saying!" He was laughing now, sounding relieved. "It's okay. This was a huge misunderstanding. I don't even like that girl. I just saw you with that guy and wanted to make you feel—"

"What Luke? Make me feel what? Like we were even? This relationship has never been about one-upping each other."

"I didn't mean for this to happen." It sounded lame, and we both knew it.

I'd come to expect a lot of things from my boyfriend. A shove, a shouting match. But I'd never considered that he might do this. I tried to control my breathing.

I got up, avoiding his face. "I think I'm going to go and find my friends now." I tried to walk past him, towards the house but he stood in front of me.

"Don't leave! We need to sort this out."

"What is there to sort? You kissed someone else, Luke. I need some time."

"It was only a kiss." I looked at him, incredulous.

His eyes were glinting with sudden tears, pleading, but all I could feel was my own pain.

"A kiss is *everything,* Luke. Do you know how excited I was the first time you kissed me? I was up for *hours* talking to Stella about how perfect the night had been. Don't tell me that a kiss doesn't mean anything."

"We can get past this. Just forget it ever happened."

"You cheated on me."

"Don't say that!" He was suddenly on me, pushing me hard against the wall of the house, my top riding up and my side smashing against the bricks beneath his weight. A stinging sensation flared in my ribs and I tried to turn around but he pressed me harder, my face centimetres from the brick. He leaned to whisper in my ear. "This is your fault. I never expected when I came to York you'd make me feel so isolated. That you would be out there with everyone like I don't exist. Is this what you were like all that time behind my back?"

I managed to slide out of his grasp, pressing my hands against my side. My ribs felt like they were on fire.

"I got to this party tonight and you abandoned me for your friends."

I thought back to his arrival, when I'd pulled on his arm to get him to stay with me, and how he'd shaken me off to go and search for beer.

"I waited for you to come back. I didn't abandon you."

His eyes were at the same level as mine. "You did. I went to get a beer, and when I came back, you weren't there. I bumped into Roxie, and she was friendly. She didn't leave me on my own at a party where I didn't know anyone."

"I didn't do anything…"

"I had no choice, Avery. You forced me."

"It's not my fault–" I stifled a sob.

Luke suddenly seemed to notice that I was in pain.

"My side hurts." I whispered.

"Let me see." He lifted my t-shirt, gently. My skin was scraped and red. "I can't see anything," he said before dropping it back. Then he put his hand over mine, his voice suddenly soft again.

"Maybe you're right," he said. "I don't know. You drive me so mad, sometimes, Avery. When I saw you with that guy–"

"I told you, he was just saying hello."

"I lost it. I just…" He pushed his hands through his hair, his voice breaking. "I'm sorry for kissing her. It was

a stupid, stupid mistake. I can't live without you, Avery."
He turned to me, brushed my hair away from my eyes and
I tried not to flinch at his touch. "Please don't leave me
because of one stupid mistake. I love you too much for
this to change everything."

And it would change everything. If I walked back inside
and left him there, things would change. I didn't know if
they would be better, or worse.

"Come on." He started walking towards the back door.
"Let's forget it. We can still have a good time."

I winced as he pulled my hands, jolting my side again.
But still, I followed his lead.

Like I always did.

Twenty Two

I waited until Luke was distracted in conversation with someone from my course to make my move.

"Just going to the bathroom." He nodded, weakening the grip on my waist that had so far prevented me from moving from his side.

"Hurry back." His lifted my chin with his finger and kissed my still lips. Connie winked at me from across the room.

As soon as I was away from him, I started to shake.

"Hey, I was looking for you everywhere…" Maia found me, steering me through the bodies and taking off her jacket. "You're really cold. Wear this."

I couldn't speak, paralysed by the fear that Luke would see me speaking to Maia and assume I was discussing his disloyalties.

"What do you want to do? Shall I call us a taxi? I was done here as soon as I walked through the door anyway." She took my nod as enough reason to call a taxi, and before I knew it, she had bundled me out of the party and we were pulling up outside my flat. I seemed to come to my senses when I realised she was poking around in my pocket, looking for the key to my front door.

"Is Eliza in?"

I found my voice. "Jack's."

Maia led me to my bedroom, switching on the light and settling me on the bed before rushing around finding me a blanket and getting a glass of water. I felt like such a fraud, that I couldn't tell her the real reason I was distraught. Luke kissing another girl I could probably get past. But the look in his eyes when he'd shoved me against the wall was replaying in my head, even when I squeezed my eyelids shut. The bruise on my chin hadn't even healed yet for God's sake.

I was my own worst nightmare. I was my own worst enemy. I'd tell any of my friends to walk away in a heartbeat from a situation like this. Now that I found myself in it, I was unable to do the same.

"What are you going to do?" Maia was sat next to me, playing with the Rubix cube that Luke had almost broken a couple of months back. It seemed everything was a reminder.

"I don't know." It was true. I didn't know. Even if we were talking about entirely different things.

"I know you love him, but he *kissed* her." I shot her a look. "Sorry. You were there, you get it. I just don't know how you're going to move past this. I don't know if I could."

I imagined her leaving tonight and going back to her house. Telling her housemates what she'd seen, what Luke had done. Revealing a side of him that couldn't be taken back. I had to do some damage control.

"Please don't tell anyone about this."

"Avery–"

"*Please*. If I decide to forgive him," Maia winced, "I really don't want everyone knowing my business. We're going through a rough patch. He messed up, but he regrets it, I know he does."

Maia seemed to be able to sense the urgency in my expression, because she backed off.

"Okay, I won't tell anyone. It's not my secret to tell."

I let out a breath.

"*But*. Please tell me if there's something else on your mind. Or if anything gets worse."

"I will. I promise." Would I go to hell for lying to so many people in my life at once?

"I have no idea what it's like to be in a relationship. But I don't want to imagine that it looks like that." The comment stung.

"He's been there for me through everything. What type of person would I be if I gave up on him when he made one mistake?" I wasn't talking about the kiss anymore.

My phone buzzed and I immediately picked it up, hoping it would be Luke. It was twisted, but right now I wanted to see him. The old him.

Beckett: Write with me tomorrow?

I threw my phone back on the bed.

"Who was that?"

"No one."

Was I being unfaithful with Beckett? I didn't want to stop writing; I'd already given up my interview for the internship, and the thought of giving up my writing sessions as well made my heart ache.

Me: I'll come over at eleven.
Beckett: Perfect.

I walked into the bathroom and opened the cupboard over the sink, grabbing some paracetamol. The pain in my ribs was intensifying. I'd Googled it in the taxi whilst Maia had talked to the driver – I didn't think I'd broken anything, but it turned out even bruised ribs hurt a ton. Maia was staring at the tablets I was taking.

"Headache."

"I'm not surprised." *Bang.* She paused. *Bang.* "Hey, is that your door?"

"Avery!" The knocks on my door had started suddenly and were persistent. "Avery!"

I knew who it was. Maia clearly knew who it was, because she'd started pacing.

"If we ignore him, he might just leave. We could have gone back to mine for all he knows."

"I'm so sorry Avery." Was he crying?

Maia sat with me on the floor, head against my bed frame, as we listened to him bang on the door for a good five minutes, never missing a beat.

"Avery, *please.*"

I stood up, wanting to see his face behind the glass. Hating myself for wanting to see him, but going anyway.

"You don't have to let him in, you know." Maia was wringing her hands.

"I know." I walked to the front door. "Luke, if you keep banging I'm going to get a noise complaint."

"Avery? Oh God there you are. Please let me in. I need to explain. When you disappeared at the party I—"

"Hang on." I turned the lock, absolute in my decision to let him in. Either way, I needed to speak to him at some point.

"Maia…"

For a second hurt flashed in her eyes, but it was gone just as quickly as it had appeared. "I get it. Call me tomorrow?"

I nodded and as I opened the door, she pushed past Luke, unwilling to even look him in the eye. I watched her go, sad that my backup had left but confident that whatever Luke was about to say, I didn't want an audience here for it. This was between us. Just us.

"Thank you." He took my hand in his own. "Thank you for hearing me out."

I didn't reply, his face a reminder of all that had happened. I wasn't sure I'd ever look at it the same way.

"I don't know what's wrong with me Avery." His eyes were rimmed red.

"You *hurt* me. Again." We weren't talking about him kissing Roxie anymore. We both knew what was bigger. I'd assumed he hadn't noticed my most recent injury, but now I knew better. He'd seen my fall and ignored it.

His hand touched my ribs lightly, and he winced when I flinched. "I'm so sorry. I just lashed out."

"I can't keep covering all of this up. The bruises, the grazes. I'm scared someone is going to find out."

"It's like I don't know who I am. This rage takes over, and I can't see straight. I'm with you one moment, and then it's like I'm somewhere else, and I don't care who gets hurt."

A single tear dropped down my cheek and he wiped it away. "It always seems to be me. Me that you hurt."

"I know." He pressed his forehead against mine. "Please don't leave me whilst I figure this all out. I can change."

"Can you?"

He was crying too now, and he nodded against my head. "Please let me stay tonight."

The fact that he was asking showed how far we'd come from the excitement I'd felt at him moving to my city. Normally, it was just expected that we'd be together most nights; I was always more comfortable snuggled up with him, my head in the space between his arm and the rest of his body. I looked into his eyes, searching for the rage I had come to associate with him. But right now, I only saw sorrow. Sorrow that I felt too. If I couldn't ask anyone else for help with this, maybe I could take support from this version of him.

"You can stay."

He pulled me to the bedroom, asking my permission with his eyes before undressing me. I kissed him back, because it allowed me to pretend that none of this had happened. We were just two people, kissing after a party.

"I love you." Luke nuzzled my neck, leading me over to my bed. I ignored the warning signs in my stomach and joined him. "I promise I can change Avery. I just need you."

I'd always thought it was quite romantic, needing someone.

"Be careful." I didn't say it explicitly, but we both knew what I meant. I felt more breakable than ever before.

"I promise." Luke pressed a light-as-a-feather kiss on my side. "I will never do this to you again."

I woke a little later, picking up my phone and looking at the screen that read 02:06. Luke was sleeping beside me, looking as calm as he always did when he slept. I opened up Instagram to pass some time, knowing that it was unlikely I'd get back to sleep any time soon. We'd drifted off some time after midnight, Luke whispering apologies into my ear until his breathing evened out and his arm had gone limp over my body.

Stella had posted an Instagram photo of her and her friends. I felt so homesick, missing her with every fibre of my being. I clicked on her profile to look at some of her old photos. There were a few of her with the same friends, dancing around at the house party she'd been talking about a couple of weeks ago. One of her pouting in our bathroom mirror. A recent one of her and Elliott at the beach, tongues blue from slush puppies. And, as much as I was trying to ignore it, the photo taken on the beach a few weeks ago, my mother cropped out except for a few tendrils of hair.

"Hmmmph." Luke rolled over and I paused, stricken, like I was doing something wrong. Staring at snippets of my mother in photos was a decidedly non-Avery activity.

I shrugged Luke's arm off my stomach and went to the bathroom, putting the seat down and perching on the end of the toilet. I dialed a number and waited, crossing my fingers that my sister hadn't turned her phone off when she went to bed.

"What time do you call this?" Stella sounded half asleep.

"A ridiculous time."

"Glad you agree." Silence, and some rustling. "Okay, I'm more awake now. What can I possibly do for you at two-thirty in the morning?"

"I just wanted to hear your voice."

"Are you drunk?"

I laughed despite myself. "No. I just miss you."

"Miss you more. Are you sure there isn't anything wrong?"

"I'm sure." We chatted for a few minutes, about nothing in particular, and I felt my insides uncurl. Talking to my little sister was a reminder of what would always stay the same.

"Mum said that I should wear the red one, but..." Stella babbled on. I couldn't place a finger on what I was feeling, but it didn't feel good.

"Can I have Mum's number?"

"Okay, where did *that* come from?"

I tried to think of a believable lie. "If something happens to you, I need to be able to contact her."

A pause. She was clearly weighing up whether to pursue her line of enquiry.

"Well, I don't really care why. I'm just glad you want it."

"It doesn't mean anything…"

"Okay. I'm going back to sleep now. Call me tomorrow? I need your advice on some homework stuff."

"And by that, do you mean that you want me to do your homework?"

"Well *I'm* hardly going to be able to do it, now am I? I'll be too tired."

I rolled my eyes. "Go to sleep."

The line clicked off and I got up, switching the bathroom light off as a text came through. My mum's phone number. I didn't think I would ever need it – there wasn't much life advice from my mum that I would trust anyway. But tonight, it made me feel better just having it.

"Where did you go?" Luke was wide awake, the whites of his eyes visible in the dark.

"Oh, Stella rang me."

"Is she okay?"

"Yeah, just stressed about GCSEs. Got to be on hand twenty-four seven." I laughed it off, hoping he hadn't heard my phone call. He had supported me ever since I'd decided to cut my mum out of my life; going back on that now would suggest that there was something wrong.

"Come back to bed with me." He patted the space beside him and I snuggled in next to him, closing my eyes to ward off further discussion.

Twenty Three

"Avery, hello?" Beckett grinned, shaking his head before turning back to the manuscript he had on the coffee table. When I'd walked in half an hour ago, five minutes early, and had glimpsed at least ten mugs strewn amidst the papers, I knew he was nearing a breakthrough. Slowly but surely, chapter by chapter, his novel was reaching an end. His deadline had been tight, but even so, I felt that the justification for our friendship was moving way too quickly. I kept looking over at him as he worked, mumbling to himself about dialogue and timelines, and found myself wishing that he would need my help for a lot longer. Lola was napping over in the next room, so we were working in the kind of silence that gave your wandering thoughts a whole lot of power.

"Yeah, sorry." I smiled back, pulling my sleeves down to cover another bruise, from where Luke had gripped my wrist two days ago. The ones on my side were lessening from last Monday, but as soon as blue turned to yellow, Luke found a reason to add new shades to my collection. I found myself reasoning with every new addition, telling myself that anything was better than saying goodbye to him.

"I can't figure out Sophia's end arc. It's been stressing me out all day long." I snapped back to attention again as Beckett gestured to the pages. I'd kept my word to his sister and hadn't mentioned what Lucy had said to me about Sophia. In fact, I hadn't mentioned Lucy at all.

"Did Lucy tell you that we bumped into each other?"

His head whipped up. "Wait, what? How did she even know what you looked like?"

"I was in The Hideaway. Lucky guess, I presume."

"Weird. What did you think?"

"She's really nice. I wasn't expecting someone so headstrong." I teased him. "*Someone* is worrying for no reason."

"Worrying about other people is unfortunately just what I do. Luckily for my sister, she isn't my latest stress. My agent wants this draft for next month, and I can't for the life of me figure it out. *This*," he looked up at me, pained, "is why you outline things. Anyway, did you hear back from the internship programme?"

He didn't see me wince.

"Yeah, I got an interview."

Oblivious to my dismay, Beckett was beaming. If there was a power cut, we wouldn't need to rifle through cupboards to find a torch. His smile was that bright. And infectious. I felt my lips turn up in the first genuine smile I'd shown in days.

"That's great, Emerson. You'll smash that interview. Tell them how you helped me find my way through all of this." He gestured to the mess on his desk and shuffled a few more papers before finding the one he was searching for underneath all the chaos. That was the thing about Beckett; no matter how messy it got, he always managed to sift through the debris and find what he was looking for. He had the first page of the whole manuscript in his hand, which he held out to me. I raised my eyebrows. "I read through a couple of chapters last night, for the first time since you touched it up. It's seamless." He blushed, realising how it sounded. "Well, the story might not be. But the writing is. You have a gift for fixing things." I almost laughed at the irony.

"I prefer the term 'enhancing'." Beckett rolled his eyes and took the page back from me, placing it in his file. Last week he'd dropped the whole file on the floor, every page out of place. The thought of sorting it out had made my chest tight but he, however, had just found page one and carried on, sliding things into place whenever he found them.

"Fine, you *enhance* writing. My point is, you can definitely do this."

"You have more faith in me than anyone else I know."

"I'm sure that isn't true."

"Uncle Beckett?" A small, sleepy voice came from the doorway to his bedroom, where Lola was standing in a Peppa Pig t-shirt and purple trousers, a blue rabbit dangling from her hand by one long ear.

"Rapunzel!" She spotted me for the first time, grinning as she wiped sleep from her eyes and shuffled over, sitting right beside me on the sofa even though there was no need for a tight squeeze. Her feet didn't touch the ground, so she clicked her heels together and slid a warm hand into mine, her tiny fingers curling. When I glanced sideways, Beckett was beaming too. What was it with this family and their never-ending supply of smiles?

"Hey Lola." I whispered, squeezing her hand. She looked up at me very seriously.

"Uncle Beckett is working."

I stifled a laugh and didn't look at him. "I know."

"It's a story." She was humming to herself, absentmindedly touching a sheet of paper next to her with the hand she hadn't tucked inside mine. "Have you read it?"

"Beckett's story? I have, it's a very good one." Beckett laughed at my confidence in his work, and it seemed like he was unable to take his eyes away from the partnership forming in front of him. This little girl was so innocent and pure, and for some reason, she'd taken to me. I watched my sleeve like a hawk, willing her not to make a split-second decision and pull it up. If Beckett saw any of my bruises, I'd have a lot more to answer for.

"Does it have pigs in it?" Lola was staring at her t-shirt.

"Yep, tons of them." Beckett placated her, and she bounced on the sofa, pleased.

"Can I have a hot chocolate?" Lola leaned forward, her blonde curls bobbing in a way that made me think of her mother. "Mummy said I could have one if I was good."

"Only if you say 'please', little miss." Beckett was already on his way to the kitchen area, pulling out three mugs.

"Pleeeease." Lola jumped out of the seat, trying to pull me up with her so that we could all make the drinks together. My heart warmed at the thought of her getting as excited about hot chocolate, as I always did, and how Beckett had just known that I'd want a mug. He reached on top of the store cupboard to get a bag of mini marshmallows and Lola started a dance party in celebration, her excitability contagious. Whilst the kettle boiled we joined in the party, two supposedly sensible adults getting ridiculously excited over a bag of mini marshmallows. The heavy feeling in my chest was slowly lifting. I continued to dance, ignoring the pain in my ribcage until at least five minutes of childlike fun had passed. I shook off the darkness, swinging Lola around whilst Beckett stirred the hot chocolate mix. I watched him, smiling to myself as he spun the spoon around, oblivious to my eyes following his ease around the kitchen. For a brief moment, I forgot that I wasn't a real member of this crazy family; that I didn't have a permanent space here, not really. That as soon as Beckett stopped needing me for his writing sessions, I would have no reason to carry on seeing him. I forgot it all for a minute, stretching my arms up over my head and shimmying with Lola. Beckett was shimmying too, scooping more hot chocolate into the mugs. He knew I liked more hot chocolate powder than the average person. Lola was going to be hyper after this.

"Rapunzel, do you need a plaster?"

Dread crept up my spine as I turned my attention to Lola, who was lightly touching the ugly fingerprint shaped bruises on my arm. She was mesmerised by the marks. I knew that kids were no stranger to the bumps and bruises you got from playing outside, but this was different. Lola could see it, and when I glanced up, so could Beckett. His expression was one of horror, and he slowly put the spoon down, abandoning the task at hand and treating the unfolding situation with caution, like he thought I might bolt. I hadn't ruled it out. Some things you could easily explain away. Some, you couldn't. I tried to plan a cover up story in my head; I'd fallen over, knocked myself. Caught my arm on a door handle in a rush to get to my seminar. Yes, that was the one.

"Lo, go take the marshmallows into my room, okay?" For a second Lola just stared at the bruise on my arm.

"Uncle Beckett has Peppa Pig plasters. I got one when I fell over at nursery."

"I'm okay. Thanks though." I leant down to her and tapped her nose. "Go and find me your favourite toy okay? That will make me feel much better."

"Okay." She took the marshmallows when Beckett pushed them into her hand, and she offered me one. "When I fall over, Mummy gives me sweets."

Despite the tension in the room, a ghost of a smile flickered over Beckett's face.

"That's just what I need." I took the marshmallow and popped it in my mouth, and she trundled off to the bedroom, singing songs to herself, the situation remedied in her eyes. From the look in Beckett's, not everyone felt that way.

As soon as she was out of earshot, he spun around and looked at my arm again, even though I'd covered it up.

"Avery. What is that?" I could tell that he knew exactly what it was. That's the thing about bad things – you never want to believe that they exist, even when they're staring you right in the face. On this occasion, quite literally.

"I was being silly really, rushing out of my bedroom. Caught myself on the door handle." I willed him to take the easy route out of this. This was nowhere near as bad as what he was imagining. Luke wasn't a monster – he was just struggling. I'd woken up yesterday after another fight the previous evening, Luke still asleep and breathing softly into my ear, with a new outlook. After scrambling us some eggs and washing the night away in the shower, scrubbing my skin to within an inch of its life, everything seemed more manageable. I could do this.

Beckett, however, looked unconvinced by my lie.

"I promise. I caught my arm on a door handle."

I wanted to turn back time to five minutes ago, dancing around the kitchen. From the way Beckett was shaking his head, I had a feeling that that wasn't an option.

"No. No, you didn't." He ran a hand through his hair, and I took a step back, knowing him well enough to recognise that that was his stress signal. "Please tell me that someone didn't do this to you."

I focused on my breathing. In, out. In, out. This was my responsibility, whilst Luke tried to fix the mess he had made. To keep it all secret. When Luke got himself under control, when he was less stressed with work, I wouldn't have to lie. I would be free.

"I just–" I stopped and tried again. "I promise. I wouldn't lie to you, Beckett."

He was sitting on the bar stool now, shaking his head. I picked up the cooling hot chocolate and forced it into his hand.

"You would tell me though, right? If something had happened to you?"

I didn't know if he thought that Luke had done this, or a stranger, but I wanted to stop him looking at me like that. "I'm supposed to be the one helping you, Beckett."

Beckett took my hand. "You seem to think that you aren't allowed to lean on me. We are equals in this friendship, Avery. You have every right to vent to me, even if you're scared."

I sat down on the stool next to him, and he gently lifted my sleeve to get another look. When he did, he winced. We both stared at it; an impasse reached in the conversation that I wasn't sure how to move past.

"I can't." My voice was a whisper, the words fragile. I was weak, and I was so tired.

"Why? You're clearly stressed out about something, even if its unrelated to these bruises. You drift off into some place I can't reach, you back out of plans, you've lost weight…" He carried on, and I stared down at myself. Had I? I supposed that meals had seemed low priority in the past few weeks, but I hadn't done anything intentionally. Was it obvious? Had Luke noticed? My heart was beating quickly, and my breath was becoming ragged. This was all too much, too loud, too everything. I got out of my chair and put my bag over my shoulder.

"Avery, don't go."

"There's nothing wrong. Luke and I haven't been getting along, but he didn't do this to me, if that's what you're thinking." The look on Beckett's face suggested it was. "I slipped."

From the doorway to his bedroom, I could see the edge of Lola's feet. There was no way I was having this messed up conversation with a three-year-old listening in.

"Please don't think about this anymore. There's no reason for you to be concerned about me. I'm fine." I was practically begging him, which made me even more upset. Beckett wasn't supposed to see this side of me.

"I have to—"

"Have to do what, Beckett?" My voice rose an octave, and I willed it to stop. "You *don't* have to do anything for me. We write, we talk, and we have a laugh. But this is my business. My life. Don't do anything to mess it up for me." I wanted to stuff the words back into my mouth as his hand dropped from my arm and he took a step back.

"Avery. I'm not trying to upset you."

"Well, what are you trying to do? I know it's your signature move, but please don't stick your overprotection on me." It was a cheap shot, and we both knew it.

"I thought you understood about all of that. I thought—"

"I think I should go."

Beckett didn't reply, and his eyes looked so sad that I took it as my cue to go, not looking back to see if he would try and stop me. Here I was again, screwing up yet another relationship that I valued. Maybe Luke was right; they couldn't both exist in my life at the same time. Maybe Luke had been right about everything.

Twenty Four

I winced at the sound of the knife scraping against my plate, and saw Luke shoot a glare from where he sat opposite at the dinner table. His mum coughed, letting us know she'd seen the exchange. I noticed she hadn't touched her steak yet, as though she was waiting for permission to begin.

"And then I thought, why let the client suffer, you know? So I told him where he could get off." Luke's dad loosened his tie in delight at his own anecdote.

Out of the corner of my eye I saw Luke loosen his own tie, almost like it was a reflex to mimic his father's actions. A lot could be said about my dad, but one issue Stella and I never had was judgement. Luke faced judgement every time he spoke to his father. I liked his mum; it was his dad that gave me nightmares. I avoided dinners like this to my best ability and being away at university had always been a welcome escape. Now though, when Luke came back to Westby, it was assumed that I would too. Which was how I'd arrived here, spending my Friday night at this grand dinner table, rather than the tiny one in my dad's house.

"Darling, that must have been hilarious." I tried to hold back the burst of laughter I felt bubbling up my throat. Luke's mum was such a liar.

"Not for the client." Mr Calkins wiped his mouth and looked at Luke. "I hear from Nathan that you're still not turning those figures around fast enough for them."

"Dad, I—"

"I mean there's really no excuses for messing up an opportunity like this." He narrowed his eyes. "I hope I didn't make a mistake in pushing you for that position."

"Darling, not now."

"I'll bloody well say what I want when I want to." He snapped and Luke's mum fumbled with the napkin in her lap, silenced. "If you don't get your act together soon, boy, there will be consequences." My heart raced. This wasn't the way you spoke to your children.

Mr Calkins broke the awkward silence. "So, Avery. How's university treating you? Not too time-consuming, I hope?"

"Dad." Luke sent him a warning glance, and I wondered what had been spoken about behind my back.

"What? I'm making conversation."

"It's fine." I nudged Luke's foot under the table and he sent me a smile. We were in this together. "Aside from some poetry I struggled with, it's going well. Just the rest of second semester to get through."

I knew Mr Calkins's position on university, and even though my boyfriend would never admit it, I knew it was the reason why he hadn't considered it. His father commended working from the bottom up and earning your place in a business. Which hadn't stopped him from meddling and placing Luke at a branch of his own firm, using his own foot in the door to get his son settled, but I kept my mouth shut. If his own wife didn't get a say, I highly doubted I would.

"I didn't know you struggled with your poetry." Luke spoke through a mouthful and then glanced at his father, self-conscious.

"You didn't ask."

His mum clapped her hands together, making both of us jump. "Right! Who's ready for dessert? I got your favourite darling." She patted her husband's arm. "Avery honey, come help me with the dishes?"

I didn't roll my eyes, knowing full well that Luke and his father could very well clear the table themselves, but again, it wasn't my place to mention.

"So, Avery," Mrs Calkins spooned crème fraiche into meringue nests. "How are things going, with you and Luke?"

I froze midway through washing the punnet of raspberries she'd handed to me, wondering if she could tell. But then she giggled, and I allowed myself to exhale. She carried on, not actually looking for a reply. A lot of questions in this house turned out to be rhetorical.

"I've had his grandma's engagement ring tucked away in the safe for seven years."

"Mmm." I was suddenly engrossed in the raspberries, making sure every berry was more than clean. I didn't want to think about the future of my relationship, focused completely on damage control in the present.

For the first time in well, *ever,* I wanted to run to the bathroom and call for help like Eliza had done to me so many times in the past on bad dates. When she'd rush home and I'd be ready on the sofa with tea and a packet of biscuits, ready for her to spill the beans on what had been said or done to make her flee. This wasn't a bad date though, it was a dinner with my long-term boyfriend's parents. And the thought of that engagement ring made me seriously worry that those mashed potatoes might make a reappearance. If she'd brought mine and Luke's future up only a month ago, I was sure I'd have been excited to chat. Now though, the thought of the future frightened me. If Luke didn't change like he promised...I didn't want to dwell on it.

Over the last couple of years we'd been messing around, joking about what we might name our children, where we'd go on our honeymoon – all the things you talked about when you were long-term. Now, the thought of raising a child with Luke filled me with dread. I could handle his anger towards me now, but with someone much more vulnerable in the house? I accidentally dropped a raspberry down the plughole.

For some reason, the question that Beckett had asked me when I'd first mentioned Luke replayed over and over in my mind. *How can you only know who you are when you're with someone else?* I was beginning to see the sadness in that.

After we'd sat awkwardly in the living room of Luke's house for an hour after dinner, we left to go and visit my own father. The difference in atmosphere had been palpable; my dad content to let us chat about our lives in York, without inserting his opinion where it wasn't wanted.

"I did tell Stella that you might pop round tonight." Dad pressed his tea bag against the side of the mug.

"I'm not bothered Dad, you know that. I want her to spend time with her friends. I don't just visit to see her, you know."

He smiled at me. "I'm so proud of you, you know. I was reading over that essay you just handed in, and my God, it's better than anything you've done yet."

I was glad Luke was upstairs getting ready for bed – the contrast between fathers would have been funny, if it wasn't so heartbreaking for him.

"How's Luke? I didn't want to ask, I know you say he's stressed. Job isn't getting him down too much, is it?"

I leaned against the fridge, sighing. "His dad is a piece of work."

"Raymond seemed decent when I met him. You just don't know what goes on behind closed doors."

You don't know the half of it Dad.

"It's a shame. Such a nice kid. Don't know what we would have done without him."

I looked down at my hands. This was the crux of my fears. If I wanted to open up to my dad, would he even believe me? Luke was everywhere I turned. Had even infiltrated my own family.

"I think I might head to bed now Dad."

"Here, have this," he passed me the cup of tea. "I'll make another for myself."

He wasn't expecting it when I reached over and hugged him, but he squeezed me tight.

"Thanks Dad."

"It's no bother."

I walked up the stairs to my bedroom, looking back to watch him humming to himself as he poured more water into the kettle. So content in his own company. Beckett had said that loneliness was where you truly found yourself. Was he right?

"You know." Luke padded out of the bathroom and met me on the landing, his mouth full of toothpaste. "Dad thinks it'd be a good idea for us to move in together next year."

"I thought we'd decided to wait until I graduated."

He was hopping on one leg as he removed his jeans, now in my bedroom.

"Yeah, but things change."

"Like what?" But it didn't take a genius to know what that meant. As far as I could see, the sole thing that had changed in our circumstance was that his dad had pushed it.

When he climbed into the double bed next to me, his breath was cool and minty fresh against my ear. I shivered.

"I like the idea of it just being us, no distractions. After everything that's happened, don't you feel the same way?" Was it just in my imagination, or did his grip on my leg tighten?

"I guess."

"I'm going to need more enthusiasm than that." Thankfully, his voice was teasing, and he flipped me onto my back, tickling me.

"It's just a complete change of plan." *Something I'd paid the price for just a few weeks ago.*

"The right change of plan this time, though." He smiled at me, so confident. "Just picture it. Our own bedroom, however you want it. We could do this," he ran his fingers down my thigh, "whenever we wanted."

I took advantage of the pleasant mood. One battle at a time. "That sounds nice."

"I knew I'd be able to convince you." Luke's lips pressed against my neck. "You're my whole world, Avery."

I smiled along and said all the right things, moving to the same rhythm as the handsome boy who wanted to offer me the world, or at least, controlled slivers of it. I bit back what I really wanted to admit to him – that we'd never been so out of tune.

Twenty Five

Maia: Are you coming to town with us today?
Me: Sorry! Got a lot of work to do.
Maia: Come to mine later then? Or call me? Haven't
seen you since the party. Worried.
Me: Don't be worried. We've talked it over. Thank you
for caring. :)

I shoved my phone in the back pocket of my jeans. That had been a stupid excuse to use. Maia, of all people, knew exactly what work I had. I shook off frustration at my poor attempt at pushing her away and manoeuvred my trolley through to the bread aisle. Eliza had texted me a list of the items she needed this week instead of coming with me for the food shop, and they were fairly simple, aside from some dairy-free ice cream that was harder to find that I'd originally envisaged. Glancing at the row of items in front of me I put some crumpets in the trolley, conscious of what Beckett had said about my weight loss.

"Hey stranger."

I jumped, startled. Beckett was standing in front of me. He smiled sheepishly.

"We really have to stop meeting like this." He gestured broadly to the aisles around us. It felt like a lifetime since we'd met here last, when friendship wasn't a cardinal sin. I was very conscious that the last time I'd spoken to him had been our argument. He'd sent a few texts, but my trip to Westby, and the simple fact that I'd been avoiding him in general, had stopped me responding.

He pressed on. "It's pretty lame to keep meeting up in the carb aisle."

I was exhausted at the thought of having this conversation. Everything was exhausting these days. Still, the things I'd said to him at his flat, pushing at his weak spots, warranted or not, were still out of line.

"Beckett, I'm so sorry. I said some pretty mean things."

He shrugged. "I was out of order as well. It really is none of my business, and if you say that you're okay, I believe you." I wasn't sure, judging by the look on his face, that he was being entirely truthful, but I was just glad to take the easy way out.

"So, what have you been up to? It's been a while."

I looked down the rest of the aisle, my heart beating so fast that I wanted to let it out of my chest, tell it to run away and never look back. Everyone I knew did their food shop here. Luke did his food shop here.

"I went home for the weekend." The shorter my answers were, the quicker I could get away.

He was smiling now, taking my path of least resistance as a sign that we were on steadier ground. "How is Stella?"

"I didn't actually see her; she was out with friends."

"Oh?"

"Besides, I wasn't really going to see my family. Luke's parents had organised a dinner."

Beckett stared at his feet, his chest rising and falling but instead of pressing me, he carried on. "That's a shame. Not long left of this semester though, is there? You'll be back home in no time."

"You're right. In a few weeks I'll have all the Stella time and Easter Eggs I could ever want."

"Keep in touch though, yeah?" He said it lightly, but when I looked at his expression, he looked pained. "I want you to know that it isn't just about the book, or the writing, for me. I overstepped the line, was a bit too pushy, but I'm still your friend. Don't be a stranger Emerson."

My heart felt heavy, a sadness I couldn't identify dragging me down. I'd wholly underestimated what I meant to Beckett, and I felt awful about it. This wasn't just my problem. Selfish seemed to be my middle name these days.

"You can come to visit the beach anytime."

He grinned. "You'll have a tough job getting me anywhere near the sea."

"What if I buy you an ice cream cone?"

"Raspberry sauce?"

"*And* sherbet."

"You spoil me."

It felt nice to resume our usual rally of conversation. Easy.

"What delights have you got in there this time?" I leaned into Beckett's trolley. There were party rings and some tinned pineapple, a block of cheese and lemonade.

"Lucy's coming over tonight with Lola, and apparently the little princess has requested another tea party. And when I say princess, I don't mean Lola. Lucy demanded cheese and pineapple on sticks, like we used to have when we were younger."

I smiled at the nostalgic expression on his face. "Don't lie Beckett Kearns, you love the tea parties just as much as they do."

"Only when I get to wear the tiara."

"Obviously."

"Speaking of, I actually do need to get back to my shopping list. I still need to get some frozen pizza pinwheels and some strawberries and cream. From the number of items on this list, I have a feeling Lucy coerced Lola into asking me for this tea party. She knows I can't say 'no' to my niece."

My heart warmed. "You're the best uncle I know."

"You think?"

"Really. Lola and Lucy are the luckiest pair in the world to have you." I meant it too.

He hesitated, like he wanted to say something, but decided otherwise. He shifted his satchel higher up on his shoulder and I suddenly wanted to invite myself to the tea party and to read his latest notes on my writing. I'd forgotten what it felt like to look forward to something instead of worrying what the consequences were.

"Unless," Beckett stared at me, "do you want to come? I know they'd be happy if you came."

I bit my lip. Luke wasn't messing around with his distaste for my friend.

"I can't. Next time though." We could both hear the lie. There was too much at stake for me now to melt into Beckett's world like I wanted to.

We exchanged goodbyes and he walked off, pushing the trolley and pausing by some cupcakes, which he carefully placed in his trolley. Lola's face would be a picture when she saw the treats he'd picked up. I shook off the feeling of jealousy that they got to hang out with Beckett, no strings attached, and walked in the opposite direction, focusing on the task at hand; to find this ice cream.

Eliza: Did you collapse in the supermarket or something?
I'm starving here, and only ice cream will do.

I fired back a response to her, laughing at her attitude, spirits lifted now that I'd patched things up with Beckett. She texted again with some exclamation points; Eliza was a nightmare when she was hungry. We were going on a double date in a few nights; her and Jack, me and Luke, and it had been worrying me since she'd suggested it. Luke's increasing disdain for my time spent with anyone else threatened to ruin what had the potential to be a nice night. I was starting to live with a constant fear that things could come tumbling down at any moment.

"Aha!" I whispered it to myself, spotting the ice cream at the back of the industrial size freezers. Next to it, I saw the mini pizza pinwheels that Beckett must have been talking about. I picked up a box and popped it into the trolley along with the ice cream. If I couldn't be a guest at the tea parties anymore, I could at least pretend.

Twenty Six

"I cannot believe that you are making me do this." Luke was perched on the edge of my bed, tying up his shoelaces.

"Eliza wants to get to know you better, and I thought it might be nice to go."

Luke looked at me pointedly. "What on earth are we going to talk about during dinner?"

"Jack is going to be there. Small talk. Wine. Nice food. The whole point of a double date is to have fun."

"Don't be sarcastic Avery, I hate it when you do that."

I looked away from him, hoping he couldn't see my expression in the mirror. I was stuck in a catch twenty-two. If I told Eliza why I didn't want to go, there'd be questions. If we went, I'd have Luke complaining to me the whole time. My time with friends was slowly receding; Beckett's writing sessions had halted, I was only seeing my course friends when we were on campus, and Eliza and I were like ships in the night, never seeing each other anymore because Luke always had me holed up in my room. It was a wonder that my best friend hadn't said anything; without Jack's presence in her life, I was sure that it would've come to a head by now. I checked my lipstick in the mirror and adjusted my tights.

"Ready to go?" I feigned enthusiasm, ignoring the weight in my chest.

"About as ready and willing to go as you would be to attend a finance meeting at my work." His expression was deadpan.

I sighed. "I thought you liked Jack."

"I don't *mind* Jack. I'd just rather not share you."

I walked out of my bedroom, hoping he would follow. I didn't know how to battle against this jealousy that Luke felt. Every contact I had with another human was becoming an attack on our relationship. It was becoming easier to just nod and not risk saying a word.

"I'm so excited, I've never been to a wine tasting before." Eliza came bounding out of her bedroom, and she lightly pushed Luke's shoulder. "Hey stranger. You finally came out of Avery's room!"

"Let's go." I intercepted.

"Yeah," Luke warmed up, flicking the switch, "I've been looking forward to this all week."

"I thought we could meet Jack there. He's on his way back from football practice." Eliza's face was one of total bliss. I envied her for still being in the honeymoon period.

A couple of weeks ago, Eliza had seen a leaflet for a wine tasting at one of the student-friendly tapas restaurants in town, and she'd been convinced it was the perfect opportunity for a double date ever since. I had to admit, sitting here now with patatas bravas and chorizo skewers, glasses of red, white and rosé littering the table-top, that it hadn't been a completely awful idea. And Luke was seemingly on his best behaviour, especially after meeting with Jack and establishing that, yes, he was completely smitten with my best friend and not in fact harbouring hopes for me.

"I like this one." Eliza gestured to the sweetest rosé on the table, hiccupping slightly.

"I think you like them all." Jack teased. Eliza had been trying second helpings of all the wines, and I was enjoying watching her relax.

"How's work going then mate?" Jack picked up a skewer as he waited on Luke's response.

"It's getting better since the last time we spoke. I'm finally gaining some proper responsibility. For the first few weeks I felt like all I was doing was making coffee and getting abuse from everyone at the business for being the boss's son." His eyes darkened.

"When I worked at that Italian restaurant last year it was kind of like that." Eliza was gesturing with her hands, a tell-tale sign that she was drunk. "People always treat the new guy like shit. It gets easier eventually."

Luke's eyebrow was raised so high that it had almost disappeared into his hairline. "I think it's probably a bit different to waitressing."

I jumped in to defend Eliza. "The essentials are still the same though. Human interaction, competition."

Jack was watching Luke carefully now, clearly annoyed he had brushed off Eliza, who hadn't even noticed. It was rare that Luke allowed his stress to be taken out on other people; why would he need to when he had his own outlet sitting right next to him?

"Did you reply to that email about the interview?" Jack persevered, this time levelling his question at me. "Eliza was so happy for you when she found out that you got one."

Luke's hand had tightened on the tablecloth at the mention of the internship.

"Yeah, it turned out that it actually wasn't for me in the end. Difficult to get to, and it was this summer. I can't leave my family for the whole year." Whilst this wasn't technically a lie – I genuinely would have felt guilt over leaving my family yet again – I felt Luke's eyes on me to make sure I kept on message. I tried not to let my chin wobble at the thought of what could have been, instead staring intensely at the nachos in front of me, picking at salsa and guacamole with my fork.

"What? You didn't tell me that." Eliza looked at me funny. "You were so excited about it. I'm sure Stel and your dad would be fine. Plus, you could go home on weekends."

"It would be a lot of pressure on Avery." Luke didn't look up from his food whilst he spoke. "I don't think she should stress herself out too much. Teaching is a great career. My mum loved it."

Until she had to give it up for a life of getting spoken down to and washing dishes.

I didn't dare look Luke in the eye, for fear that he might be able to read my mind. Again, Luke had removed me from a conversation about my own life, talking *about* me instead of to me.

"I think if you want something enough, it would be worth the stress." Jack picked up his glass.

"Sorry if I'm the only one with real life experience here." Luke snapped at him, and the three of us – Eliza, Jack and I – froze.

"That's not fair." I put my hand on Luke's, willing him to calm down, and then looked at my friends. "He doesn't mean that. He's just worried about me having too much on my plate."

"Yeah, sorry about that. Must be the wine." Luke shrugged. "Uncool of me. I just meant that I really want to be an accountant like my dad, it's just a lot harder getting started than I thought it would be."

Eliza laughed, brushing his snap comment under the rug. "We're all existing in our uni bubble. We'll understand once it bursts, I'm sure."

Jack still didn't look impressed. "Yeah, I guess."

"I'm really sorry. I've just remembered I've got to make a call." Luke stood up, clenching and unclenching his fists. I could spot the beginnings of rage in his eyes, so I stayed put, even though I knew I was expected to follow. Once he was out of the front door, his phone in his hand, Jack turned to me.

"What's his problem?"

"He's just stressed. Probably hangry too." I tried to laugh but it fell flat.

"Are you sure you don't want to just go to the interview?" Eliza poured me some more of the white wine. "It wouldn't hurt to see what happens. Heck, if you need me to FaceTime Stel every night, I will. You should do the internship."

"I probably wouldn't have got it."

"You'll never know now." Jack had a point. I never would.

"I'm sorry about Luke, he was out of order. He's never usually like this."

"We know that," Eliza patted my hand. "His work is obviously getting him down. No hard feelings."

Even after patching up relations, I could see Luke pacing on his phone outside, and my throat filled with panic. What would happen once we got home? I'd been careful to avoid mentioning my application when we were alone, but surely I couldn't be held responsible for topics that my friends brought up.

"You good?" Jack looked at me.

"Fine. I think I'm just going to go and reapply my lipstick."

"I'll come with!"

"Eliza you can't leave Jack on his own. If Luke comes back there'll be too much testosterone at the table." My heart was racing, and I felt sweaty even though the weather was cold and there was a distinct lack of heating in the restaurant. I couldn't shake the fear of what might happen when the night was over, and it was just Luke and I, alone. He would never touch me in front of my friends, but when we were on our own it was an entirely different ball game.

Once in the bathroom I took out my lipstick, pretending even to myself that the reason for this trip to the toilet hadn't been full blown panic. I couldn't get the look in Luke's eyes out of my mind – the one I associated with him before he turned. He was unrecognisable, too many moods to pin down just one. When I'd first fallen in love with him, it was the safety and security that had kept us afloat. It was unravelling around us now, and I'd never felt so insecure. So unsafe. I wiped the tears from my eyes, fanning my face so it might look less red. I didn't need any extra attention.

"There you are. I needed a wee too much to wait." Eliza came into the bathroom and stopped when she saw me fanning my face. "Are you crying?"

"What? No." I wanted to let her hug me, but I resisted. "I was topping up my mascara and I accidentally poked myself in the eye with the wand."

"Oh my God I do that every time I apply the damn stuff. One second, I really am desperate." She went into the cubicle. "He's so dreamy, isn't he?"

Despite everything, I laughed. "Jack?"

"Who else?"

She was right. There was absolutely nothing dreamy about the other man sat at the table.

"I just feel on top of the world. I'm so glad I decided to ditch my bachelorette ways."

"I think that might be the wine talking." I ignored the jealousy I felt deep in the pit of my stomach.

"Probably, but I'm just so happy that you're here too." She washed her hands, hugging me. I tried not to sag too much against her. "I've missed you lately."

Why did everyone keep saying that? I was *right here*.

"I've been around."

"Yeah, I know. I've been busy too. I guess you never could have known how hard it would be to juggle everything when Luke moved here, huh?" There was no accusation in her voice, but the confirmation of my neglection of our friendship caused new tears to brim, which I blinked away. Eliza had no idea how much I could never have been able to predict.

I steadied myself, letting her lead the way back to our table. Luke eyed me as I sat down, and his eyes held a warning. Say anything to anyone, and there will be consequences.

Twenty Seven

Considering it was only March, it was hot.

"I mean, I know it's warm, but *really*?" Eliza gestured with her ice cream to the group of boys walking around shirtless. In fact, when I turned my head to scope the full extent of the park, I noticed that a lot of men had followed suit. Eliza rolled her eyes.

"And I bet, if I stripped to my bra right now, it would be considered indecent." The ice cream was pointed in my direction, and I held my hands up.

"Don't point that Cornetto at me, I'm with you."

After the other evening, I'd made a conscious effort to separate my time with Luke from my time with Eliza. The two were not compatible anymore; if I was with them both, I was stressed about what happened after. Luke had completely turned the night back around when he'd returned to the table the other night, apologising for his rudeness and charming my friends again. When we'd got home though, Eliza's slip about the internship had earned me a shove. It was too risky to be with both of them at the same time; Eliza was a chatterbox, and I had no idea what she'd say.

"If you were an ice cream, what would you be?" I threw my head back and laughed at her question.

"How did you just go from feminism to Cornetto-talk?" I watched a group of dog walkers stride past our picnic blanket, half-walking, half-dragged across the grass. A beagle eyed Eliza's ice cream hopefully; a leash away from bounding over to us.

"Because, my friend, true feminism is making talk of equality so normalised it can be brought up casually. Now answer the question." She cocked her head whilst she waited for my answer, clearly deep in thought about her own. "I think I'd be a Fab." I raised my eyebrows. "For obvious reasons."

I threw my hair forward whilst I pondered the deeply philosophical question, desperate to tie my long hair out of my face. It was the kind of heat that leaves you sticky, the humidity that I associated with early September in Westby when nipping to the newsagents meant you needed to take a shower when you got home.

"Honestly, I have no idea."

"I'm thinking maybe an orange sorbet or something. You're sassy."

"Pfft." I didn't feel sassy right now. I felt more like vanilla; plain, boring.

"Hi Rapunzel." I felt a small tug on my hair, and when I lifted my head backwards again, I saw Lola standing in front of me. After a moment of sunshine-frazzled brain melt, it occurred to me that a three-year-old probably wasn't supposed to be wandering around the park on her own. I knew Beckett's flat wasn't far, but still. When I swivelled my head to glance around my immediate surroundings, I couldn't see him or Lucy.

"Lola." She grinned when I tickled her ribs, and she plonked herself on the blanket between me and Eliza, who was beaming. Eliza loved kids. "Who are you with?"

"Uncle Beckett." Her tiny fingers reached for the punnet of strawberries that lay beside our assortment of magazines, and she started to eat one, the red juice staining her mouth. I still couldn't see her uncle, so when Eliza mouthed "where is he?" behind Lola's back, I could only shrug.

"Who are you?" Lola pointed at Eliza.

"Avery's best friend."

Lola blinked before nodding, grabbing a second berry. I hoped that she was allowed them, since there was no hiding the mess on her face.

"Uncle Beckett said we could eat ice cream." She'd clocked the Cornetto in Eliza's hand.

"My favourite flavour is chocolate, what's yours?" Eliza picked a daisy from the grass.

"Strawberry. Pink like Peppa. Do you watch Peppa Pig?" She took the daisy from Eliza, rubbing it between her tiny fingers. Phewf. Crisis averted. I sent a thankful look Eliza's way and then left them to chat whilst I scrolled to Beckett's number in my phone.

"Lola!" I whipped my head around and saw him jogging over, the concerned expression on his face melting away when he realised who she'd wandered over to.

"We do have our own picnic blanket." He looked exasperated – the unruly hair being the main giveaway I'd come to depend on as an indicator of his mood.

"It's fine." Eliza shrugged and offered him the strawberries. He seemed to visibly relax, because he took one before offering his hand to Lola, who seemed hesitant to leave our blanket. Who could blame her?

"I like it here."

"Well, I like it at our own blanket. What are you laughing at, Emerson?"

I laughed even harder. Eliza was looking at me weirdly, raising her eyebrow. I hadn't even realised how much I'd been missing him. There was a Beckett shaped hole in my life at the moment.

"Beckett! Did you find her?"

I turned around in the direction of the shout to see a girl jogging over to us. She arrived, out of breath.

"Oh, sorry Iz." His cheeks flushed and his eyes flickered to me. She was beautiful, this girl – all red hair and green eyes. I'd always loved my own green eyes, but they suddenly seemed a little dull in comparison. Eliza was flicking her head between us like she was watching a tennis match.

"Guys, this is Isabelle. Iz, this is Eliza and Avery."

Why had he said my name second? Lola was singing to herself as she shuffled off the edge of the blanket, picking daisy after daisy. The only one of us not feeling awkward. Besides Isabelle maybe, who was beaming at me.

"Hi! I've heard a lot about your writing."

"Yeah?"

Isabelle started some small talk, but I was too distracted to give her my full attention. Beckett was avoiding eye contact whilst I tried to stare him out. I needed details. He'd never mentioned a girlfriend, but had I ever asked? He was an attractive and intelligent young man. Why wouldn't he have one? But at some point over the two months we'd been friends, he definitely would have brought it up, I was sure.

Especially after our last conversation at his flat.

I became unable to concentrate on much besides the sinking sensation within my stomach. I'd pushed it away time and time again over the last few weeks, the butterflies I'd felt with Beckett at our dinner party. The butterflies that hadn't, I knew, occurred on a one time basis. In fact, I could feel them hammering against my chest right now.

"Avery? You okay?" Eliza nudged me. I smiled at the others, too consumed by my thoughts to contribute. I could feel Beckett's stare burning a hole through my skin, willing me to look around, but I was worried what my facial expression might convey. That I'd realised that as much as I loved Luke, or at least, as much as I knew that I needed to love Luke, I didn't want Isabelle to be Beckett's girlfriend. I had no idea what that meant for me.

"Yeah, I know exactly what you mean." I didn't know what Eliza was talking to Isabelle about, but I nodded along, trying to keep up.

"Oh it's the best place to study, but we're probably biased." the girl was saying, putting her hand on Beckett's arm. "We were on the same course." She knocked him with her shoulder and I tightened my grip on the edge of the picnic blanket.

"It's…good." I forced out a reply.

"Shall we go and find our abandoned blanket Iz?" When she nodded, Beckett pulled Lola up from her spot next to me.

My eyes finally met Beckett's, but I quickly looked away. What I was feeling made me want to hang my head in shame. I couldn't claim both Luke and Beckett, and I'd chosen my side.

"Bye Eliza. Bye Rapunzel." Lola waved in the way three-year-olds do, a quick curling of her fingers. She bent close to me and hugged my neck before wandering off with her uncle and Isabelle. I watched their heads bent close together as they walked away; deep in conversation.

"That was weird, right?" Eliza had sat up, hugging her knees. "I had no idea he was seeing someone."

"Do you think that's who she was?"

"I mean, I'm no romance expert but…*wait*. Do you care if he's seeing someone?"

"I mean, I don't know."

"Shit."

All I wanted to do was open up to her about the feelings I'd discovered. That maybe I'd been ignoring what my heart was trying to tell me. That my boyfriend scared me, but the boy from The Hideaway made me feel safe. Amidst everything that was going on, I was one hundred percent sure that Beckett would never lay a finger on me.

I picked at a hangnail, deep in thought. Beckett and Isabelle were almost out of sight now, barely a speck in the distance, but they were definitely not out of mind.

"What are you going to do?"

"Nothing. I have Luke." I'd mentioned to Eliza that we were having a rough time, but as far as she was concerned, it wasn't enough to abandon my relationship. Even in my own shoes, knowing all that I did, I still wasn't sure that it was enough. Luke and I had been through too much together.

"I'm sure it was just all this random heat today. It can do things to a girl." She stood up and brushed the grass from her trousers. "If I got myself down every time I checked out a guy at the park, I'd never give myself a break. What Luke doesn't know won't hurt him."

At least we were on the same page in some respects. What Luke didn't know *wouldn't* hurt him. But if he found out what I was feeling? It would end up hurting me, no doubt about it.

"I know what'll cheer you up." She reached out her hands to help me up.

"Yeah? What's that?"

"A rom-com and a slice of pizza as big as your head."

It was going to take a lot more than that, but I let her lead the way.

Twenty Eight

Eliza hadn't been kidding about the pizza.

"Make sure you get one half barbecue, one half tomato." Even though we'd only separated ten minutes ago, she was already on the phone. I couldn't decide whether it was because she thought I was too distracted to remember our pizza order, or because she wanted to check that I hadn't freaked out as soon as I'd walked in the opposite direction. I'd known for days that she had coursework due next week, but after our conversation with Isabelle, Eliza had told me that it could wait. She was rushing back to the flat to work on it while I went and collected dinner.

"Yeah, yeah. You don't need to check up on me." I hedged my bets that *that* was the reason behind her call, and her mutterings went silent on the other end. "Caught red-handed?"

"Maybe. I also just really don't want you to get the order wrong. Sun makes me *hungry*."

It had taken us a while to find our favourite Italian takeaway place, but once we'd found the cheesiest pizza with the thickest crusts, we'd never looked back. The only downside was that I had to pass Beckett's flat building on the way, but I was planning on walking as fast as I possibly could with my eyes on the ground. I didn't want to think about what might be going on in there.

"I can be trusted with pizza. See you in a few." I hung up on her despite her protesting and shook my head, still smiling when I passed the window of The Hideaway. I knew I shouldn't, but I couldn't help it; I looked inside. This was ours, and it would feel like I'd been sucker punched if I glanced through the window and saw him sitting there with her, discussing literature over a slice of cake. Thankfully, almost every seat was empty; the waitress turning the 'Closed' sign on the door.

The light was fading and all around me on the street people were pulling on their hoodies and coats, remembering that despite the weather, we lived in Yorkshire. I crossed the road to avoid the entrance to Beckett's flat, looking straight ahead, not wanting to risk bumping into him. Or her.

Standing in line ready to collect the order, I barely noticed my name being called.

"Avery?" I jumped, suddenly freaking out that it might be him, and blushed when I realised that it was just the waiter, pizza box in hand. "We threw in a slice of our new brownie. Let us know what you think!" I smiled with fake enthusiasm and weaved my way through the line of people still waiting for their order, reaching the door just as someone pushed it open. I gasped and almost dropped the pizza box.

"I thought I saw you heading past my building."

I quickly noted that Beckett was on his own and tried not to make it obvious that I was relieved.

"Yeah, we wanted pizza." I held up the box in explanation, and he laughed.

"Well I didn't think you'd come here for fish and chips." He was teasing me. It was all a bit *too* normal, considering.

"Do you have a few minutes to come up?" His eyes looked into mine searchingly. "Please?"

"I have pizza. If it arrives cold then Eliza will flip." It was true, but it was an excuse.

"I'll put it in my oven to keep it warm?"

"I don't know if…"

"I will buy you a new pizza if it's cold, Avery. Please let me explain. I don't want to leave things awkward between us."

A pause.

"Please?"

I nodded.

As soon as the door closed behind us and he'd put the pizza box in the oven on a low temperature, he spun around and started pacing. "I want to explain."

"You don't need to do that." I started to reach out a hand to still him, but pulled it back quickly, unsure of where

I stood. I had a boyfriend and of course he didn't need to explain. But I wanted him to. More than anything.

"We aren't," he gestured between us. "Me and you. There's nothing going on here. I know that. But there's nothing going on between Isabelle and I either."

I paused, stumped. It hadn't been what I was expecting. I'd assumed I was about to hear a long-winded story of how he and Isabelle had met and instantly clicked, but it wasn't going to impact our friendship. Now, I was even more confused. I could tell by the expression on his face that I wasn't being very discreet about it.

"She's my ex-girlfriend." Somehow, that was even worse.

I kept quiet, desperately waiting for confirmation that what I'd seen in the park wasn't some sort of rekindling. Not that it should mean anything to me.

"How long ago did you–"

"Two years. We met here, at university."

"Why did you break up?" He raised his eyebrows. I backtracked.

"Sorry. I know I'm in no place to question." We hadn't exactly been in constant contact the last couple of weeks, particularly after our argument. I was in no place to interrogate him, so I stopped the inquisition and waited for him to tell me whatever he'd brought me up here to say. I felt my phone buzz in my pocket, and was confident that it was Eliza wondering where on earth I was.

"It's fine, you can ask." After a moment of agonising silence, Beckett waved me off. "We broke it off not long after we graduated – she travels with her job, and to be honest it just wasn't working anymore." I'd never understand that phrase. If a story I was writing wasn't working, I'd work as hard as I could to fix it. I was trying everything I could to hold on for dear life to my relationship with Luke. Broken words and all.

"But she does still feature in my life quite a bit. We're friends. She understands me, and my family, and Lola loves her. We were too close to cut each other out, so we keep in touch. That's why we were together today, at the park. It wasn't… Christ what am I saying." He rubbed his face. "I don't know why I feel the need to justify this."

I wanted to reach out and take his hand from his face, to reassure him that he hadn't missed the mark. He hadn't been the only one noticing the chemistry between us. There was a gentleness to Beckett that I'd never found in anyone else, and I wanted to tell him that. But I was terrified of the consequences.

"She seemed nice." It sounded weak, even to my own ears, but I had to make at least a feeble attempt to not sound the pathetically jealous friend. And after all, she'd done nothing wrong. Upon reflection, she *had* seemed nice. It made sense now why she hadn't found the situation awkward. For one, she hadn't known that there was even a situation and two, she genuinely wasn't a man stealer. Not that he was mine to steal. *Oh God.* If I hadn't been in the company of another human, I would have put my head in my hands.

"She is." There was an awkward pause, although I wasn't sure whether it was just my interpretation.

I turned to go and retrieve the pizza, thinking that this conversation had probably run its course. "Well, I'd better get going." I blinked, stuck between not wanting to leave and wanting to run as fast as I could. This was something, Beckett and me, that I was never going to be able to have.

I turned to leave, my heart aching.

"Avery, wait." Beckett grabbed my arm, and instead of backing away like he usually would, he pulled me closer. "I need to tell you something. The reason I didn't want you to get the wrong idea about Isabelle," he stared at me, "is because of how I feel about you."

Even when you suspect that something might be true, it still takes your breath away.

"I don't know what to do Avery." He took his hand from my arm and started pacing again. "I've never met anyone like you." A blush crept up to my cheeks as the words that I hadn't realised I wanted to hear left his lips. It was so unfair for me to crave this. I knew that, and yet…

"I don't know what to say." It was more than that though. I wasn't sure what I *could* say.

"You don't have to say anything. I just want you to know."

"I–"

"No wait, I have to say this. I know you seem to want everyone to turn a blind eye, and I don't think I know the extent of it, but I can just feel that something isn't right with you and him. He's affecting you, and even as a friend you won't let me in enough to see it. But I want you to know that I do. I want you to know that I won't be silent about it anymore; every time you're upset, or *bruised* – God, I can't believe I didn't follow that one up – I will be here to tell you that you are worth so much more. And even if you don't want me, I will always be here for you. Whenever you're ready."

He was directly addressing my worst fear, remembering it from that day in the bookshop. When we'd sat in between millions of stories, without realising that we were in parts, writing our own. I bit back the confession that sat behind my tongue.

"He gets angry, he doesn't mean it." Despite the tingle that climbed my spine at the thought of his feelings, I couldn't get rid of the sharp instinct in me to protect my boyfriend.

"I fully believe that when he looks back on it, he doesn't. But he's not good for you. You're on edge every time I see you. I can't ignore this Avery. What if next time, it's even worse?" He'd stopped pacing now, and was perched on the arm of the sofa, leaning forward and pleading with me with his eyes. He was offering me help.

It didn't quell the pang of fear. And sadness. And loyalty. My mind was a spider's web of emotion, too many paths that crossed and intersected to know which one was the right choice. Beckett was honest and wouldn't think twice about supporting me. But we had a long way to go, and he didn't know me like the back of his hand. Hadn't seen all the crooked parts of me that you couldn't explain. Luke had never left my side through the ugly parts. How could I abandon him through his?

"He's the only one who's ever been there."

Instead of getting angry, Beckett's expression softened. "I know. But I care too much not to tell you that you are strong enough on your own."

Twenty Nine

Luke was sitting less than a metre away from me, and the guilt was eating me alive. After getting back from Beckett's the evening before, I'd eaten pizza with Eliza and although she pretended not to notice how distracted I was, I'd caught her watching me several times. I felt like a fraud; I was keeping secrets from my best friend, and now, sitting here next to Luke, my boyfriend too.

"You're quiet." We were sat in the smoking area of a pub; Luke wanted to be away from all the people inside. He'd always been like that, preferring enough quiet for us to talk, but nowadays it came with its own risk.

"I'm just kind of in my own head." I forced myself to lean over and kiss him. "Sorry."

"Anything you want to talk about?"

"Nope." I wasn't drinking tonight – too confused without alcohol making things blurrier. Beckett had called me earlier, worried after my mad dash from his flat, but I'd smoothed things over, telling him I needed some space to think. I didn't want anyone to know I was having feelings for someone else. Someone other than Luke. And the truth of it made my heart shatter. I had to bury those feelings for now. I had to get through one thing at a time.

I stood up. "Do you want anything?" I asked but Luke gestured to his still full beer and I went inside.

"On the hard stuff tonight, then?" The bartender joked when I asked for another Diet Coke.

The front door opened, sending a gust of wind through the pub, whipping my hair in front of my eyes. I went to brush it back behind my ear but instinctively thought of Luke, who might be watching. Touching my hair could easily be mistaken for flirting so instead, I just let the hair get in my eyes.

"Hey, are you okay? I didn't mean anything by the drinking comment." The bartender's brow was furrowed.

"I know." I grabbed the glass and fled back outside.

"I could have got you that." Luke nodded to the Coke.

I knew by now that it was probably better to stay quiet.

"Took you long enough. Chatting to the barman were you?"

Again, I stayed silent. There was another group of people outside; three students that had been laughing over pints of cider the whole time we'd been there. I wished it was me, sitting over there with Maia and Eliza. I'd never felt this way before: like I had no reason to want to be with Luke.

"Are you even listening to me?"

"I am."

Luke had been going on and on about the new responsibilities he'd been delegated at the office, and I was trying to listen, but there was a buzzing in my ears. I could feel my heart beating erratically. Beckett's presence was the opposite to Luke's; like waking up in the morning and knowing exactly where you were. Luke's was like waking up alone in the dark. I quickly brushed the thought away, scared that Luke would read my mind and label me exactly what I was. A traitor.

"God you really know how to make me feel like shit don't you."

I startled, Luke's eyes zeroing in on me.

"What are you even thinking about?"

"I'm sorry," I said. "I'm just tired."

"Do you know why you're tired? You're stretching yourself way too thin. I told you that you shouldn't be seeing so much of your friends." Luke's words were slurred. "You have enough on your plate with your course work."

"I don't see my friends that much anymore. Aside from on campus, and–"

"I don't care."

"What?"

"I," he said each word slowly, purposefully, "Don't. Care. I've said it once and I'll say it again: your friends aren't worth it. Once you're done here, we'll be going to London. Think they'll make the effort to stay in touch with you?" He laughed and shook his head. "Sometimes I think you like spending time with them more than you like spending time with me."

"That's not true Luke. I love you."

"Do you?" He snapped.

"*Yes*. Please stop." I glanced anxiously at the group of students, who had stopped chatting and were now staring.

"What are you looking at?" Luke squinted drunkenly at the other table.

"Oi, Mate!" He pointed to one of them. "What's your problem?" They shook their heads and got up to leave. How had I got here? My boyfriend was the charmer, the crowd pleaser. Even when he'd been different behind closed doors, he'd been on his best behaviour out here, in the world. I didn't recognise him anymore.

"If you love me so much," Luke shifted, slopping beer onto the floor, "why do you still see Beckett?"

I froze. Did Luke know about last night? About Beckett admitting his feelings for me?

"You know what?" Luke's beer bottle slapped against the table. "I don't want you to see him anymore."

"What?" My voice was a squeak. I'd purposefully stopped hanging out with my friends, and I was seeing Eliza less and less. But Beckett? Even though I couldn't think about my feelings for him right now, there were other reasons for our friendship. "My writing…"

"If you're a good enough writer, then you don't need him." His voice was soft now. "I believe you can do it without him. And there's always the teaching to see you through. If you love me, you'll stop seeing him. You know how much it upsets me."

My silence angered him. I saw the switch in his eyes.

"When did I stop being good enough for you?" He leaned in and stared at me. "What do I have to do to keep you here with me?"

Before I could answer he pushed his lips against mine. This wasn't what I wanted. My hands went up in defence against his chest.

"Lu-uke…" I tried to force the word out past his lips but it came out strangled. He didn't pay any attention to my discomfort. He pulled away, but his face was still close.

"Avery." He cupped my chin. "At least *show* me that you still care." And then he was back again, aggressively, insistently covering my mouth with his while his hands travelled up my leg.

I focused all my attention on pretending it wasn't happening. Squeezed my eyes tight.

He snapped back. "What's wrong with you?" he whined. "Am I that repulsive?"

But before I could answer he was on me again, gripping my thigh. I tried to focus on something else; the sound of customers inside the bar, having fun. The warmth of my jumper around my shoulders. The feel of the loose thread on the ripped knee of my jeans.

As he grew more persistent, he dug his fingers into my skin but the harder he pushed, the further my mind disappeared.

But then I felt his hand go around my neck and I suddenly tensed.

"Please," I said around his mouth. "Luke. You're hurting…"

He pulled back and slumped in his seat "I wanted to come here after work with you…unwind, relax. Forget about everyone breathing down my neck and just be myself. You're the only person I can be myself around, did you know that?"

He said it like it was a good thing.

"You're the only person who sees someone worth saving." He brushed my hair away from my eyes. "You're my person."

I felt bile rising up my throat. How were you supposed to reply to something like that?

"I'm just going to go to the toilet."

I kept my head down as I entered the pub through the back entrance, making my way to the bathroom without drawing attention to myself. No one was looking at me, and it didn't seem like anyone had noticed our argument outside. The group of students must have just pegged us as an overly dramatic couple. Was that what we were? Was I being overdramatic about this?

"Hey." A hand stopped me before I entered the toilets. "Come this way." I didn't dare look up in case they noticed the tear tracks on my face. I was led into the kitchen of the pub.

"Let me get you a glass of water." The voice was calm, soothing. When I finally did gather the courage to look, I realised it was the bartender who'd served me before. He passed me some ice water, and I took it, taking a small sip. My eyes flashed to the door.

"I'm not kidnapping you." He smiled, but it fell kind of flat.

We stood in silence for a moment. I had no idea what he'd seen. "I'm Tom. I'm the assistant manager here."

"I'm Avery." My voice was barely a whisper.

"Is that your boyfriend you're with outside?"

I nodded, my heart pounding.

"I saw what just happened on the CCTV."

I swallowed and stared hard at the floor.

"Avery," he continued. "What I saw was pretty worrying. It didn't look like you wanted him to be doing that to you."

Like a rabbit caught in headlights, I was frozen, unsure what to do.

"You can tell me."

I hesitated. "What would you do, hypothetically, if I did tell you?"

Tom sighed. "I'd have to tell my manager. Then they might need to report it, you know, just in case."

"In case what?"

"Well, he's in a public place. And what I saw... is that the first time he's done that?"

"Done what?"

"I'm training to be a social worker," he said. "And part of that is spotting signs of abuse."

I rolled the word around on my tongue. "Abuse."

"Yeah. Like your boyfriend hurting you. Or if someone forced themselves on you without your consent."

I thought back to the bruises on my body, some still there, some long gone. To the graze on my hands when he pushed me over outside the restaurant that first time, and the mark on my chin when he'd hit me with the beer bottle. To the pain in my ribs that still zinged if I moved too quickly. I'd known that it was wrong, but abuse? That was something you only heard about. It didn't happen to people like me. And consent? He was my boyfriend. Did that not equal consent? After everything, my instinct was to protect Luke.

"He was annoyed. We were having an argument. He tried to make up. That's all. Happens in all relationships." I laughed even though I definitely wasn't finding anything funny. "Do you always kiss your girlfriend when she kisses you?"

"If I didn't want to, I wouldn't." His tone made me stop in my tracks and I was suddenly crying. "Look," he was saying. "Do you want me to go and say something to him? Let him know that I saw what…"

"No!" I exclaimed. "Please don't say anything! It was just a stupid argument." I wiped my face. "I need to go, he'll be wondering…"

"Okay. I don't feel great about this." He grabbed an order pad and a pen from his apron, "This is my number. Just in case."

I looked at the slip of paper before finally taking it from his hand and sliding it into my pocket. "Just in case.

Thank you." I went to leave, my heart rate calming down now that no one was planning on marching over to Luke and confronting him.

"Avery?"

"Yes?"

"Tell someone. If what I saw tonight on the cameras is only a snippet. Tell someone."

"I will," I said. But I think even Tom could tell that was a lie.

Thirty

I dropped my bag on the couch, getting a glass of water and leaning against the sideboard in our kitchen, finally letting myself breathe. I hadn't been able to shake the memory of last night from my mind all day. The way Luke had forced himself on me.

I'd stashed Tom's number inside my copy of *To Kill a Mockingbird*. Maybe I would need it someday; maybe I wouldn't. Either way, it was comforting to know that it was there.

"Where did you come from? I've been in my room all day with cabin fever and I didn't hear you." Eliza pulled some raspberries out of the fridge and started munching.

"I was out getting a coffee."

"Did I tell you who I bumped into yesterday?" Eliza wasn't looking in my direction, just chatting as she typed on her laptop. "Maia. I think her date went well!"

Shit. I'd never called Maia back.

"Erm…"

"You know, her date with that girl from the Scrabble society?"

"Yeah, I know." I was lying through my teeth, and it was probably obvious. I desperately needed to call her; I'd just been so scared of what she might say. "Did she say anything exciting?"

"Well you probably already know, but they went to this really cute open mic poetry night and got late night coffee after."

My heart warmed at the thought. Especially after she'd been hung up on Connie for so long.

"So it went well then?"

Eliza looked at me weirdly. "Didn't you guys talk about this? She said that as far as dates go, she thinks it went well."

Which in Maia-land, meant it went extremely well. I added calling her to the long to-do list in my mind.

"Anyway, what are you doing tonight?" Eliza continued. "I thought we could have a study party, put some music on, cook something nice enough to make us forget about the work we have to do…"

I paused. I wanted to stay here with her. I wanted to relax and chat to her about things that didn't have to matter. Maybe even things that did.

"I think I'm going to Luke's."

"*Again?*"

"Yep."

"How are you not getting bored of him yet?" She laughed. "I'm kidding. I just need to break up my time with Jack with other things. Clearly I'm not in love yet."

I wanted to scream at her that I wasn't sure I was in love anymore either.

"Have you spoken to Beckett since we saw him the other day?" She had pink berry-juice on her lips, just like Lola had that day at the park.

"I haven't." It was an outright lie. I hadn't told her where I'd been whilst I was getting pizza, pretending that the wait for takeaway pizza had been ridiculous. I'd wanted her, of all people, to challenge me. She never had though, not since our spat that day when we'd bumped into Maia and Connie. I'd pushed her away, and it had worked.

"I was thinking about it. I do think you'd make a cute couple. He was great at our dinner party, and Stel wouldn't shut up about him after the ball."

"Slight problem there." I raised my eyebrows.

"Yeah I know. But you don't have to be stuck with Luke forever, Avery. If you're having doubts, that's okay."

I hated how wrong my best friend was.

"I'm going to go and get a shower before I head to Luke's."

During the earliest days of the family fallout, before the reality set in, the part that got to me most was the cooking. Mum had never been the most extravagant of chefs, but she was the one who accumulated recipes and put food on the table. On the rare occasion that Dad cooked, it was always something simple, like bacon and eggs, or spaghetti.

In those first few months, whilst Dad was emotionally absent and before he stepped up, it became apparent that mine and Stella's knowledge on cooking was limited. And that despite what our father might have been believing, we couldn't survive purely on beans on toast. Our first meal, with me on meat and veg and Stella fixing up some condiments, was fajitas. The first meal that we'd sat down as a three for, the first time Dad hadn't eaten on his lap in months. The first time that we'd accepted that despite all the things we might wish we could change, our story now featured one character less. It wasn't long before Dad began to add to our recipes, but fajitas always took me back to that first night where things weren't suddenly so bleak.

"You're definitely chopping that wrong."

Luke had invited himself around for dinner despite this being the umpteenth night in a row I'd seen him. When he'd suggested that we make some fajitas, completely forgetting the significance, I'd agreed out of nostalgia. If Stel had been here, she'd have taken over the condiment task from Luke; there was a way to make guac, and a way not to make it. I kept my mouth shut in fear of causing conflict. He was less worried about that though.

"Luke, I've been cooking these for years. I think I know how to chop an onion."

He rolled his eyes and continued to lay the table, lighting a tea light in the centre. He'd even nipped out to the supermarket whilst I was preheating the oven to buy Quorn for Elisa, which spoke volumes, since lately he'd been trying to avoid contact with my friends to the best of his ability. I assumed he was feeling bad about the incident at the pub, because for the past few days everything had been eerily rosy. Apart from needing to see me every evening, which was becoming the norm, there had been no arguments, no possessive phone calls and no 'accidents'. I watched him as he focused on his jobs. He was complex, and he was frustrating, but he was Luke.

He caught me looking at him. "I love you." He said and made his way around the table to put his arms around my waist and tickled my neck with his kisses. I squirmed, eyes watering partially due to the onions. He knew all the spots that made me laugh the most.

"I love you more," I said, trying to ignore the guilt in my chest. I felt strongly about him, but it was shifting, changing. Was it even love anymore? "Cut this up would you?" I handed him a pepper and he saluted me, sitting at the table with a chopping board whilst I began to add everything else into the pan on the hob.

"How was uni today?" He mentioned it casually, like neither of us would recognise that this was the first time he'd taken an interest in my studies since that night at his parents' house. I shrugged, not wanting to admit how awful I'd been feeling about my PGCE. That I wasn't sure if I wanted to take it. That I was still upset about the internship. That his moods were distracting my studies and that instead of my usual first, I'd got a third on my last project.

"Good," I said. "Did I tell you that Maia had a date?"

Luke turned around in his seat to look directly at me, for once paying attention when I spoke of my course friends. "As in, *Maia* Maia?"

I smiled at the genuine interest. Things were suddenly running so smoothly between us that if you waltzed into the conversation, you wouldn't believe we had a problem.

"That's nice. I'm imagining a Pictionary genius."

I bent over in laughter and Luke raised an eyebrow in response. "It's Scrabble, actually."

"Close enough."

"Oh my God A, *what* is that smell?!" I'd been so busy laughing that I hadn't heard the sound of her key turning in the lock. Eliza burst into the room, laden with textbooks, which she immediately chucked onto the floor in pursuit of the hob. "Oh, hi Luke!"

"Hola."

She clocked the fajitas. "Spanish. I like it."

She plugged her phone into one of the sockets by the kitchen table before heading into the hallway to hang her coat up. I followed.

"I'm sorry that he's over here again." I knew she'd been feeling neglected.

"You know I don't mind. Have you mentioned anything that we've been talking about?" She was whispering. "You know, about *him*?"

"I don't actually know how I've been feeling. That's the issue."

"But Beckett–"

I shushed her, desperate for this conversation not to be overheard. I'd kept to my word about not seeing Beckett over the last few days, but I was still paranoid. Any mention of him and the night could be derailed. I didn't think I had it in me to stomach another fight.

"Why do I have to shush?" She rolled her eyes. "He thinks you're just friends."

"We are just friends."

Eliza shot me a look. If only she knew the half of it.

"He bought Quorn for you." It was a weak attempt at defending him, but I stuck with it.

"Everything okay?" Luke was trying to play it cool from the kitchen, and I couldn't figure out whether the tone in his voice was worry about what we might have been speaking about, or anger that we'd done it in private.

"Just talking about our rent for this month! Be back in a second."

Eliza's eyebrow was raised. "This month's rent?" She shook her head. "So, just to be clear, what can I speak about over dinner, and what is a no-no?"

I didn't want Eliza to think she had to tread on eggshells, but I couldn't deny that I was happy that she'd brought it up without me having to tell her. There was a long list of inflammatory topics, but I stuck to the main one.

"Do not mention Beckett."

"Got it."

Smash.

I rushed into the kitchen. Luke was standing with his hand braced on the fridge. Salsa was all over the wall, the bowl smashed on the floor.

"What happened?" Eliza moved toward the mess but I put my hand out, suddenly protective. I knew that look.

"Luke?"

He slowly turned around. I was surprised to see tears in his eyes. Angry tears. Had he heard us talking?

"What the hell is this?"

I put my hand to my mouth. In his hand was the strip of photos from the ball that Stel and I had taken with Beckett. The drawer that I'd shoved them in was open.

Luke gripped the photos. "Are you going to explain this?"

Eliza laughed nervously. "They bumped into him. It was no big deal."

"Was I talking to you?" Spit flew from his mouth and Eliza stepped back, startled. "Avery." His voice was almost a growl. "I'm trying to figure out how I fell in love with such a liar."

"I didn't lie, I just didn't think–"

"*Do you ever think?*" He stepped towards me and I braced myself. Eliza had her hand on my arm.

"Shall we all just calm down? Let's just go into the living room and–"

"For God's sake Eliza!" Luke threw his hands up. "This is none of your bloody business."

When I didn't offer anything up, he shoved past me.

"I haven't seen him since you asked, Luke." I grabbed his arm. "I cut him out, like you said."

"Avery, what?"

We both ignored Eliza, who was hovering behind me.

"I love you." I tried to touch his cheek but he pushed my hand away.

"The damage is done. I trusted you." The angry tears were back in his eyes. "I've spent all of our relationship protecting you. Just think where you'd be without me."

"I promise. I've not been over to his since you said…"

Shit.

"*Over to his?*"

"I mean–"

"You've been going to his flat?"

There was no point denying. I focused on damage control. "I've been round a couple of times to talk about writing, Luke. That's all."

"Shut up Avery."

"His *niece* was there. It was harmless, we had a tea party…" I didn't mention the other couple of times I'd been there for our writing sessions.

"You barely talk to me anymore, but you have tea parties with him? He deserves everything that's coming to him."

I saw in his eyes that he wanted to hurt Beckett. I darted in front of the door.

"Don't, Avery. I'm warning you." He gestured for me to move aside, a threat hanging in the air that only disappeared when an arm yanked me backwards. As Luke thrashed around putting his shoes on, I tried to hurriedly send a text to Beckett.

"What did I just say? Whose side are you on?" He plucked the phone out of my hands and shoved it in his pocket. "Cheating bitch." The door slammed behind him.

"*What* is going on?!" Eliza held my arms, but her touch was gentle. "What on earth have you not been telling me, Avery? This is so much more than an argument!"

"We have to warn him." I was only worried about Beckett. What if Lola was there? I grabbed my shoes.

"When we catch up to him," Eliza grabbed my hand, "you have to tell me what's going on. Is this why you've been so distracted lately? Is this why you've been going to his flat every night?"

A tear fell down my cheek. "I will."

"Okay. Come *on*." Eliza pulled me by the hand, out of the door, and my heart shattered when I looked up and saw that her eyes reflected the fear that I felt. What had I done?

Thirty One

I'd told Luke where The Hideaway was when I'd been feeling guilty about spending time there. And then with horror I realised as we followed him in Eliza's car that my stupid, stupid mouth had also mentioned that Beckett lived above the bakery opposite.

Luke knew where he lived.

Beckett hadn't answered any of the calls I'd made on Eliza's phone.

"Babe, *please*." I tried to grab Luke's arm as we followed up the stairs to Beckett's flat. I'd hoped that by the time we reached the block of flats, he'd have had time to calm down.

I was wrong. If anything he seemed angrier.

"I'm telling you Avery, back off." He started going along the corridor, ringing on bells and pounding on doors. Luckily, no-one else seemed to be in. Unfortunately, Beckett was.

"Hey." Beckett saw me first, and then stiffened when he realised who had been knocking.

"Sorry—" I tried to get in first, but Luke overpowered me, shoving Beckett to the side and barging into the flat. Beckett stumbled back in surprise.

"I don't think I said you could come in, mate."

"And I don't think I said that you could have Avery."

For someone that had been raging, he was suddenly eerily calm when faced with Beckett.

"What?" Beckett's laugh was incredulous. "For some reason, Avery is unbelievably loyal to you."

Luke shook his head. "Coming here is loyal?"

"She doesn't need to *ask* every time she wants to spend time with someone." Beckett was sneering.

"Beckett, don't." I met his eyes. "Don't." Panic had flushed my cheeks.

"Don't even say his name." Luke narrowed his eyes.

"I think you need to leave." Beckett crossed his arms.

Luke was taken aback, so used to me bending to his will that he wasn't used to defiance. He stormed in my direction and grabbed me around the wrist a little too roughly, pulling me to the door. I'd never seen him give up a fight so easily.

"Come." This time, though, when he ordered me around, I froze.

"No." I dug my heels in as he pulled me harder. Beckett stepped forward, and out of the corner of my eye I saw Eliza jump towards me as well. They exchanged a look.

"I'm not going with you."

The look he sent when he turned around to face me wasn't just one of anger, but of pain too.

"Avery?"

"I'm staying here. With my friends."

His nails dug into my wrist hard enough to draw blood. His cheeks were red. Eyes so wild they were unrecognisable. I didn't want him to lash out at them. Desperate, I turned back to Beckett.

"Give me a minute."

Beckett immediately began to protest. "I don't think that's a good idea."

"Please."

Without waiting for confirmation, I grabbed Luke and pulled him outside.

He was crazy. Pacing. "You've been c*heating* on me. God I thought I was going mad."

"Luke, stop." I grabbed his chin in a moment of bravery, directing his eyes to mine. "He's just a friend."

"I don't believe you."

"You have to! This is ruining us." I swiped at a tear.

"How *dare* you accuse me of being the reason for this." His fists were clenched.

"You need to calm down. I can't carry on with…"

CRACK. A sharp, hot sensation stung my skin. His eyes were burning with untamed anger. He'd slapped me.

"Never threaten me again, do you hear me Avery? Do *not* humiliate me in front of these people any more than you already have."

He released me and I pressed my hand against my cheek, letting out a sob. When I didn't respond, he launched. I was pinned. Pain in my leg as he trapped it against the exposed brick.

"Luke!"

"I said, *do you hear me?*"

"Get away from her." Beckett's face was bright red as he approached us, his voice low. "Get your hands off her."

Another guttural sob. *They'd seen.* All of this, trying to cover up his violence, and two of the closest people in the world to me had seen it.

Luke's expression was suddenly one of fear. "I didn't mean that, I—"

Beckett shoved him against the opposite wall, his arm against his throat. "This is none of your business." Luke struggled against Beckett's hold. "Avery knows I didn't mean it. Don't you?"

I was leaning against the wall, hand on my cheek, trying to catch my breath.

"Don't you?"

I jumped. My face was on fire. Eliza had disappeared into Beckett's flat again, only to return with a cold tea towel that she pressed against my cheek.

"How could you?" She directed the question at Luke. "How could you do this to her?"

I witnessed the change. The moment when he snapped back to reality. Blind panic not unlike my own. He was reaching for me. "Avery, Avery you know I love you. You know I don't mean it. Please. Avery."

Eliza put her hand to her face at his admission that this wasn't the first time. Beckett winced but didn't break his stare with me, asking me with his eyes if I needed him.

I knew he would get Luke out, but he was giving me the space to be my own person.

"You need to go." My voice shook.

"Don't do this," he said, his voice breaking. "Don't turn your back on me."

"I'm not," I said. "You've done that to yourself."

I turned so I wouldn't see him leave, touching the skin that was now red hot with the imprint of a hand I knew so well.

In the silence after he'd gone, everything hit me.

"I think I'm going to be sick." I tried to act casual, but my hands were shaking so much that I struggled to stand as I stumbled to the bathroom, head over the toilet, unearthing all of the fear I'd felt in the last twenty minutes. Stumbling to my feet, I looked in the mirror. I saw myself for the first time; really saw myself. Dark circles under my eyes, pronounced cheekbones – how was it possible that I was paler than before?

Eliza's voice was muffled in the living room, Beckett shushing her in hushed tones. "I had no idea Beckett. I knew they were fighting. I feel guilty, so guilty. If only I had *known*."

"I thought I knew." Beckett sounded broken. "I will never forgive myself for this."

"Do we call the police?"

"I don't know. We can't do anything without asking Avery. I hope he gets put away for this, but we shouldn't do anything she's not okay with."

They didn't know I was listening, and my heart broke at their shared guilt. I'd pushed everyone away. This was no one's fault but my own. I flushed the toilet, washed out my mouth and pushed open the door to the living room.

"This is my fault. I hid this."

Eliza rushed over, hugging me. "I'm so sorry A. I've been so distracted with Jack and I genuinely thought it was just an argument or two."

"One hell of an argument." Beckett was pacing, barely looking at me.

"What's been going on, A?"

"I can't…I don't have the words." My voice was stronger than I felt. "I need to show you."

"Are you sure?" Beckett took my hand and squeezed it. Eliza nodded. "Anything."

I fought the instinctual part of me that had ruled for so long and reached down for the hem of my t-shirt.

"Avery…"

Beckett knew what I was about to do.

"Do you need me to go?"

"Stay." My eyes pleaded with him. I lifted the hem all the way, over my head. Stood there in my bra.

"Oh my God." Eliza put her head in her hands.

"I want to *kill* him."

I turned to Beckett's mirror, to see what they saw. I was a mess of yellow, blue and black. Across my ribcage, down my arms. *How had I let this happen?* In tears, I grabbed my t-shirt and yanked it back over my head.

"I'm so sorry, A." Eliza was crying again, and she hugged me gingerly, like she wasn't sure where she could touch me.

My eyes felt wild. "I don't know what to do. I care about him." I felt nauseous again. Sick that I couldn't help but love him. Sick that I hadn't fought this harder.

"I know you love him. That doesn't mean it's right." Eliza brushed my hair back from my face, where it lay plastered to my clammy skin.

"He's always sorry."

"He'll be sorry every time." Beckett took my hand again. "It doesn't mean he deserves your forgiveness."

Luke needed help, but it wasn't the kind that I could give him. His anger was bigger than me, than us, and I wasn't enough to support him. If I tried to be enough...

"I promise you are not alone." Eliza's hand on my spine, which all of a sudden felt entirely too prominent, startled me. Not with shock, or fear, but with clarity.

"I have to let him go, don't I?"

Beckett hadn't said much whilst we were leaving, which I put down to residual anger – both at Luke and maybe towards me. I felt that it was my weakness that had caused the scene, and it was weighing me down that I'd taken so long to finally listen to what he had been saying.

"Beckett was angry."

"Not at you, A. At *him*." Eliza couldn't even bring herself to say his name. I wasn't that eager to hear it either. Her shock at the whole situation was still evident on her face. "I can't believe I didn't see this. I'm supposed to be your best friend."

I smiled at her. "I didn't want you to see. You weren't supposed to."

"He's a monster. Beckett told me about the bruises he saw the other week. He feels awful. Was there anything else…" Her voice caught. I knew what she meant.

"The other day…" my voice shook, "I didn't want it, didn't want his hands on me, and–" I couldn't get the words out.

A sharp intake of breath. "I hate that man. He is a liar and a coward."

"Is that not what I am? I've done both."

Eliza pulled over in her car and turned to face me. "God no, you're the bravest person I know. He put you in a position where you had to lie for him. He fooled all of us."

I stared out the window, realising how true it all was. I was a victim.

"I think I want to go home. To Westby." I hadn't realised until I'd spoken the words out loud, but it was true, I needed to go back to Westby to see things in the clearest light possible. The idea that Luke was somewhere on his own thinking about what he'd done, maybe only a matter of miles away from me, was too much. If I stayed here, there was a chance I would run back to the very thing I should be running from. That was the thing about addiction; it offered no mercy.

"I think that's a fab idea. Stel will be over the moon."

"It's *killing* me Eliza." I was talking about the pain, the actual physical pain. Not from the marks on my skin, but everything else. I didn't know who I was without him. And there was nothing romantic about that. "Four years is a long time to waste." There, I'd said it. It had been circling around in my mind every time I tried to convince myself that it was a good idea to walk away. If I ended it, I was ending years of work, and effort. Years of trying to fix myself with someone else's body, when I should have been caring for my own.

"It's not a waste Avery. You wouldn't be you without him, just like you wouldn't be this version of you if your mum was still living at home, and like I wouldn't be me if my dad had stayed. Even if people come into our lives and change it for the better, there can still be an expiration date on it."

For some reason unknown to me, I started laughing, and after a second, she joined in. She pulled the car in and we both doubled over, tears running down our cheeks that had nothing to do with Luke, for once. It might have been delayed shock but I didn't care.

"How did you get so wise?"

That made Eliza laugh even harder.

"I have no idea," she slapped the steering wheel. "It's not funny. None of this is funny. I don't know why we're laughing."

"Because you're my best friend. And that's what we do." I looked at her, and she grabbed my hand and squeezed it. "I know I'll always have you."

"Don't make me cry you idiot." She started driving again, since we'd calmed down enough to finally get home. I wanted to get under a blanket on the sofa and not move until morning; Eliza had already said that she was on hot chocolate duty.

"What do you want to do about today? Do you want to report it? We saw it, we can back you."

"I don't know. I want to go home." I was sobbing now, clutching at my stomach. This was way out of my league. I thought about the bartender and what he'd seen, the number he'd given to me. "I don't know what to do. I've been holding it together for so long and I just," Eliza held my hand as I spoke, "I just want my mum."

As I said it, I knew that what I was saying was right. For the first time in years, I was ready to give up the chip on my shoulder. This was bigger than my residual anger. I just wanted my mum.

Thirty Two

There's something about sitting alone at a table on an overcast day, sipping cheap watered down coffee, that fully allows you to analyse a situation. I'd survived two trains so far, my weekend bag packed in a hurry and thrown over my shoulder in my haste to get away from York. This morning, during another long chat with Eliza, she'd booked me some train tickets. I hadn't yet told anyone at home that I was on my way, hadn't stopped long enough to think about the repercussions of packing up and going home for the weekend without my boyfriend. *My boyfriend.* The label felt bitter on my tongue in a way that had nothing to do with the Styrofoam cup in my hand. I was beyond excited to sit by the sea and breathe in the fresh air, a rite of passage that I did every time I came home. No matter where you go in life, if you've spent a childhood by the sea, it's a sigh of relief to return. Nothing is as fresh, or freeing. And that was exactly what I needed. Beckett had texted this morning to wish me a good journey, obviously filled in by Eliza. At around midnight last night, about an hour after we'd gone to our separate rooms, Eliza had snuck in and peeled back the duvet to lie next to me. I was glad of it. I wasn't one hundred percent sure that I trusted myself either.

My cheek had looked a lot better when I woke up this morning, the red mark faded to what could pass as a spot of blusher. If I didn't want my family to know, it could remain unnoticed. I hadn't yet decided what I was going to tell them, if anything. One word of violence to Dad and I knew he would react strongly, handling the situation drastically and irreversibly. But it was so much more than a slip of Luke's hand; and that wasn't a story that would be easy to tell.

"How's it going?" My phone had buzzed with an incoming call, and without hesitating I'd picked up straight away.

"Baby steps. I'm currently sipping train station coffee."

Beckett laughed, and while it suddenly felt like our usual rhythm, it had an aura of forced positivity around it. "Ah. If I ever come to Westby we're taking a flask."

My cheeks warmed with the meaning behind his words, but I'd done a lot of thinking overnight. Now wasn't the time to try and sort out my feelings for Becket. I pushed his comment to the back of my mind.

"You're okay though? Going alone?" The word 'alone' stirred butterflies in the pit of my stomach, and I couldn't be sure if it was with newfound excitement, or the return of the one fear that plagued me. Beckett knew all about that. I closed my eyes and took a breath.

"I'll be fine." I paused, and then tacked another phrase onto the end. "Thanks though." I wasn't sure what I'd done to deserve friends like these, but I was eternally grateful.

I took a deep breath and dragged my fingers through the sand. This had been the best idea I'd had in a while. After arriving in Westby my first port of call had been coming here, where the waves met the sand. Usually I brought headphones and sat on a sand dune for hours, sometimes with a notebook in case inspiration struck. Today, it was all about the soothing sound of the waves. I'd been so desperate to escape the memories of this town when I'd moved to York, but now that something even worse had happened, it was the only place I wanted to be.

Once I was done, instead of running straight to my house and settling on the couch to watch *Friends* reruns with Stella, I knew where I wanted to go. I was terrified that I wouldn't be wanted there, but I had to try. As it had turned out, four years was enough for something to run its course, but I was also learning that it was enough time for something to rebuild itself.

Me: At The Point. Avery x

I knew that Stella would turn up. She was a busy teenager, but it was unusual for me to arrive in Westby unannounced, and especially for me to arrive back in Westby without Luke. I'd already had a torrent of angry texts from Luke since letting him know that I'd gone home for the weekend. It hadn't gone down well, but he needed to get used to it. I'd decided that making my own decisions was going to be a common theme from now on.

"You know The Point means business."

I grinned at Stella as she plopped herself down next to me, her arms crossed over her knees as she drew them to her chest. It had taken her all of ten minutes to reach the destination on last minute notice. The Point was the part of the beach that crossed over into the next village. There was a path from our house that led directly onto the sand, and we'd found this spot when Stel had been about seven. We'd built a thousand fairy houses out of sticks and shells and sat for hours waiting for magic to happen. To everyone else in Westby this was The Point, but for us it was *our* point.

"Fairy houses and all." My voice carried on the sea breeze, and Stella giggled.

"Fairy houses and all." A pause. "Are you going to tell me why you're here on such short notice?" Part of me was surprised that Eliza hadn't given her a heads up, but she would have known that this was delicate news to break. Stella loved Luke as a brother.

"It's Luke, isn't it?"

I was pretty sure my mouth was open. "How did you know that?"

She stretched back on her hands. "Sisters always know. You've been weird for ages. I tried to bring it up with Eliza when I came up for the ball but you came back from the bathroom too quickly." For fifteen years old, she could produce quite the stare. "I have no idea what's going on, but you can tell me. You know I'm on your side, forever."

Tears welled up in my vision and I pushed them back, not wanting to cry and ruin the moment. A tiny part of my brain had said that even if I did choose to tell it all to Stella, she might not believe me.

"It's…complicated. He isn't who I thought he was."

"How so?" She was trying to be brave, but her chin wobbled. "What has he done to you?"

I lifted up my sleeve, revealing a collection of bruises new and old. Stella cried onto my shoulder.

"I don't, I don't know what to—"

"It's okay." I held her hand in mine. "I know you love him too. We'll get through this together."

She nodded. "People keep disappointing us, huh?"

"Seems that way." We were both being brave for the other.

"I love you so much, Avery." She lightly ran her fingers over the marks. "He was so special to us, but you're my *sister.*"

I'd underestimated everyone around me but I think, most of all, I'd underestimated myself.

"You're a gem, little sis."

Stel nodded. She seemed to get that I wasn't ready to trash his name completely just yet. "Well, I'm here indefinitely. Or at least until I get bored."

I burst out laughing, laying my head on her shoulder. We chatted and laughed together for over an hour, watching the sun move through the sky, comforted by the fact that our little town was safely behind us.

There really was no place like home.

Stella had errands to run anyway, but I told her that this was something I needed to do on my own.

When I knocked on the door, I took a step back and readied myself. I was nervous, wiping my clammy hands on my jeans. This visit had been a long time coming.

"Steve, hang on, I need to get the door." I heard her before I saw her through the frosted glass, and from the confident way that she strode to the door, I could tell that she had no clue what was awaiting her on the other side.

Stella was still a huge part of my mum's life, had forgiven when she was ready and jumped back into arms that welcomed her without a second thought. I was the trickier of her daughters – a grudge holder, a more hesitant version of my vibrant younger sister.

"Steve, *one second.*" The door finally opened, and my mother's mouth dropped open.

"Oh my goodness." Time stood still before she pulled me to her fiercely. "Avery." I had been expecting surprise, but there were tears running down her cheeks. She pushed me back and stared into my face. There was a second of silence before a smile took over the entirety of her face.

"My baby girl. *Look at you.* You're so grown up!"

A tear rolled down my cheek. I wondered what she was seeing. If she recognised me enough to see the changes Luke had inflicted on my body.

"Your hair is so long." She reached out tentatively to touch it. "Everyone used to tell me that you and Stella were polar opposites but now I *see it.*" She grabbed my bag off me, depositing it by the entrance to the hallway and drawing me in for another hug. "I am so glad that you're here. Are you staying? Are you okay?"

This time I pulled back so I could look at her properly. She had crinkles near her eyes that hadn't been there the last time I'd seen her, and her hair was shorter. She also looked happier, like the world no longer sat on her shoulders.

"Who was it?" Steve came round the corner, and I fought the urge to glare at him, settling with a small smile. "Oh!"

"Are you staying for dinner? We'll do anything you want to do." She looked at my face and for some reason I knew that she *knew*. Like she'd read it on me.

I tried not to barrel into her arms and start sobbing. "Thanks Mum."

She hugged my frame even tighter before picking up my bag again and taking it to the bottom of the stairs, gesturing for me to follow and then she stopped and said: "Whatever the problem is, we'll sort it. Okay?"

At that I couldn't help it; a single tear escaped. The relief was palpable. I was doing at least one thing in my life right.

Thirty Three

I'd told her that I was starving, although it was a lie. I feared opening up to her; my defense mechanism from the past four years was still my automatic response. Luckily, Stella had arrived just after me and was chatting enough for all of us.

"Mum, this is amazing." Stella shovelled risotto into her mouth, sighing happily.

It was weird seeing Steve, so aware of how he'd betrayed my dad. He wasn't smug, like I imagined, or annoyed that I'd dropped by. He'd gone out of his way to make me welcome, and almost seemed nervous. He was no Paul Emerson, but he was Steve. It could be worse; he could have been Raymond Calkins.

"I've come a long way since I used to cook for you two." Mum laughed, and I was once again reminded of the dishes she used to present to us, smile on her face, knowing it looked nothing like the picture in the book. The thought surprised me with its sadness.

"We never minded Mum." I smiled at her, and she reached across to squeeze my hand. We hadn't yet spoken about why I'd come to see her after years of silence – rushed into preparations for the evening meal by Stella's prompt arrival. I knew that we'd have to talk after dinner but, for once, that didn't make me feel afraid.

"You kids were fed with good intention, if not good skills." Steve chuckled, shaking his head. He had no children. I knew that from when he'd been friends with Dad.

"We gained some skills between us when we had to." I'd meant it as a joke, but a swift kick from Stel under the table let me know that it had been poorly timed. Mum's cheeks were red, and Steve was looking at the table, awkward. I backtracked.

"Do you remember that time we tried to make pancakes that Pancake Day?"

Her face immediately brightened with the memory.

"I didn't even realise that pancakes *could* get stuck to the ceiling!" Everyone laughed, even Steve, who hadn't been there. I'd spent years assuming that discussing our previous life with her would feel painful, but I only felt happiness. That had been a great Pancake Day cramped around the table, excitement in the air because dessert for dinner only happened once a year. We *were* happy, once.

And Mum and Dad were both happy now, in their own way. I imagined Dad sat at home, probably in front of the TV eating spaghetti hoops from his lap and watching the football. When I tried to imagine Mum, once the core of our home, sitting in one of his old t-shirts with her legs over his and a book in her hand, I couldn't. They were so far apart now that I didn't feel resentment anymore. There was no need. We all ate in silence for a minute or two, before

Stella started chatting about her latest date with Elliott. It would most likely be a fleeting love for her, that she'd look back on fondly as she grew older. That was the way it was meant to be. My orbit should never have been someone else. It should have always been me.

"So Avery, what are you thinking of doing when you graduate?" Steve pointed his fork in my direction. "Stella constantly tells us that you got all the brains."

I poked Stel. "Liar."

"Okay, she got all the *motivation.*"

Steve chuckled, looking at Stella fondly.

"I'm considering going into publishing, perhaps as an editor. I've applied to a few publishing houses for internships already." As soon as I said it, butterflies stirred in my stomach. My relationship might have been coming to an end, but my future was just beginning. My *own* future. "I've been asked to interview for one for this summer, which is pretty exciting." Fishing the internship email out of my trash folder had been the first thing I'd done when I'd woken up, finally accepting the interview for a few weeks' time. Now was the time for focusing on what I wanted.

Mum smiled softly. "Gosh. I remember you sat at the kitchen table writing stories when you were five years old. This is perfect for you darling. I am so proud of the woman you've become." Her words made me glow.

"Thanks Mum." Steve was watching the exchange like a tennis match, smiling. I was surprised that I didn't mind him whatsoever.

"Oh, Stella." Mum turned to my sister. "I hear that you introduced this new boyfriend to your dad the other day."

Stella coughed on her lemonade. "Ah yes. What a ride."

I couldn't remember whether Dad had been protective over me when I'd introduced Luke, but then again, he hadn't even been in a state of mind to protect himself.

"It was intense, but I think he liked him."

"I'm glad. Your dad is a good judge of character. No one better to approve a boyfriend." She only spoke of Dad warmly. I wondered if I'd ever understand.

"And how about your boyfriend Avery? There's so much I want to know."

Stella shot me a concerned look.

"We have a lot to talk about Mum."

After dessert Stella had gone out with some friends, which she claimed was a planned excursion, but I suspected was a reason to leave me here alone. Stella had always been a brilliant teller of what I needed, even when I hadn't admitted it to myself. Mum and I were on the chair swing that sat on her patio. Her house was nicer than our home, and I tried not to think of it as a pie in the face to Dad. He was quite happy where he was. Taking it all in, I was impressed. The garden wasn't huge, but it was immaculate. I often wondered what Mum had been doing in her spare time after she left, no longer two girls to take care of, but it was evident when you stepped outside. Plants and flowers were *everywhere.*

"Beautiful, aren't they?" Her voice was low, as though she didn't want to wake them. "I needed something to take care of." The confession made the breath catch in my throat. I couldn't have led myself here earlier. I needed those years to find my way back, but I didn't like to think of my mother, weeding her garden to get over her loneliness. I'd abandoned her in the exact same way that I assumed she'd chosen to abandon us.

"I'm sorry Mum. I couldn't–"

"I know." She patted my hand, and then shifted in her seat so that she was looking directly at me. "Are you going to tell me why you came home so abruptly?" There it was. Sitting in front of me, the opportunity to tell her everything. For the first time in four years, I took it.

"It's my boyfriend." Mum nodded, taking it in her stride. She had no loyalty to Luke. She'd probably only heard of him through snippets from Stella. She hadn't been dragged under by his charm like the rest of us. "I've been so stupid."

She wiped away my tears at the admission. "You could never be stupid, Avery, that's your best quality. But everyone can be drawn in by a façade." Without even admitting why Luke wasn't right for me anymore, she'd got it. Or at least, enough of it. "The charming boys are always the most dangerous. When I was a teenager I dated someone for a couple of years, and he drew me in slowly. It didn't take long before I was looking in the mirror and not recognising my own reflection." I didn't know what to say, so I stayed silent.

I wanted her opinion, honest through and through. Parents are sometimes the only people that can offer that luxury.

"You are worth so much, and I'm sad for every second of your life I've missed. I am so proud of who you are. If he doesn't allow you to see that, or even worse, discourages it, then you have to think about yourself. What's good for you."

"It's so hard." I let her pull me in to her side. "I know it's going to hurt to let him go."

I didn't mention the violence. I wasn't ready for that just yet. There were some things you couldn't take back. It was scary enough already.

Instead of sugar coating it like I was expecting, Mum gave me a squeeze and then laid her hands out in front of her. I remembered this from years ago; how she talked with her hands when she was passionate about something.

"Life hurts honey. All of it, every decision. I promise you, that as long as you keep living the way that you're supposed to, it will hurt, because it's meant to."

I was full-on ugly crying now, thinking of the way it was going to feel letting Luke go. Sleeping alone, eating alone, just generally being on my own. I knew I had people around me to support the new chapter, but they weren't Luke.

"You can't help who you love." I wanted her to understand, to justify my mistakes. I couldn't imagine any of my friends being so stupid or weak, and that hurt the most. "But you can help when you choose to walk away from it." We sat in silence broken only by my sobs. "That's the bravest part, honey, don't deny yourself that. It takes a brave woman to walk away from something that no longer makes her sparkle."

There it was. My chance to ask something that had kept me up at night, every night, for the last few years.

"Is that how you felt about Dad?"

"In a way, yes. But it doesn't sound like Luke's much like your dad."

"How so?" I already knew how, but I wanted her to leave nothing out.

"He would have supported me through anything, and I loved that about him. But I'd changed, and I needed something different. I wasn't the best version of myself when I was with him."

I considered it, this truthfulness. I couldn't say I quite understood it, but at least it was there.

"If he supported you, then what else did you need?"

"I was growing to resent our relationship. I wasn't getting what I wanted out of it – he wanted to sit and watch football, I wanted to talk about the latest novel I was reading. We had nothing in common anymore. Apart from you girls. But I didn't want to hurt him. Although I guess that was what happened in the end." Her face was sad. "It will haunt me, the look on your father's face when I left. It will haunt me for the rest of my life."

I didn't say anything. I wasn't quite ready to forgive on Dad's behalf yet. There was something I did still want to know though.

"What about us?" My voice cracked on the last word. "Why weren't we enough?"

"You were always enough. But you needed a happy mother." She said it like it was a matter of fact, like Stella and I hadn't sat up in our pyjamas for nights on end, trying to puzzle it out. "You two were the best decision I've ever made."

"You didn't make me feel like that."

She fiddled with her hands. "I thought I was doing the right thing."

I tried not to let it make me feel angry. I wanted her to know about the fajitas, and the late nights, and the days spent sitting outside her old bedroom, waiting for Dad to stop sobbing so that we could go in and try to make him eat something. And deep down, but closer to the surface than I would ever admit, the idea that without the emotional turmoil, I might never have fallen into the trap. Might never have needed the support that Luke gave me – a fast track to co-dependency.

"Why didn't you fight for me?" She didn't reply, because there wasn't much that she could say. What was done was done. I got up from the patio seat and went inside. Repairing this rift was going to be a long haul, and whilst I was fully prepared to commit, it wasn't something that could be put back together in one night alone.

"Grace, is that you?" I cringed, wanting to hide myself in the gloom of the living room. Steve poked his head around the door, drying his hands on a tea towel, the dishes done.

"Oh, Avery. Hi." I wondered if he was waiting for a big moment, a reconciliation.

"She's outside." I gestured to the patio doors, and Steve nodded.

I grabbed my bag and climbed the stairs, looking for the toilet so I could freshen up before going home. Checking behind me in case I'd been followed, I pushed gently on a door, trying my luck. By the matching robes on the back of the door, I could immediately tell that I'd guessed wrong. At that point, I should have walked away and tried another door, but for some reason I felt compelled to tiptoe in. I used to bounce on Mum and Dad's bed in the morning, yelling for them to wake up. This room was completely unfamiliar, another man's aftershave set on the dresser next to her Chanel. I could tell my mum was happy with this life which was so different to the one I remembered, and despite the curling in my chest I was happy too, for her.

"I missed you." The whisper hung in the air as I lay back on the duvet, breathing in the lingering scent of her perfume. We wouldn't always get on, but I wasn't sure I knew a mother and daughter that did. And when I glanced up at the ceiling, I couldn't help but smile. Hundreds of glow-in-the-dark stars staring back at me, welcoming me home.

Thirty Four

"Now, I was doing some thinking…"

I put my head in my hands. "That can't be good." I felt the oven glove swat me on the back of my head.

"Oh shut up. I'm giving you a free pass to be sad, but not to be rude to your best friend."

It turned out, when Eliza wasn't sure what to do in a situation, she turned to baking. For the past two days since I arrived back from my trip to Westby, I'd had several batches of baked goods brought to my duvet fort. I might have taken a step forward in patching things up with my mother, but Luke? That was still raw, and I was still processing. Hence, the blanket fort. I'd emailed my tutor, claiming family emergency, so I had some time to wallow.

Eliza moaned. "Oh my days Avery, try this."

"I don't think my stomach can take more sugar."

"What was that? You're excited to try these caramel brownies? Sounds good to me, open up!" She shovelled a fork of brownie into my mouth, and I had to agree that it was good. My appetite had dwindled over the weeks and months, but now that Eliza was constantly hovering, I wasn't getting out of my three meals a day.

"Okay, the brownies caught me off guard." She put the tray down, picking up the wooden spoon from the bowl and licking the batter before pointing it at me. "So anyway, I was thinking, and I thought of the perfect way to take your mind off things."

"Oh?"

"Uh huh. So I don't know if you're aware, but there's a book signing for your favourite author at Waterstones tomorrow."

I'd had it on my calendar for months. Rosaline Green almost never did signings. I desperately wanted to go, and yet…

"I don't know if that's a great idea. Luke knows that I was looking forward to it, and if he comes to find me I–"

"It's a public place, lots of people." When I didn't respond, she pointed the spoon in my direction once again. "You know you want to. How often do you get to hear your favourite author speak?"

It was true, I did want to.

"We could ask Beckett…"

"No." That was one thing I was sure about, even if my head was spinning about the rest of it. I might not have been able to decide whether I was going to report Luke's violence, like Eliza was pushing me to, but I knew I had to distance myself from Beckett. He'd done nothing wrong, but I needed this time to reflect. I couldn't do that with him around.

"No?"

"I need distance. One life-changing issue at a time." I thought for a moment. "Plus, if Luke finds out that I went somewhere with Beckett…"

"We're through with that Avery. Luke is never going to get you alone long enough to say anything, or *do* anything," I tried not to notice her crumpled facial expression, "ever again."

The idea that I would never be alone with him again had me crying for a different reason.

"I didn't mean to make you cry A."

"I know. I'm scared to be with him, but I'm scared to be without him. He's my best friend."

"I'm going to ignore that because I do understand what you're saying, but let's get one thing straight. *I'm* your best friend."

I laughed through my sobs.

"Avery, it's going to be okay. I don't know how yet, but it will be."

"What if no one believes me?" I felt myself pale.

"I believe you. Beckett believes you. Stella does too. That bartender who saw Luke lose his temper believes you. We saw it, he saw it."

"I'm scared."

"I'm scared. We can be scared together. Build ourselves a double duvet fort and live off these brownies I made."

"I thought you said we had to get out of this flat."

"We do. And tomorrow, we will. But if you want to get back into your fort straight after, I will support that. Screw the seminar prep."

"Wow." I said, laughing. "You must really love me."

"More than I love these brownies." Her eyes were wide. "And that is saying something."

I'd always valued Eliza, but never as much as I'd valued her these past couple of days. I wasn't sure I could do this without her. As soon as I'd returned to York my resolve had broken, and I'd almost got a taxi straight to Luke's flat. If Eliza hadn't dragged me back inside, I wasn't sure where I'd be. Luke hadn't pestered much, calling briefly and telling me that he knew I needed time, but that I shouldn't let 'them' get into my head. I couldn't deny it; his lack of presence was eerie. I held my breath, fighting back another sob. Why was I upset that my controlling boyfriend hadn't come to find me? This was all kinds of messed up.

"What are you thinking about?"

Now was the time to be honest, if I even had any of it left in me. "I just don't know if I'll ever feel that again. That all-consuming love."

"Would you want to?" I blinked at Eliza. And then blinked again. Maybe it was that simple. The type of love you read about, the *'I can't live without you'* kind of love – maybe it wasn't something to fight for.

"Look Avery. I can feel it here," she pointed to her own heart, "how much you love him. But he is bad news. Awful news. The worst kind of news."

"Maybe he'll change." It was desperation, and we both knew it. "Maybe he was just frustrated a couple of times and–"

"I get frustrated when Jack forgets to put the seat down after he uses our toilet. I get frustrated when you take my grapes out of the freezer–"

"It's weird Eliza."

"They taste *better*. Anyway, I get frustrated at that too. But I would never get frustrated enough to hit someone, or cheat on them and make them think it's their fault, or push them so roughly that they bruise." She grabbed my shoulders. "It's time to wake up. I woke up when I saw Luke hit you. Everything has changed, and there is no going back."

I knew it, and yet it scared me half to death.

There was no going back.

I had to wake up.

I was practically bouncing in my seat.

"We can't even see her yet! Why are you freaking out?" Eliza was tapping on her phone whilst we waited for Rosaline to come out for her panel.

"Because I'm about to be in the same room as my all-time inspiration." I paused. "It's almost exciting enough to forget about the shitshow that is my life."

At that, Eliza looked up. "We're not thinking about that this afternoon, remember? Even actively not thinking about it counts as thinking about it."

"I know. What are you looking at?" I leaned in to see her screen, where she was watching a video with the sound turned off.

"It's the new choreography for practice on Thursday, so I'm getting prepped. I think it's going to be a real–" she halted, attention caught. "Oh my God."

"What?"

A tap of the microphone. "Hi guys, and welcome to the Rosaline Green event. I'll be moderating…"

"Wow."

Eliza grinned. "Yeah, I know. Even when you're trying to avoid him."

Beckett was at the front of the room, addressing the rows of seats.

"Welcome to the stage…Rosaline Green!" The crowd clapped and I sunk in my seat, unsure whether I wanted to catch his eye or not. He looked the part. Same goofy smile and glasses but he'd ironed his t-shirt and his hair was relatively tidy.

A tall red-haired woman took a seat angled towards Beckett's. "Hi everyone."

"Rosaline's new book, *Caught Up,* was published last month, with rave reviews so far." He smiled at her. "That must feel incredible. What's been the craziest moment of this process?"

And the panel began. I took notes, trying to forget how fast my heart was beating, focusing instead on the advice that Rosaline was giving. Beckett was responding animatedly, and clearly hadn't seen me, sat in the fourth row back.

"And you have your own second novel in the works I hear…" Rosaline turned the spotlight on him and he grinned shyly, revealing dimples.

"If I ever get there, yes. Second book syndrome is a real thing." The crowd tittered. "I've been lucky enough to have had some great help on the novel though, so I have faith."

I half-coughed; half-choked. He glanced up, finally clocking me. He grinned spontaneously, his cheeks pinking as he pushed his glasses back up his nose and turned back to Rosaline.

Eliza sat up in her seat. "Well this just got one hundred percent more interesting."

As soon as the signing was over, Beckett walked over to us.

"Wait for me? I'll walk with you."

I didn't have the strength to say no, so we milled around as he packed up and said goodbye to Rosaline. As he stood in front of her, he waved me over and I tensed up.

"Oh my gosh, go go go!" Eliza pushed me in his direction.

"So, as I was saying,' he said as I arrived. "This is Avery. She helped me with a lot of the second book."

Rosaline turned to me and beamed. I died. Right there on the spot.

"Hi!" I squeaked.

"I'm so pleased to meet you, Avery. Do you write yourself?"

"I'm working on it. I *loved* this." I held up my copy of her book.

"Thank you so much! This one really took it out of me. You know, Beckett certainly rates you… Here's my email," she scribbled on a piece of paper and passed it to me. "If you ever fancy another writing buddy, let me know!"

Rosaline said goodbye and went off to find her publicist. After she had gone, I grabbed Beckett's arm.

"Did that really just happen?"

"It really just did."

"You didn't tell me that you were moderating the event!"

"There hasn't really been time to bring it up." He'd acknowledged the elephant in the room. "For a minute there you reminded me of the girl I first met. How are you doing?"

"I'm doing okay. This," I pointed to the scrap of paper, "has cheered me up massively. It was definitely worth leaving my duvet for."

"You guys ready to go?" Eliza walked over. "I am *starving*."

We followed her out onto the cobbled streets, looking for the nearest place to satisfy her requirements whilst I filled her in on what had just happened with Rosaline.

"Wow Beckett, look at you. Mr hotshot author getting all the connections."

He scratched his head. "I don't know about that."

"Finally, a Tesco Express." Eliza got out her purse from her crossbody. "Do you guys want anything? I'll be right back."

"I wouldn't say no to a Kinder Bueno." Beckett pulled out some change and offered it to Eliza.

"That's the most random request in the world."

"Alright Detective Emerson. What are you asking for?"

"Will you two hurry up. I'm hungry and need snacks." Eliza was stomping her feet.

"Actually, a Kinder Bueno does sound kind of nice. We'll split it."

Beckett smiled. "You're impossible."

We watched Eliza run off, suddenly awkward in our own company. I hadn't been alone with Beckett since our conversation about his feelings, and I had barely seen him in person since the awful incident with Luke last week.

I walked over to the nearest bench to sit down whilst we waited, and he followed my lead.

"How are you really doing?" His touched his pinkie finger on mine, the slightest touch. "And you don't have to pretend that you're fine. I know you aren't."

"I wasn't going to pretend."

He gave me the side eye.

"Okay, maybe I was. I don't know how I feel. I'm scared." I waited for Beckett to interject, but nothing came. Beckett always gave people time to talk; time to think things through and say their piece. "I'm scared that Luke will come find me. I'll either bend in a moment of weakness, or he'll hurt me again."

A minute of silence.

"I understand what you're saying."

"And?"

"And what?"

"What do you think?"

"I don't know if you need someone else in your life trying to tell you what to do. I'm with you whatever you do. I just want you to be safe, and happy."

"About what you told me…"

"Avery." Beckett was fully holding my hand now. "When I said those things, I had no idea the extent of what was going on."

My heart dropped. I wasn't ready to think about the things he'd said yet, but I knew how I'd feel if he tried to take them back.

"Oh, okay. I know it was in the heat of the moment."

"Don't be silly Emerson. You're the best thing that's happened to me in a long time. I don't take what I said back, but I do wish that I'd had better timing. You aren't obligated to say or do anything. Being your friend is more than enough."

I knew what he was saying. I didn't have to tell him how I felt; although I imagined he probably already knew. My hand was still perfectly fitted into his. Beckett knew the damage that being with Luke had done to me. That feeling of a foregone conclusion, of being trapped. He would never do that to me. Especially not right now.

"I'm really glad that you sat in my seat that day." I squeezed. Tight.

"You do realise that it technically isn't your seat."

"You've never taken it since that day though."

"I know… Emerson, you're shivering."

I looked at the goose bumps on my forearm. "It's fine."

"Now this, I do insist on." Beckett took his jumper off, leaving him in just his t-shirt. When he flashed his upper arm, I caught a glimpse of his tattoo again.

"What are you—"

I hadn't even realised that I'd touched it absentmindedly. I blushed. "I'm sorry."

He touched it too, lost in thought. "Don't worry about it." I could see clearly now that it was a horseshoe; a detailed black drawing inked on his bicep forever. The permanence of a decision like that scared me, but it intrigued me in equal parts.

"Why a horseshoe?"

At first I couldn't tell if I'd overstepped the line, but Beckett smiled and lifted the sleeve down, covering it up once again. I liked the idea of a tattoo that people could only see if you wanted them to.

"When my dad died," I must have inhaled loudly, because he raised an eyebrow at me, "I was way too young to understand. I didn't know him, not the way I wish I had. I was about ten when I first saw the horseshoes, lined up on the wall of our garage. There must have been over a hundred." I couldn't quite believe that he was opening up about this, so I kept my mouth shut and listened intently. I didn't know if he knew that Lucy had already told me about their father, or if he thought that this was the first time I was hearing it. "Mum told me that they were Dad's collection; he loved horses. He volunteered at sanctuaries. I have vague memories of him taking me to visit some before he died. When I was old enough to want to memorialise him, the solution seemed obvious."

I was touched that he'd told me this, but even more so that he'd had the capacity to think of something like that in the first place.

"I like that." I squeezed his shoulder to let him know that I cared, because I knew he wouldn't appreciate an apology.

Eliza came jogging back, Kinder Bueno in hand.

"Yum." I snatched it off her, only to have it snatched from my own hands by Beckett.

"Sneaky."

He broke it in half. "The sneakiest."

"Can we go to your Hideaway?" Eliza rubbed her shoulders. "It's cold and nothing seems better than a hot chocolate right now."

"Sounds good to me." Beckett stood and we all fell into a line, walking the few minutes to my favourite place in the whole world.

Whatever happened, looking to either side of me, I had support. I suddenly knew what I wanted to do. And if I didn't do it now, I might never work up the courage again.

"I'll meet you guys inside, okay? Stella needed me to ring her."

They both nodded, blissfully unaware as I walked off. As soon as I was out of sight, I began to run.

Thirty Five

Me: Meet me outside my flat?
Luke: I've missed you so much. Be there in ten.

Even though I knew what I was about to do, I still felt the same pang that I had done in our first few months, when a simple good morning text was enough to make my whole day. I popped the phone in the pocket of my coat and sat on the steps of our building, fiddling with my zip to pass the time until he arrived. Across the street a couple were walking hand in hand, whispering to each other in total comfort. I knew Luke and I would never find that peace again; it was all or nothing with him, and that was the very root of our problem. In time, I hoped he would realise too that he had become toxic.

Whether or not I decided to get the police involved would depend heavily on his reaction. I knew his heart was a good one, deep down. I had to try to appeal to that part of him. The boy from the chemistry lab who just wanted to make the sad girl happy again. Except this time, I didn't need him. This time, I was letting him go.

Eliza: You okay? You've been gone a while.

I ignored the text as Luke's car pulled into the car park. When he got out he leant against it, not noticing me crouched on the steps. He hadn't seen me yet, and in his trademark jumper and jeans, he looked so beautiful. The kind of beautiful that could lead to bad decisions. I stared at him for a few more moments, wanting to savour it. The way he looked before the anger. The boy I remembered falling in love with four years ago. I allowed myself to let my heart go out to him once more. When I was done I pinched the bridge of my nose, steeling myself and standing up.

"Avery." He stood up straight when he finally saw me, his face breaking into a smile as he walked over. "I'm so sorry baby." When he pulled me in tight to him, I stiffened instinctively. The last time I'd seen him was still fresh. Taking a deep breath, I pulled back and returned the smile.

"Are we alone?" Luke looked up to the window of my flat. I knew what he was asking.

"Yep."

"I'm so glad you texted. I was worried for a while, but I knew you'd agree. It's us against the world. No one else matters." He pulled me in again, squeezing me tight. "I would do anything for you, Avery. Anything."

Except the one thing that matters most.

"We can just leave everyone else. Start our lives together. I know it feels bad now, but those people?" He was almost frothing at the mouth. "Those people trying to split us up don't know what they're talking about."

Looking at him now, so high on the idea that I'd ditch my friends and family to be with him, I felt sick. Sicker than I had when he'd slapped me or pushed me. This was different; I was seeing him. Actually seeing him.

"Luke…" It was a now or never moment.

Luke pulled back from where he had me against his chest. I could so easily scrap my plan and go home with him; continue life exactly how he had it shaped for us. He'd control every moment of it, every person I spoke to. That wasn't a real life. And I so badly wanted one of those.

"I'm sorry baby, I'm not giving you a chance to speak." He laughed. "Go on."

I shook off the guilt. "I'm not here to play happy endings Luke. I want to finish." He stared at me blankly, despite it being more than obvious what I was trying to say. "Us."

"I don't think you mean that." He spoke so calmly that it was almost eerie. His tone was so soft; a siren at sea, waiting to drag me in. I'd expected this though, steeled my heart for the eventuality that he rejected my choice.

"I do. I promise I do."

I'd expected anger. Rage like I was used to. I wasn't expecting him to cry.

"You want to leave me?" He looked so broken that I almost caved. "After everything I've done for you?"

"The things that you've done Luke," I choked on his name, "they can't be undone. I'll never be able to forget."

"It was a mistake, a stupid mistake."

I swiped at the rogue tear that had betrayed me. "If it was one time, I might believe you right now. But it wasn't. You know that. I don't feel safe around you anymore."

He ran his hands through his hair, turning around in a circle. "What about what I want?"

"I have to put myself first."

A split second passed. Just one moment. I knew by now that that was all it took. Luke's face contorted into one of fury.

"This is because of him."

"No."

"So this is what you do then, huh?"

I recoiled. "What do you mean?"

"I was there for you when you cut your mum out of your life. I stood by you, defended you. All I've ever wanted was what's best for you, tried to be there for you."

"What—"

"Is this what you do Avery? Cut people out as soon as they make a mistake? You did it to your mum – *which I never agreed with, by the way* – and now you're going to do it to me? I can't believe this." He ran his hands through his hair. "I cannot believe you."

My face dropped, and I didn't bother to swipe the tears away this time. My history with my mother was my weakest spot, and he knew it.

"You don't have to push everyone away, Avery." Luke grabbed my hand and squeezed it, using the other to hold the car door open. "Come home with me. I'll forgive you. Let me love you the way you're meant to be loved. Don't abandon me the moment the balance switches and I need you more than you need me."

His voice broke on the last five words.

"You are the only one who can help me change. Remember what you always said? That I saved you?" He pleaded with his eyes. "This is your chance to save *me*."

"You're right." He smiled as I spoke. "You did save me."

"Of course I did. I'd do anything–"

"But if you hadn't been there, I would have learned to save myself."

"Get in the car, Avery."

I looked at him. "No."

With that one tiny word, everything changed.

"You're deluded if you think that this is just it. You belong to me."

Cold sweat dripped down my back.

"I don't belong to you. I don't belong to anyone."

I'd been kicking myself for depending on him, but he'd been thriving on it.

"Yes. You do, Avery. You're *mine*."

I felt his arm around my throat before I even registered it happening.

Smash.

He slammed me back into the bonnet of his car. My head spun. The world tilted.

Smash.

This time the back of my head hit the bonnet. Vision blurry, I tried to speak, to plead with him, but I couldn't get the words past his vice like grip.

"You're mine, you're mine, you're mine." He was chanting it, like a mantra. He had my hair wadded in his hand.

"Get off me!" I clawed at his hands. He kicked my shin. I tried to scream.

"See how you depend on me." He released his grip and I fell. Legs too wobbly to stand. Luke was laughing. He dragged me back up.

Smash.

I couldn't think. Couldn't breathe. The smell of rust filled my nostrils.

"Shut *up* Avery." Was that me? Screaming? "Shut the fuck up!"

He yanked my hair again, throwing me on the floor.

I sobbed. Prepared to give in. My whole body was burning.

"Remember who you belong to. Remember you are *mine*." He kicked out, connecting with my stomach. I slumped over on the tarmac.

Breathe Avery. In, out. In, out.

There were two voices now.

"Get away from her, I'm calling the police."

"Laura stay back, he could be dangerous…"

"Look at her Phil! Phone the damn police."

A car door slammed and an engine revved. I knew he was gone.

"Give them that registration Phil."

Hands were on my back, rubbing.

"Stay calm."

I spat out blood. Panted. "Who…"

I could only see braids. My vision was still blurred.

"We've got an ambulance coming, okay?"

Hysteria clawed up my throat. I couldn't catch my breath.

I was about to tell her my name when the scream of rubber on tarmac commanded our attention. The crushing of metal. A sudden, deadly silence.

And then I screamed.

At the hospital, Laura would tell my parents how I'd staggered away from them to get to Luke's car, the front end of which was completely crushed. That Luke was in the driver's seat, unconscious. How I'd lain down on the ground next to him, body exhausted. Blood. So much blood. They thought I was dying. I'd felt like I was already dead.

Thirty Six

"Avery?" I wasn't sure where I was for a second. I blinked. "Avery look straight forward please."

My mind refocused and I winced at the bright light shining into my eyes. I grabbed at the sheet I was lying under.

"Don't panic Avery. I'm a doctor in A&E. Now look forward? That's perfect."

"Where am I?"

"York Hospital. You were attacked."

I sucked in a breath, and then winced. My throat. I remembered now. Remembered the paramedics who had peeled me from the ground and lay me down on a stretcher.

I had no idea where Luke was now; where they'd taken him. I'd heard something about surgery, but I'd been kept separate, taken straight to a doctor myself. I hadn't looked in the mirror yet, but I had a feeling that I didn't look great.

"Your reflexes seem fine. I'm going to take some photographs of you, if that's alright?" The doctor stepped back, holding up her gloved hands so that my photo could be taken. I didn't ask why.

"So I've cleaned the cut on the back of your head and given you some stitches. It was deep, so I'm going to give you some pain medication for that and the bruises around your neck will hurt tomorrow, so you need to take your meds every four hours." She patted my hand. "And let everyone give you some proper TLC. You took quite a bump so we're going to keep you in overnight to keep an eye on things. Sound alright?"

I nodded at the doctor, still completely unable to speak. What if Luke died? I was the last person he'd spoken to, the reason he'd driven off.

"*Avery.*" Eliza stepped into the room, sobbing.

"If you're going to be in here, I need you to keep calm. I don't want her to be frightened."

I found my words, throat hoarse. "It's okay. I'm okay."

Eliza barrelled past the doctor, hugging me gingerly, like I might break. "I tried calling you, and this stranger picked up and told me that you were in the hospital, and that Luke was in surgery, and that he'd attacked you..." She put her head against my shoulder. "I wasn't there. Again. I'm so sorry."

"It wasn't...There was nothing you could have done Eliza. I wanted to do it on my own." I turned to the doctor, who had paused, looking a little sad herself. "Is he going to be okay?" No one asked who I was talking about. No one had to.

Eliza huffed. "You shouldn't care."

"You know that I still will."

"Please tell me that you're going to press charges. *Please.*"

I wasn't sure what I was going to say; or confess. The control, all he'd ever craved, was in my hands now. And I had no clue what to do with it.

"I got croissants. And pain-au-chocolat. I feel like all I ever offer in times of crisis is a selection of baked goods." Eliza gestured to the pastries, which she put on the side.

I didn't laugh. Didn't take my eyes off his body, which hadn't moved since they'd brought him in an hour ago. He looked as bad as I felt. There were tiny cuts all over his skin from where the glass had shattered; apparently that's where all the blood had come from. He'd been in surgery for three hours for the bleeding inside.

"They should be getting here soon." Eliza was referring to my family. I'd asked her to call them – all of them – as soon as I'd come out of my temporary daze. And then I'd moved from my room to Luke's bedside. I hadn't moved an inch since.

"That's good."

"Beckett has been in the waiting room this whole time."

I still didn't look up. "I know."

I couldn't go out and see him, Beckett, until I knew that Luke was going to be okay. I couldn't have it end like this. Eliza was watching me like a hawk, like my grief was a sign of my ignorance. I wasn't going to go back on my word. But after everything, he was still Luke. I was still me.

"I have to see this through."

"I understand." I could tell by her voice that she didn't.

I waited another half an hour, until the doctor came into the room and checked Luke's injuries.

"He's going to be okay. Lost a lot of blood, but he'll be okay. We had to take out his spleen, reset the bones in his arm." The doctor pushed her glasses on top of her head. "The police have arrived. You shouldn't be in here. Don't worry, his parents have been informed."

I nodded, having gotten all that I needed to know. He was going to be okay. Whatever happened from here on in wasn't my fault. When I finally went past the waiting room on my way back to my bed, I noticed that there was no sign of Beckett. I ignored my heart.

"Honey." Mum jumped up as I walked into my cubicle and grabbed my hand. "I have *worried*."

At that, I broke down. She caught me in her arms, holding me to her as I cried.

"Your dad wanted to go in there and get you out. He wanted to hurt that, that *monster*." I looked up. "But I told him that it was something that you needed to do." Mum lifted my chin with her finger. "You should have told me how bad this was. I thought I knew what you were talking about, but I had no idea."

Her voice broke, but she held it together. For the first time in a while, I realised that I admired her. I'd thought of my mother as the weakest figure in my life for years, but I was beginning to see her strength as it really was.

"Did you all drive up together?"

"Avery. Some things are bigger than the past."

I tried to imagine it, all three of them together again for the first time. Not all families were conventional, I was learning, but that didn't mean that they weren't worth fighting for.

"I love you. So much. You don't even know." Mum fished around in her handbag. "I'm just going to call Stella. She's with your dad and Eliza in the cafeteria getting coffee. Since when did Stella drink coffee? You're all growing up way too fast."

"Mum?"

She sent off the text before giving me her full attention. "Mhmm?"

"I'm sorry. For icing you out."

"Avery." Her fingers touched my cheek softly, avoiding all the places I was hurt. "You were fifteen years old and I just left. I don't blame you in the slightest. For anything. We're both here *now.*"

I leaned into her hand.

"Now let's talk about your best friend, Eliza. I *love* her." She'd moved on quickly, the best way of letting me know that everything was going to be fine between us. I might have lost one of the important relationships in my life, but I'd also gained one back.

I felt a body slam into me. "You scared the *shit* out of me."

"Watch her injuries." Mum patted Stel's shoulder.

"You aren't allowed to leave my sight ever again." Stella still had her arms around me, trying to look stern, but unable to stop her lip from trembling. "I knew. You *showed* me what he did. And I let you come back here. I let you come back."

"Stel, it's okay." I stroked her hair like I'd done so many times. "It's all over."

I looked up at the sound of my dad crying.

"Dad…"

His hand hovered over my arm, unsure where was safe to touch. I had a lot of bruising, from today and all the other days. "You're my daughter." His breath caught in a sob, and Mum squeezed his hand. "I'm your *dad*. I should have known. I should have known."

We were all crying now.

"I was worried," I took a deep breath, "that you might take his side." Saying it now, watching my dad's horrified expression, it seemed silly. It hadn't at the time.

"If I could go into that room, if the police weren't there…" Dad gritted his teeth. "Avery he was your *boyfriend*. We had to accept him. Don't you ever forget that my daughters will always come first." My dad pulled both of us into a hug, and a second later, Mum too. I had never felt prouder of him. "You can tell us anything."

We stayed there until my nurse broke us all apart, ordering me back to bed. I was staying in overnight so that they could monitor my concussion. My family never let me out of their sight.

A while later, Stella lay beside me on the bed. Our parents were in the corridor, talking to the police and to Laura, the girl who'd found me. Apparently her and her boyfriend had stopped walking when they'd heard the noise, retracing their steps to where Luke was attacking me in the driveway.

I'd been quietly weeping for about an hour. Eliza had left the croissants on the side, promising me that she'd be back after dinner. I hadn't been able to speak.

"This ceiling would look a lot better with stars." Stella smiled at me. "I know that you loved him." She leaned her head on my shoulder.

"I couldn't see past it."

"He had us all fooled. Eliza told me that Beckett was the only one who could see through it."

"Even then he felt guilty for not seeing the extent of it. It seems impossible now that I hid it. That I was able to hide it."

We sat in comfortable silence, like we'd done so many times over the years. Most of the time I'd felt that I had to be the emotional rock for my sister; someone to lean on, a role model. I didn't feel that way right now.

"I saw the way you looked at Beckett. It's okay if you have feelings for him."

I looked at my sister, for once, the one of us standing solid. She'd grown up a lot since I'd moved to York. Maybe all along she'd been solid, and I just hadn't realised.

"I need time. Time on my own. I don't want to spend my whole life moving from one crutch to the next. I don't want to be someone's *girlfriend*. I want to be me."

"Have I ever told you how much you inspire me?"

I nudged her. "I highly doubt that I look like an inspiration right now." I could feel the crusted blood in my hair from where Luke had slammed me into the car. I desperately needed to get in the shower and wash this day away.

"No, I'm serious. I want to be you when I'm older."

I raised my eyebrow.

"Maybe not exactly like all of this. I mean it though. I was inspired by you before Luke, and I'm inspired by you now."

"Aren't you meant to get all moody on me in your teens?"

"Har-dee-har."

Mum poked her head in.

"How are you feeling?"

"Sore."

Stella squeezed my hand.

"When you're ready, there's a police officer here who wants to speak to you. I can tell her to come back tomorrow if you want…"

"No."

I sat up in my bed, ignoring the pain. Stella adjusted my pillows.

"I want to do this now."

"Okay honey. If you're sure." Mum left, soon returning with the policewoman. I was sure.

"You ready for this?" Stella looked sceptical.

For the last four years since Mum had left Dad, I'd been searching for strength in other people. I'd convinced myself to stay with the first person who showed me support when I was at my lowest. Convinced myself that I wasn't strong enough on my own. This moment was the beginning of the rest of my life. I was ready to start searching for strength somewhere new.

I was ready to find it in myself.

Thirty Seven

One year later

The dinner table wasn't your traditional spread of food – that was for sure. All of my favourite dishes, from mashed potatoes and gravy, to gummy bears and lemonade, layered the table. The best part though, were the people sat around it. Dinner at Mum's was a regular thing now, and one that I'd been coming home every month for during third year, sometimes on my own, sometimes accompanied.

"May 11th." Dad was slightly tipsy but going for the speech anyway. No one had even suggested it; the past year had turned him into a soppy sort of father. Stella pretended that she hated it, but secretly we all knew that she loved it. "This day twenty one years ago," he paused to take a sip from his glass pre-toast, "we brought the most wonderful human into the world."

"Hey!" Everyone laughed at Stella, who was watching the whole thing with endearment as she helped herself to more gummy bears (which was clearly a genetic thing).

"Honey, we didn't know you then. We didn't know that there were two most wonderful humans at that point."

"Three most wonderful humans." Eliza piped up through a mouthful of potatoes, Jack nudging her in laughter.

"Okay, let me start again." My dad waved us all off, his speech needing a little tweaking. "May 11th." He cleared his throat. "This day twenty one years ago, we brought one of *many* wonderful humans into the world. Better?" Eliza stuck her tongue out at him.

I smiled. I *was* surrounded by wonderful humans. And I hadn't taken them for granted in a long time. Stella was sat beside me, grinning at Mum as they made faces at each other across the table. After Elliott broke her heart, she'd made a pledge to grow her hair as long as mine, and she was sticking to it. First love had wounded her, but it hadn't consumed her like mine had, and I couldn't be happier that she'd found the right way to do it. God knows everyone was hoping that *that* tendency wasn't genetic. It had taken a few days after the dumping, armed with a lot of Ben and Jerry's and cosy blankets, for her to see the light, but she'd bounced back pretty quick. That was the way it was supposed to be; I could see that now. Jack and Eliza were getting stronger by the day, and I couldn't have been more supportive of my best friend's relationship choices. He wanted her to succeed, in a way that my boyfriend never had. Sure, they fought; shouting so loudly that I'd spent nights with my pillow over my head, but then they listened. And got quieter. Until all that I could hear was a quiet murmuring. There was nothing to fear in conflict, I was learning, if there was respect.

"Who wants more carrots?" Steve passed the bowl around, tipping some on Stella's plate as she narrowed her eyes at him. I accepted him now, just like I accepted that my dad wasn't interested in finding another woman. One had been enough for him, and he'd found peace on his own. We'd had a lot of conversations this year about that. It had been weird, at first, to see Dad at the head of this huge dining table, our big mixed up family coming together once a month to talk everything out. Eliza had become a huge part of our routine, and on the odd occasion, Maia came to, bonding unexpectedly with Steve over her science fiction obsession. She'd visited me as soon as she'd heard about the crash, and had been the only one not to cry. Instead, she'd taken a criminal law textbook out of the library, coming to our flat armed with chocolate buttons and her technical advice for the battle ahead.

Once upon a time every person sat around this table had been the type to bottle things up, but not now. We'd learned our lesson there. And I was on my way to classing this mish-mash of people as a definition of complete. I'd craved conventional, but it wasn't what I'd ended up with. And conventional wasn't perfect anyway. Luke's mum had tried to contact me once following the hearing, a small voice reaching through the answerphone to ask me a million questions. It was hard to imagine her sat in that big house, a victim, maybe not of the things I'd experienced, but still the product of control. It could have so easily been me in that house, leading that monotone life under someone else's shadow. Eliza had deleted the message, knowing that it wasn't necessary for my recovery. It had been a recovery of sorts, training myself to look at all the pieces of my life differently. I no longer jumped every time I heard footsteps behind me, or felt a wave of guilt when I texted my friends. It was a new way of life, for everyone, but it was a good one.

"So, cheers to Avery, our beautiful little girl." Stella scrunched up her nose and make a gag sound, Eliza pushing her until she admitted defeat. "We are so incredibly proud of the woman you've become." He wiped his eye. "Oh look, something is in my eye." We all laughed, equal parts caught up in the emotion as well, and making fun of my father.

"Thanks Dad." He winked at me as Mum left the room, presumably to get the cake that Stella had attempted to smuggle inside the house inconspicuously.

"Quick. Go!" Dad whispered back to the shadows, and then the room glowed with the light from a line of candles, stuck into a Colin the Caterpillar cake that reminded anyone of being five years old and completely carefree. They all sang along, six voices trying to match each other and failing miserably; my family coming together, just for me. Mum grabbed my hand, squeezing it. I'd never felt so lucky, or so complete.

***

Eliza, Stella and I were sat on the patio seat, looking out over Mum's garden. I'd been helping her with the planting now and again, as she taught me to understand what the last few years had been like for her.

"I feel so happy, that my toes are tingling." Stella swung her legs to the rhythm of the music still drifting in from the house.

"I feel so happy that I might just spontaneously combust, right on this spot." The three of us giggled – sisters even though we weren't all joined by blood.

"I feel so happy that I might cry." I smiled at them. Eliza grabbed my hand.

"We've all done enough of that. Now comes the best part."

"What's that?" Stella put down her phone, on which she'd undoubtedly been texting her 'girl squad'. The idea of it made me beam every time she recounted a high school drama to me whilst we sat eating cereal.

"The part where we laugh. Constantly. All the time."

That sounded nice. It had been a complete rollercoaster of a year, starting with the hearing. I'd decided to testify against Luke, if only to quench the fear that plagued me whilst I lay in bed at night. He didn't deserve to walk about unscathed. After his immediate recovery he'd woken up to questioning and the news of the charges I was pressing against him. He hadn't tried to argue, and the one time I had seen him since the accident, in the courtroom, he'd looked so defeated. He got six months for domestic violence; a sentence based on the marks he'd left that you could see. I knew I'd spend years trying to fix the ones that you couldn't; I hadn't slept with the light off in a long time, but it was slowly getting easier.

The last I'd heard he'd lost his job and was stacking shelves in a supermarket, no longer in York but back home, living with the Calkins. I'd half expected him to try and find me, even after Eliza and I moved into a different flat, but he knew the risk. I couldn't imagine that Luke had fared very well in prison, even if only for a short time. Nothing compared to the time that I'd spent trapped.

"That sounds good. Let's start right now." I tickled Stel, watching her face light up. Eliza shook her head at us, trying not to join in but failing miserably.

"I wonder where we'll be in another year."

"I'll be applying to university." Stella paled. I didn't think she'd end up going down the traditional route, but for now she seemed set on it. Knowing her, she'd probably have changed her mind by tomorrow.

"We'll be free in a post-graduate world." I spoke directly to Eliza, a question hanging between us that had started at the beginning of third year, and never really lifted. I had ended up doing the internship last summer and was fast approaching the beginning of my adult career. I was undecided on whether the feeling I got in my stomach whenever we discussed it was fear, or excitement. Definitely a different sort of fear to the one that I was used to. Maybe a mixture of both.

"Do you think you'll ever contact him?" I knew who Stella was referring to without having to ask her to specify. I'd thought about him a lot over the past year. We'd emailed a couple of times, but I hadn't seen Beckett since our conversation the day of the book signing.

"He's probably moved on by now." I'd avoided looking at his social media, afraid of what I might find. I did however, have several copies of his second book dotted around my house in Westby and mine and Eliza's flat in York. I'd never had the chance to officially edit his work, but that had been for the best. He shone through the pages without any help from me.

"You *were* just friends before." Stella reasoned.

"I couldn't do that now." As I let the confession slip out, I realised it was true. I didn't have it in me to deny my feelings a second time around. He'd been the first man to show me what I couldn't yet see in myself.

"He doesn't have a girlfriend." Eliza's voice was so quiet, it was almost inaudible. Stella's head whipped around.

"How do you know that?"

"I kept in contact with him." She looked at me apologetically. "Of course I did. We were all involved in something so big, that it would have been awful to lose contact."

"I don't blame you." I didn't. How could I? They had both been my best friends at the same time, joined by a period of my life that was almost too terrible to look back on. But I did sometimes, if only to revisit the memories I had of him. "How is he?"

Eliza looked relieved, and hesitated, sipping her wine. "He's well, obviously. Being a bestseller was all he ever wanted." There was a moment of agonising silence, and I could tell Stella wanted to rush Eliza, but I put a hand out in warning. "Until he met you Avery. I didn't want to tell you this and hold back your progress, but I think he still cares about you."

I felt the blood rush through my ears.

"It's up to you." Eliza shrugged. "You know we all have your back, and I can keep being friends with him no matter what you choose. But he still lives at the same address, FYI."

I thought of Lola, Lucy and Beckett. I wanted so badly to see them all again. I wondered about Lola, who must have been getting ready to start school. I wondered if Lucy's relationship had worked out, if he would be there at the school gates with her.

Most of all, I wondered about the boy from the window seat in the café. I hadn't been back there this year, too scared to come to terms with all of the decisions that I'd made. It was a good thing that we lived in a world where, if you were lucky, second chances came along every single day.

Thirty Eight

The bell chimed as I walked in, still so familiar after all this time. I ordered my usual hot chocolate and took our spot, pulling out *To Kill a Mockingbird*, if only for sentiments sake. The plan was to gather my thoughts here before making my way up to his flat.

"There you go." The waitress smiled warmly. She'd told me that Emma had finally got her freedom and was off studying management when I'd asked after her earlier – I asked the waitress to send her my love.

As I settled into my seat, my confidence was wobbling. I could definitely do this, I told myself. It was no big deal.

When I turned the page, a movement in the corner of my eye made me look up. I'd been trying to stop myself from even looking at his flat window, afraid that it might lead me to chicken out. Now, when I lifted my head, he was standing right there on the other side of the glass. He held his laptop, and his expression was just as shell shocked as mine. His hand pressed lightly against the window and I put my book down, lifting my own to match. Beckett grinned, *oh God how I'd missed that grin,* and then as soon as he'd appeared, he was gone. I'd looked behind me to see if anyone was watching our moment, and before I knew it, I was alone again. He was nowhere to be seen.

"Well." I wasn't even embarrassed that I was talking to myself. "I guess that's that."

Eliza was going to be just as confused as me when I told her about his reaction. I pretended to read in silence for a few minutes, putting off the task of calling her, despite promising that I'd call as soon as I had news.

"Avery." I turned in my chair, overwhelmed with relief to see his hands resting on the back of it. He held up a paper bag. "Had to make a pit stop."

I nodded. He'd never particularly been a mystery to me, but in this moment, I couldn't predict or control a single thing. Control had been such a theme throughout the last five years of my life. And I was learning to be okay with knowing that you never really had it. Not completely.

"*To Kill a Mockingbird*," he nodded at the book in memory of our first meeting, "good choice."

"I like classics, what can I say?"

He bit his lip, trying to hold back a grin.

I pushed forward. "I have five copies of *Sophia*."

He beamed, shaking his head. "It's been an even better ride second time round. I've loved it. Every single second. You'd love it too, Avery, you really would."

We had so much to catch up on for two people that had once been so close.

"I ended up getting that internship last summer."

He sat down next to me, grabbing my hand. "You did? And how was it?"

"It was amazing." It felt so good, talking to him after all this time.

"You're going to be incredible in this field. I am so excited to see what happens–" he broke off, suddenly unsure.

"How's Lola? Lucy?"

"They're great, better than great. I don't even mind her boyfriend anymore."

I raised my eyebrows. "Are you thawing Mister?"

He rolled his eyes. "Ha ha. I'm trying to accept that my little sister will be fine on her own."

"Ditto."

I clung to every word he said. There was so much that had happened that I could never put into words for him. Like standing up against my ex-boyfriend in court and trying not to burst into tears, or the first night in my own bed after the accident, and the panic attacks that had followed. We had both been changed by our experiences. I was just hoping that we hadn't changed to the point where we didn't fit together anymore. The paper bag still lay on the table between us.

"What's in the bag?"

Beckett rubbed his hands together. "I was beginning to think you've never ask." He peered in and pulled out a cupcake that I knew he'd bought from the bakery beneath his flat. And then from his back pocket, a candle.

He lit the single candle and placed the cupcake in front of me, the sweet scent of the white icing mixed with the burning smell brought back memories of birthdays past.

"I missed the big two-one. There was no chance I was letting that milestone slip past without wishing you a happy birthday." Beckett leaned over and kissed my cheek. "Happy birthday Avery."

I was so touched by the gesture that I almost started to cry. Did this mean what I thought it meant? He'd moved on, oblivious to what that simple gesture had meant to me. I blew out my candle and closed my eyes, taking a moment to make my wish. When I opened my eyes, he'd moved to sit next to me.

"I missed you Emerson. The last few chapters of my manuscript were a dogs dinner without your touch."

He was joking, like he always did. I didn't think I had it in me to joke around.

"I missed you too. Every single day. I'm sorry for the silence." There, I'd said it. I almost winced at the thought that he might not feel the same way. I waited a second, and another. And then he grinned wider than I'd ever seen him do before.

"You never have to apologise. You needed that." I was so glad that he understood, but I wanted to make sure.

"I didn't want you to put me back together. I wanted to be the one to do it."

He considered this for a moment, and I held my breath. Some people would never be able to understand that. Why would you want to be your own hero? I was lucky, because I was pretty sure my person did.

"And now you have?"

I threw my arms around his neck, unable to wait any longer. "I have." It was a whisper in his ear, but from the way I felt goose bumps cover his skin, you would have thought it was a scream. I kept my lips at his ear. "Do you want to know a secret?"

"More than ever."

"I think I love you."

He let out a breath. "God, I *know* I love you."

We pulled back. Our eyes locked.

And then he reached in and he kissed me.

It had taken a while for me not to flinch when people reached out to touch me, and sometimes I still faltered, but here with Beckett everything felt right.

He wasn't mine, and I wasn't his. I was done with that.

But he was what I wanted, and who I loved. And that would be enough for as long as we wanted it to be. Even if that didn't mean forever. It was all up to us.

And so... I kissed him back.

The End

If you have been affected by the topics described in *Mine*, you can visit www.saladpages.com/support where we have information on organisations and charities who can offer help and support. You are not alone.

Acknowledgements

Firstly, my biggest thank you is to Claire. You took a chance on this book, and me. I'm so thankful to be part of the Salad Pages family. To Lucy, my editor, this book would be full of boys wearing baseball caps and animal figurines if it weren't for you (if you know, you know). I learned a lot about writing from our work on this book, and your attention to detail is second to none. Kate, you designed a cover that is beyond my wildest dreams. Your art is incredible.

I'm a big believer in the little motions that set you on the right path, so Robbie, thank you for forwarding me that email. To everyone at *The Gryphon,* being part of our newspaper gave me confidence in my writing, which could have easily dwindled when I was querying for this book. Beth, you are the kind of friend I aspire to be, and you have supported me every step of the way. People like you are few and far between. Rosie and Mariana, being part of blogs with you is on my highlight reel. To my friends from home – you know who you are – you make writing friendships so easy. Thanks for checking in on me when I retreat to my writing fort and being there to listen when I finally emerge from it. Growing up with you has provided endless inspiration. Han, my tendency to write love stories certainly comes from all the nights we stayed up listening to Taylor's songs on repeat. To Bradley, I sat down on our first date and told you about the story I was writing, and you have never doubted me. Our hot chocolate breaks have fuelled this journey, and I value our team more than you know.

Every member of my family is unbelievably supportive. I am truly blessed. Thank you, Fiona, for reading my manuscript and reigniting my hope for it. To my grandparents; it is a dream to have three extra parents in my life. Rachel, it was extremely easy to write about a feisty little sister. Thanks for leading the way at parties when I'm too shy to do it myself. To my parents, I know how extremely lucky I was to end up being your daughter. Mum, your excitement for *Mine* rivals my own. Thanks for being honest and saying that my first chapter needed work. It was a very nice way of telling me the truth. And thanks for showing me that books are my happy place. How many hours do you think we've spent in Waterstones? Dad, it is so rare to have someone that you know you can call anywhere, anytime, for support. Thanks for walks on the beach and dropping everything to come and get me from uni when it got tough. Thank you for jumping on board with this book and telling everyone you know.

And finally, to Avery. I hope you have the most wonderful fictional life.

About the Author

Emily started her debut novel, *Mine*, when she was eighteen years old. Emily is a gifted and whole-hearted writer. She grew up in a coastal village near Liverpool, and recently graduated with a degree in Geography from The University of Leeds. At uni, Emily was a regular writer for the prestigious student newspaper *The Gryphon*.

Emily is a passionate reader, book reviewer and vlogger. You can follow her on Twitter, Instagram and YouTube @alittlewriterem.

Emily now lives in York with her best friend, pursuing her dream career as a writer. She can most likely be found in a café with a great book and a hot chocolate!